Fear in Fenway

FEAR IN FENWAY

A Duffy House Mystery

—— Crabbe Evers ——

WILLIAM MORROW AND COMPANY, INC.
NEW YORK

Library of Congress Cataloging-in-Publication Data

Evers, Crabbe.
    Fear in Fenway : a Duffy House mystery / by Crabbe Evers.
        p.   cm.
    ISBN 0-688-11468-7
    I. Title.
    PS3552.R33F4   1993
    813'.54—dc20   92-37664
                                                                         CIP

Printed in the United States of America

First Edition

1   2   3   4   5   6   7   8   9   10

BOOK DESIGN BY LISA STOKES

To Julie Fallowfield . . .
"Peck's bad boys, *indeed.*"

Our thanks to the Boston Red Sox Baseball Club for its cooperation and hospitality. We also tip a '67 Red Sox cap to Tom Shaer, broadcaster extraordinaire and Fenway aficionado, for access to his storehouse of Boston lore.

And special thanks to Dr. Jeremy C. Hewens and his fellow physicians—Ken Kutcher, George Hartpence, and John Zapp—at the Hunterdon Medical Center in Flemington, New Jersey, whose toxic imaginations rival only their appreciation of natural turf.

"Boston fans realize that death is lurking in the background of every celebration. It can't be avoided. Their city is filled with famous old cemeteries. Every corner you turn, there's John Adams or John Hancock. And they're all dead."

—BILL LEE, *The Wrong Stuff*

Prologue

Watching a guy go down with food poisoning is no picnic. You clutch your own innards, the lower intestines. A grip of vicarious indigestion radiates upward, burning your heart and corroding your throat. In the meantime, the fellow stews there, green, seized with a bowel-wrenching ache that saps the color from his face and splays his legs. Sick to his stomach pretty much says it all, which is not pretty, and there is nothing much you can do but watch him suffer and hope that it will pass. If there is ever a case for euthanasia, for sticking a fork in, it is in times like these. Even dead, the guy would thank you for it.

So it was with Ossee Schreckengost, his well-fed body of six decades cradled in a director's chair in a major-league clubhouse, when he suddenly took ill. He gagged, he choked, he clutched at his gut and at his throat. His eyes bugged in terror, then rolled in pain. His massive belly, the caldron of this sudden onslaught of dyspepsia—hell, of the Mother of all Gutaches—heaved and buckled and fairly roared with pain. Worst of all, he looked up at me for help.

Schreckengost was an Old-Timer, a former ballplayer who had come back to Fenway, home of Boston's beloved but cursed Red Sox. A celebration, three innings of nostalgia, hoisting of several toasts to old times and old buddies, and bellying up to the buffet table. I figured Schreckengost had done too much bellying already, and that was what had precipitated this attack. I hoped as much. I held my stomach, for I too had sampled the buffet.

"Ossee . . . ?" I said in a feeble gesture of aid or comfort.

Others crowded near, for Schreckengost was more than a mere visitor to the Red Sox clubhouse. He had played for and later managed the Sox. The latter stint had earned him thirty-two more victories than losses, no championships (true to Red Sox tradition), and an honorable mention among Boston managers. Not a beacon in Red Sox history, Schreckengost had, nevertheless, lit a small, memorable light. And people, including me, had always liked him.

Yet the rotund figure who was writhing in misery in his chair was more than just an affable, overweight cud chewer. For Schreckengost had left the Red Sox and baseball and gone on to make some significant money in New England real estate. He could buy and sell today's players, even at their bloated salaries, which was exactly what he wanted to do. His money had brought him power and position in Boston, and when the venerable, family-held Red Sox franchise seemed up for bid this year, Schreckengost formed a syndicate that boldly announced an intention of winning it.

First, however, he had to survive what ailed him. And to me, that prospect looked dicey. In his agony, Schreckengost suddenly slid off the chair and flopped onto the floor. His stomach heaved and his legs stiffened. Not getting the needed response from me, perhaps in a frantic zone of their own, his eyes rolled back once again, his head lolled, and suddenly a rivulet of blood coursed from his nose. It was an eerie, hideous sight, one that mocked my hopes that Schreckengost's attack was due to indigestion, some bad potato salad, maybe too many oysters. I am no physician, but I know all too well that people with upset stomachs do not bleed like that.

By now the Red Sox trainer had been called in, and he did not like what he saw. There were shouts, hurried motions, a justified panic. The air was clammy, almost as much as Ossee's hide. An ambulance was summoned, and its arrival could not occur too soon, for Schreckengost, half dressed in his Red Sox colors, his heavy legs now twitching involuntarily in front of him, looked more awful than anyone should ever look. I felt terrible for him; my eyes stung.

Just then he exhaled with a shudder, and he choked. The

sound—Death's gurgle—is one that should never buffet your ears. With it his eyes widened the way they used to at an umpire's bad call, or maybe as they do upon seeing the final one. And, ever so reluctantly—I am positive of it—they closed. Then, except for a few haunting tics and contractions, Ossee Schreckengost was still.

—1—
Hub Fans Bid Us
Bonjour

SHE WAS ANTSY, SHE WAS GIGGLY, SHE WAS BUZZING AND charged and as excited as a kid with her first whoopee cushion.

"For cryin' out loud, Petey, calm down," I said as our plane climbed out over Lake Michigan and banked eastward.

"Scrape me off the ceiling, Unk," my niece Petey said. "If you can."

"A visit to *Old Ironsides* and a trip down the Freedom Trail will do that to ya."

"The three Fs," she said.

"I'll bite—Freedom Trail, Fenway, and . . . and—"

"Filene's basement," she quickly put in.

We were buckled up and wedged into what passes for airline luxury nowadays. A year-old bald kid with four teeth and a moon-pie face looked at me over the seat back as if he'd seen his twin brother. Petey mugged at him and made things worse.

"I've just about clipped the Rs from my diction, as in 'I'll have the clam chow-dah,' " she said.

"Good choice, so-so delivery," I said. "Don't think the natives won't be onto you in a syllable."

"I tried to find a Berlitz tape of old Bobby Kennedy speeches," she said. She had settled instead for a tape of something by the Cowboy Junkies, a copy of *The Sporting News*, and a novel by Linda

Barnes. She could work on all three at one time and not miss lunch.

We were headed for Boston, Mass., and therein lay the reason for Petey's being pumped. It was midsummer, just after the time when baseball likes to pause and hold an all-star game, put everybody but Nelson Fox in Cooperstown, and generally take a breather before the trophy run begins. The Red Sox were having their own affair, an Old-Timers' Day; only this time they were spreading things pretty thin by also inviting coots from the press corps.

The Red Sox franchise buttering up the wretches of the press was like the board buying roses for the darts, the Christians sending bonbons to the lions. So you could have knocked me over with a Fenway frank when a nice young lady from the Red Sox called my home number and asked if I'd include myself among their fourth-estate guests. As soon as Petey, my niece and a would-be law-school matriculate, got wind of the invite, she moved like a rookie sniffing a spot on the roster.

Now, I love sister Betty's carrot-topped daughter, and from the moment she came to Chicago a few years back to bunk in with me until her dormitory room at the proper and pricey Northwestern Law School came available, my life was elevated. Hell, I was retired from the *Daily News* and a widower, mixing my Metamucil with beer and spending too much time in the lounge. Suddenly I had some tension on the old rubber bands.

My daily excuse is that I'm hard at my memoirs, a collection of postcards and yarns mixed in with a look at how the game was played back when I started writing about it, which was in '51, compared to the spectacle of today. Oh, it's a serious project, and if I ever get it out of the chute I have enough devoted readers and faithful subjects still respiring to lunge at it. Or at least that's what my publisher hopes.

Well, Petey came along and insisted that I put a cork in it and show her all my old haunts. I bellyached for a few minutes, then turned over some old Chicago sod with her. I closed some places that I hadn't haunted since Durocher was still the Lip. I said to hell with it, and drank too much and told bawdy stories about guys with double joints. Look at it this way: The brain will fog and arteries will clog in no time if you let them, and Petey was not going to let them.

On top of that, she was an unadulterated fan of mine, just

a walking glossary of my better stuff. She'd read my columns more carefully than I'd written them and had a memory like a scorekeeper.

Then, of course, big-league baseball put murder on its schedule; Granville "Grand Canyon" Chambliss, the current commissioner of the game, put me to work. In sagas recorded elsewhere, Petey served as my Watson, and she hasn't set foot in law school yet. That's a damn shame and sister Betty isn't pleased. Wait until this year, I've promised.

"How much of a feel for the Red Sox do you have in you?" I asked her.

She thought about that one, nibbling a bit at an unpolished fingernail.

"Let me say for the record and not to rub it in or make you feel that you're some kind of fossil, Unk—you know, dug up by Louis Leakey at Olduvai—that I was only in the third grade when Fisk hit his home run in '75. But I remember it better than my birthday, okay? Mom let me stay up and watch it on TV even though it was way past my bedtime. But we were in good ol' Cincinnati, don't forget, and I loved the Big Red Machine even more than I did Jonah Gaster and I had a mad passionate crush on Jonah Gaster. And whew boy, did I bawl when Fisk did it. We were all crying—my mom, my brother—crying like mad for the Reds."

"But you still had the seventh game," I said.

"You got it," she said. "We didn't cry after that one."

"Boston—no, all of New England—did."

"So what," Petey said, "It was our turn."

"No, it wasn't," I said.

In what seemed like no time at all we touched down at Logan International and were soon, bag and baggage, in a cab headed downtown. The Red Sox had wanted to put me up in a glass and chrome hotel in Copley Square. I said nothing doing. We were registered instead at the Parker House, home of the rolls by the same name, a grand, magnificent old place. I communicated as much to the cabbie, a coal-haired Caucasian, and his whistle was an editorial comment that needed no footnote. He took us for a pair of swells.

That impression was not dispelled by Petey's luggage. Where normally she travels with a backpack and a canvas bag that looks like a Red Sox equipment satchel, this time she had a full-fledged garment bag and a matching suitcase. Dress up, I had said, or you may not go to Locke-Ober's with me. Obviously, she'd taken that warning to heart.

It was midafternoon Boston time, warm if not a little muggy, the sky bright. We cracked the cab's windows.

"Good day for a ball game," I ventured.

"Yeah, if we only had a team," the hack returned, and I knew we had a live one.

Once we were out from under the canopy of Logan's arrival area, the cab's radio crackled with some red ass from a guy named Eddie Bindleman or something, who was moaning about, what else? the Red Sox.

"We got thirty-three thousand *votes* each game, you with me?" he yelped. "Every time you walk down Yawkey Way and into the *pahk* you cast your vote. Affirmative. So how 'bout we staht changing our votes, for cryin' out loud? They ain't gonna play no bettah until we staht stayin' away! I mean, the joint is sold out in February so it don't mattah if they do good or not!"

Petey pumped her fist in the air.

"Aw—right," she said.

"Welcome to Boston," I said.

The hack heard me and cocked his head in the direction of the dashboard static.

"The guy's a moron. Fahget him," he said.

"It's the *pahk*," the radio Eddie went on. "Everybody knows it's Fenway *Pahk*. The future of Fenway is *mawbid*. It's archaic. If they had a biggah pahk you wouldn't see the seats all sold out, and then management would staht to worry. Now they don't. It's a day at the beach for them!"

A specious bit of reasoning, I thought, but I didn't have to say as much. By now we were past the low lights of Callahan Tunnel, which runs beneath Boston's Inner Harbor and into the streets of the North End. Petey was wide-eyed.

In minutes we were winding our way past Faneuil Hall and what is called the Government Center until we hit Tremont and School streets. The Parker House stood there like an old hat, unchanged, a proud edifice saved from a wrecking ball that swung too close for comfort.

Through it all, the radio complainer kept up his cavil.

"Listen to him," the cabbie snapped as he pulled up in front

of the hotel. "The idiot wants to teah down Fenway Pahk. Fenway
Pahk! Proves what my fathah always said to me, 'There's nevah
a shortage of morons in this world.' "

He handed our grips to a bellhop and shook his head the
whole time.

"Wants to teah down Fenway Pahk. Can you believe that?"
he groused. "Can you believe that?"

I could not.

The next day, we arrived at Fenway and were joined by dozens of participants in the arthritic three-inning Old-Timers' frolic
before the varsity millionaires showed. Now I never thought much
of Old-Timers' games until I became one. In my early days as a
smart columnist I thought they were a sorry excuse for a lot of
potbellied pensioners—as small as baseball's dole was back then—
to come back and belly up to the buffet table. Age blurred the
gap in talent and pay between them to where fat guys who hadn't
been up for much more than a cup of coffee sat next to fat guys
who were Cooperstown residents. Ike Delocks, of which there
were many, sat next to Ted Williamses, of which there was one.
Age also added dozens of chins, softened the lines around the
eyes, and hardened the arteries.

Oh, I had liked the old guys, but they weren't deadline stuff
as far as my paper was concerned. Then my eyebrows grayed and
hair started growing in my ears, and, like a slap on the cheek, I
got a little perspective on things and decided that sentiment is the
real glue to this game. So what if nostalgia games had no effect
on league standings? Take away Old-Timers and their memories
from baseball and you've got soccer.

The more I saw old Fenway faces I had not seen since the
Nixon-Kennedy debates, players I'd written of only sparingly, if
at all, the more I wondered why I was here—a Chicago scribbler
who got to Boston only with the White Sox and an occasional
postseason series. The sponsors of this affair had even said they
wanted me to take a bow next to New England names like Curt
Gowdy, who was a talker, and Bob Cunningham, who wasn't.

And the topper was an intriguing phone call I'd fielded a few
days earlier. It came from Mrs. Tom (Patsy) Dougherty, the
Grande Matron of the Red Sox, widow of the team's owner, and
a woman who had become a power among the men of baseball.
Currently, however, because of bad estate planning and a share-

holder rebellion, she was fighting to keep the team from hostile bidders in a struggle that was shaping up as Boston's nastiest franchise battle since the passing of Tom Yawkey.

"We must talk, Mr. House," Mrs. Dougherty said, "about things more important than the ball club."

What things? I had wondered.

By eleven o'clock, two hours prior to the main event, the clubhouse and the infield were an Elks convention. Dozens of old Red Sox were indulging twice their number of scribes and cameras. No dearth of gab in this group. Hyperbole was stacked like Ace bandages. Statistics were tossed around so carelessly you could have caught a spike on them.

Ducat holders for the day's game got to witness the geriatric proceedings for no extra fare, and at least twenty thousand of them had shown up early and jammed the front-row seats and aisles. Cameras clicked and whirred, and guys who hadn't signed an autograph on Fenway's grounds in twenty years were putting chicken scratches on pennants and programs older than Burma-Shave signs.

An Old-Timers' Game is like any reunion: You spend half your time eating, drinking, forgiving, and trying to figure out who's who. Guys who were as skinny as Eddie Bressoud twenty years ago come back looking like Smead Jolley. Throw in too much gray hair and too much collar and you can't believe some of these birds are who they say they are. All that was alleviated some by a nifty scorecard full of old-time photos and statistics, and in no time you were warped right back to the days when the Green Monster shilled for Gem blades and Lifebuoy soap.

While Petey stayed around the batting cage, I headed for the clubhouse. Even though it would be full of reporters, radio guys, and uncounted hangers-on, more old ballplayers were coming in all the time, and I felt comfortable there.

The Red Sox clubhouse was a dressing room in keeping with Fenway Park itself: small, cozy, a little worn, a little tacky. Clutter was the dominant theme, the red carpeting was worn, a soft drink machine was whining in the corner. Players dressed in front of wooden cubicles the movies would bring in if they were doing *The Doc Cramer Story*. An old-fashioned mail station with pigeonholes stood in the middle of the room.

Today the place seemed to be divided in two halves, each side attracting a scrum of reporters and leaving a hole in the middle. It did not take me long to see what the fuss was about, and it did not have anything to do with an Old-Timers' Game. On one wall sat Ossee Schreckengost and Lou Criger, two former Red Sox and current millionaires who were partners in a syndicate that wanted to buy the club. On the other wall sat Jack Slattery, one of the greatest former Sox of them all, who had announced his own bid for the team. So right here in this shabby locker room was a miniature franchise fight, with big egos and millions of dollars, and newsies eating it all up.

Such concerns were too lofty for my taste, so I turned to the food. A pair of tables was heaped high: mountains of roast beef, ham baked in honey, fried chicken, and shrimp the size of prawns. There was a crock of chowder and tangles of clams and crab claws. A great bin of baked beans bubbled and beckoned, along with cold cuts and cheese, pickles, and potato salads. Let the others worry about the sale of the club; I attended to the trough. While I was spreading horseradish on my roast beef I got a whiff of a fragrance three octaves sweeter than Old Spice. I looked up to see the arrival of Herself, Patsy Dougherty, the Red Sox's principal owner.

Mrs. Dougherty swept into the clubhouse like somebody who owned it, not bothered by the prospect of seeing an Old-Timer in a state of undress. She was an elegant-looking lady, an ex-model who had kept her fine facial lines. Her hair was dyed blond and swept back. Her ears and neck and fingers glittered with ice. I do not remember exactly what she was wearing—something peach-colored and silk, I think—for my eyes were drawn to her lovely countenance. I was a gawker at an air show, and my pocket could have been picked while I glommed.

At the sight of her, the two clumps of reporters stopped their pens and recorders in midsentence and turned her way. This was drama in a bottle: All the contestants in Boston's home version of *The Price Is Right* assembled in this humid, liniment-stained dressing room.

"As you were, boys," Mrs. Dougherty said, her voice as sharp as a drill sergeant's. "I'm sure those gentlemen"—and with the word she turned to each, to Jack Slattery, her former superstar, on her left, and to Schreckengost and Criger, her onetime employees, on her right, and fixed them with a sharp, momentary glance that could have seared flesh—"have *important* things to tell you."

With that she moved to the buffet table, looking over the arrangement and the supply as if she had personally catered the feast. She repositioned platters, rearranged the fruit, and occasionally plucked a tidbit with thumb and finger and nibbled. When a reporter approached, she waved him off. The rebuff kept the others at bay.

I kept my eyes on her.

"*Imposters*," she said under her breath.

Just then she turned in my direction.

"There you are!" she said, and swiftly glided over.

She offered her hand and I managed to grasp about three fingers of it. They were not ample digits as she was a very slender woman. But she radiated like a scoreboard and seemed genuinely pleased to see me. She had a gorgeous smile. I generally give wide berth to ownership, but Mrs. Dougherty, who wouldn't see sixty-four again, was what rakes in my day called "handsome." I kept a smile pasted on my face. If there was roast beef stuck in my teeth, all bets were off.

I was just about to say something awkward when a figure loomed over my shoulder and captured Mrs. Dougherty's attention.

It was Jack Slattery, the big slugger, reporters hard on his elbows.

"What say we break bread together, Patsy," Slattery said, grinning, "and may the best man win."

A few of the reporters laughed. Mrs. Dougherty stood her ground and looked up at Slattery as if he were a pox upon the ballpark. She did a burn as slow as they make them.

"It's a woman you have to beat, Jack," she replied.

That got a bigger laugh, even a smirk from Slattery. Mrs. Dougherty, however, cracked not a slice of a smile. Instead, she turned to leave, sending a promising nod my way before she went for the door. She had to pass within a few feet of where Ossee Schreckengost and Lou Criger were sitting, however, and when she did she paused. Again the glow I had seen in her eyes only moments earlier drained, and she was all hard edges.

"Eat well, fellas," she said.

Schreckengost, the ex-manager, bobbed his head almost good-naturedly; Criger scowled like a bail bondsman. For long seconds you could have cut the clubhouse air with a proxy. I was struck by it, at the rancor here, the kind of bile that rises in the throats of family members involved in blood feuds.

Then Mrs. Dougherty took leave with little more than a parting sniff and a turn of the hip—and a nice hip it was, I must add. Looks do not kill, and Messrs. Slattery, Criger, and Schreckengost remained with their vital organs intact. But the situation was obvious, the regiments had formed. Boston was in revolt again.

"Ah, to hell with her," Ossee Schreckengost suddenly exclaimed. "I'm gonna fill the tank."

With that he got up and came my way, waddling over in his socks.

"Hey, Duffy House, you old freeloader!" he barked. He slapped me on the back before grabbing two plates with one hand.

"We eat this well if you get the club, Os?" I asked.

"Every day'll be Mardi Gras!" he said, and laughed with his belly. It was a favorite line of Bill Veeck's, and Ossee knew I'd appreciate it.

I gave him a wide berth as he stabbed cold cuts and cheeses, scooped salads and soups, slathered bread and stacked pickles like cordwood. He finally departed from the table, returning to his cubicle across the way with enough food to feed a farm club.

I worked on building my own plate, taking my time and selecting well. I wondered if I should locate Petey and ask her to join me. I decided to let her fend for herself, and I found an open chair on the far side of the clubhouse, where, for the next several minutes, I practiced gluttony. That is when I heard the growl from across the room. It was a fearsome bellow, and it came from Schreckengost's cubicle. I stood up to take a look, and that is when I saw Ossee begin his fateful gag. Watching a guy go down with food poisoning is no picnic. . . .

When the trainer said Ossee needed some air, I moved back and decided to get the hell out of there. Right now Ossee certainly did not need me. As I went out the clubhouse door I pushed against a dozen reporters who wanted to get in. An ambulance was nigh, and they were chasing it. It was a mess. Somehow I made it down the plywood-laden tunnel into the Boston dugout.

"Hey, where you been?" Petey said, elbowing me. Her press pass had a dozen autographs on it, and a similarly scratched baseball bulged from her back pocket. She was having a time.

"Dammit, Pete. He collapsed right in front of me. Ossee Schreckengost," I said. As I spoke, the faint sound of the departing ambulance's siren could be heard. I filled her in on what I had witnessed.

"Food poisoning?" Petey suggested.

"Worse than that," I said. "Much worse. Ossee's—ah, shit, he's gone, Petey."

Her expression dropped. She squeezed my arm.

"I'm in no mood for a festival," I said. "Have half a notion to get the hell out of here."

"C'mon, Unk. This is your hour," she urged, tugging at my sleeve like a nine-year-old. She was all health and longevity. "I know how you feel—"

"No, you don't," I said, because young people know nothing about mortality. "You come to these Old-Timers' games to see these birds once again and you forget that it's probably the last time you'll ever see them."

Petey frowned. "Stop it," she said.

Just then our words were interrupted by a commotion in the infield. We looked up to see Buck Freeman, a former player whose chief claim to notoriety was that he had been nuts, prancing into view. Freeman reminded everybody of Jimmy Piersall, the legendary Red Sox manic depressive, in the battiness category. By my yearbook, Freeman was about fifty, but he was still vigorous in his blousy Red Sox uniform. Grinning, chattery, and full of shit, he skipped around the infield in his polished spikes, clopping butts and pulling down visors. He was higher than a kite.

"A man possessed," someone said, and I turned around to see the craggy face of Chick Stahl, an old scribe I used to run into now and then.

"Hope he drops dead," Stahl said blankly, not bothering to say hello.

"Don't say that, Chick," I said, about to inform him of Ossee Schreckengost.

Stahl growled. "They did a bypass on Freeman a couple of years ago and they shoulda killed him then."

"A bypass? He's tearing around like that with a bypass?" I said.

Then Freeman grabbed a fungo and ball and whacked a can of corn out to left that thunked off the Green Monster like a hailstone.

"I could hit these bastards. These hotshots. Call 'em pitchers!" he screamed. "Hit three hunnert blindfolded!"

"Run the bases backwards!" someone shouted.

I turned to see a thick-chested, black-haired young fellow holding a cassette tape player in his outstretched hand in an attempt to record some of Buck Freeman's yelps.

"Jesus, Jake," Chick Stahl grumbled at the guy with the recorder. "My own kid falling for Freeman's crap."

"Huh?" I said.

"Yeah," Stahl replied. "I raise a ballpark rat who turns into a radio jockey. Makes a living talkin' sports. *Talkin'*. Can't write a word."

In the meantime, Buck Freeman was indeed pedaling backward around the bases. It was all wild fun, the fans got a good laugh, and Chick's son, Jake, was getting it all on tape, presumably for a replay on his radio sports show. I marveled at the job of the mechanics who had sutured Buck Freeman's ticker. The chuckles descended from the stands and rippled through the press and players dotting the infield. For the most part, that is. As much as Buck Freeman's antics had always been a diversion, they could not erase what had just happened in the clubhouse to Ossee Schreckengost. Not for me, anyway. I caught the looks of a few of Ossee's old cohorts, and there wasn't a lot of merriment there either.

Just about the time I was going to take a pass on this whole affair, Curt Gowdy stepped to the mike with a script longer than the book of Genesis. The superlatives started flying like "begats" and "thou shalt nots." I had a ribbon in my lapel and had no choice but to pay attention. I was ushered onto the baseline. When it was my turn for kudos, Gowdy rehashed the usual baloney and got most of the facts right. I heard the boos when my Chicago affiliation was noted, and who could blame them? They neglected my best attribute, which is the fact that I've managed to dodge the embalmer all these years. Stick around long enough and everyone forgets his grudge.

But I enjoyed the nod; I'm not above that. I never thought that what I wrote about games would add to the world's store of literature, but it meant a lot to a lot of people. Don't undervalue diversion. And if these folks wanted to throw a bouquet or two my way, well, I'd catch it and smell it. And I savored niece Petey's glow from her perch just behind the dugout, God love her. I tried not to think about my departed Wilma, the good woman who had tended the store when I was away. And Commissioner Grand Chambliss, a good man, sitting in his front-row box, applauded. So I can't debunk the proceedings altogether.

Finally, with a brief but somber mention that Ossee Schreckengost had taken ill in the clubhouse, the game commenced. It did so with pepper and tobacco juice and umpires who called a wide strike zone. The Red Sox opponents were has-beens from a dozen different clubs in both leagues, and there were enough Gaylord Perrys and Dick Allens to put some attention on the opposite dugout. But for the most part it was a Red Sox affair, and the crowd doted on its old Fenway faces, mugs the fans had grown up with. By this time there was a crowd so thick you would have thought it was a playoff game.

You had to hand it to these faithful, for with all the mention of feats and records and derring-do, with all the sepia-toned images and last-minute heroics, with all of this and The Sixth Game too, not once did the man say the word "championship" or point to a World Series ring. For not a soul motoring on the Fenway field this day had ever brought one of those to this park while in Red Sox flannels. But still the fans from South Boston and Framingham and Pawtucket cheered, cheered their lungs out. And how do you like that?

When the game got going, a few old hurlers who once threw smoke burned one in now and then. But mostly they threw batting practice, because the crowd wanted to see the old hitters hit. The trim alumni took their cuts and smacked line drives. Jack Slattery hit a rope to right center and stood up at second, giving everybody a dose of déjà vu. If you had a quarter for everybody who said he could still own the pitchers throwing today, you could play the slots at Atlantic City until you dropped.

There were good-natured collisions and brushback pitches, leaping stabs and plenty of boots. It took no leap of imagination to see that every one of these guys had once had the fluid coordination necessary to be one of those elite athletes who play major-league baseball. That many of them were once trim enough to do it required a greater leap.

The game went on with the usual lack of drama until Lou

Criger came to the plate. I had last seen him sitting next to his partner Ossee Schreckengost in the clubhouse, and I was a bit surprised that he had decided to come out and play after what had happened. But that was Lou Criger. He dug into the box and waved his bat, his expression as rigid as the wad of tabacco in his cheek. His appearance evoked scattered catcalls and mutterings in the crowd, and they reminded me of what Criger meant to these Red Sox fans.

Lou Criger was as lean and austere as Schreckengost was congenial. Still in his forties, he was solid and unsmiling, with dense, dark eyebrows that ran unbroken across his forehead. He was clean-shaven today, and you noticed that, because in his playing days Criger had a mustache as meaty as the Marlboro Man's. Thick and downturned, it matched his demeanor. He always looked like the guy who refuses you a car loan.

Criger had been a scrap-iron catcher but not a big ox, not a wide, oak-legged backstop. His strength was in his hands and arms. He had a peg that he snapped off at his ear and blistered down to second so low a pitcher had to step aside to keep from losing his navel. Criger had played like a snarling rat killer. The plate was his until you moved him off it, and then he made you pay with a shin guard in the chops. A play at home involved a cloud of dust and fists. The guy fought like a pit bull.

I admired that, though I never cared for him personally one way or another until he made that big error in the Series. With two outs in the ninth, Sox ahead in the sixth game and up three games to two, an opposing batter lifted a foul pop fly. Criger got a late start, made a bad read, then stumbled over his mask—and the ball fell in front of him like a contaminated piece of space junk.

He didn't drop it exactly; he just didn't catch it. The crowd gasped, incredulous at opportunity so quickly lost, then clutched its collective throat. It put off going berserk in hopes that the pitcher would simply retire the lucky bum, get the out and end the damn game, and finally bring championship glory to Fenway. But the batter singled, as did the next batter, and the next, and the Red Sox had once again snatched another morbid loss from the jaws of victory. Naturally, they lost the seventh game and the Series the next night.

Criger never did atone for his muff, and after a creditable career, he ultimately left the club with that sour, unforgivable legacy. Still, the stain, the curse, the old Fenway voodoo had not lanced Lou Criger badly enough to keep him away from the premises. The fact was, he had returned to conquer. Ten years out of baseball, Criger had made himself a rich man in the import business. Liquor, spices, electric shavers, just about anything he could get on a boat. And with his money, he had tossed in with Ossee Schreckengost in a bid to snap the Red Sox away from Mrs. Dougherty.

His visibility, many believed, was important if he was to have a chance to buy the club. Another, less charitable, interpretation held that Criger was probably so bitter about the scarlet letter E burned into his sternum that he wanted to buy the Red Sox just to change its name and move it to St. Petersburg. If time cannot expunge the memory—and it cannot—then pack up the evidence and move it south.

With all that running through my noggin, and before the crumbums along the left-field line could tar and feather him, I saw Criger lace a screamer between the outfielders. It smacked the wall on one bounce. Criger could have walked to second— that is, if he could have walked. Instead, he stumbled going around first base, and then dropped to the ground as if the umpire had lassoed his ankles. He rolled once and held not his knee or his foot or some long-ignored string of a muscle in his thigh, but his chest. I swear, he held his chest.

The crowd roared at his fall. People stood up. Infielders rushed to his aid. Alas, he lay there as if he'd been downed by a sniper, his knees pulled up, his arms wrapped around his chest. And just before he was cut off from my view, I spotted a pained, pinched look on his face that I'd seen only once before. Trouble was, I'd seen it only a few minutes earlier, for it was that same horrid mask of pain that Ossee Schreckengost had worn.

And then I myself, decorated scribe, veteran of the ink wars, began to feel queasy. Or maybe it was pure dread, as if I had sensed the reappearance of that hovering devil of death in the ballpark. Fenway Park this time, where I was in the front row. If anyone in the seats as close in as mine did not know that Lou Criger was a bubble away from his maker, then he was shelling a peanut.

I swallowed, stroked my wattles, and caught a look from the commissioner a couple of boxes over. I didn't like what I saw.

—2—
Daily Fee

THAT NIGHT IT BROKE. LOU CRIGER HAD BEEN POISONED, according to news reports. His system had been laced with enough nicotine—*nicotine?*—to bring down a tobacco farmer. I did a double take at the news. Nicotine, that drug central to cigarettes and plugs and snuff, was as plentiful in a baseball park as bubble gum. And yet it was poisonous? I thought of Don Zimmer and Ralph Houk and Luis Tiant and just about three thousand other spitters and wondered why they all had not keeled over on the dugout steps. But that was it: Lou Criger had died from a nicotine overdose.

With Schreckengost, they still were not sure. He had been ailing from a variety of maladies and was on so many medications that the crime lab was working overtime to analyze his juices. But the word on Criger was enough, and in hours Boston became San Francisco during the earthquake series of '89, minus the fissures and the collapsed double-decker highways. Logan Airport bustled with incoming news teams and journeymen reporters. The grubby side streets around Fenway Park were soon clogged with broadcast trucks. The fight for the local ball club was now a national affair. Murder has a way of expanding things.

My phone at the Parker House rang within minutes of the newsbreak on Criger. Commissioner Chambliss was still in town, and he hated it when the Game became undermined by foul play. I knew he wanted to talk daily fee.

While his office has its share of investigators, Chambliss has taken me on from time to time when things got nasty in the clubhouse. I'd done some work for him in Chicago and on the coasts, and he felt comfortable asking me to look into the Fenway mess. I could tell him the baseball side of it, talk to the cops, and if my luck held, mount a case against somebody. My cover was a natural: An old sportswriter could nose around and nobody would think twice about him.

"I'll come to you," Chambliss said. "I like that old Boston inn you're staying at. Maybe we can recite some good poetry."

He was referring, of course, to Lowell, Longfellow, and Whittier, those bards who hung out at the Parker House in the century when rhymers were the rock stars of their day. I marveled: a baseball muckety-muck well aware that this hotel had been a home to poets as well as Irish politicians. Before these back rooms were filled with smoke, they were flooded with meter, and Chambliss appreciated that. Not a bad man to be working for, I told myself.

I had just enough time to gargle before he'd be downstairs. I changed my shirt and put on a bow tie. I slipped a piece of stationery under Petey's door telling her of my doings and suggesting that she join us. She'd gone out on her own to walk around town and I did not know when she'd return.

Chambliss, who never looked good even when he was, looked even worse against the soft glow of the Parker House mahogany. He was noticeably haggard, the glare of the press having hollowed his eyes and weighted his brow. Yesterday he'd swung into Boston from his place on the Cape for a quick few hours of baseball and baloney, and he'd been stuck here ever since. Probably had not brought a change of clothes. His shirt fared badly against the spotless table linen. His blue blazer looked as if a goat had grazed on it.

"I never wear bow ties," he said. "They don't give you anything to spill on."

I gave him that one and draped an arm on his shoulders as we were led to a corner table. Grand needed all the privacy and moral support he could get. He didn't need the fracas that was the commissioner's job. He could retire on his CDs and spend his time fishing for bluefin on Cape Cod Bay. Instead he fought the sharks looking to feed off baseball's latest carcasses.

Now, I knew Chambliss from his days in Chicago when he was a rich bean trader with a baseball jones. He was one of those American League zealots, the kind who remembers where he was when Williams hit the three-run homer to win the '41 All-Star Game. The fact that Chambliss, a shrewd, hard-nosed guy, was hired on as commissioner when baseball was amok with cocaine, gambling, and umpire's strikes was a turn of fate that the paying fan is blessed with now and then. He never felt comfortable in Manhattan, much less on Park Avenue, which is where they locate the office itself, but he fit into the job like a hand into a glove. A boxing glove or a rubber one, take your pick.

A cross between Judge Kenesaw Mountain Landis and Happy Chandler, with a touch of Bart Giamatti thrown in, Chambliss ran baseball like a good dog handler heels a mutt. The owners who belonged on used-car lots resented him and wanted to fire him. The ones who knew the business of baseball—and who also would not feel out of place on a used-car lot—knew they had a keeper and let him do his job.

The only thing he did not expect was that his tenure would involve murders in the ballpark.

"I was reading the curio cabinets out in the lobby," he said. "Did you know Ho Chi Minh was a busboy here and Malcolm X was a waiter? How do you like that?"

"Amazing . . . and it's only been here since 1854," I said.

"I bet those commies stole a lot of flatware," he said.

What could I say to that?

"Hey, where's your beauty—my sweetheart?" he asked.

"Went out before you called. Left her a note to come down and sup with us," I said.

"She's on the payroll, I hope."

"You couldn't keep her off."

"Good. She's a damn fine operative and she keeps you jumpin'. You're lucky to have her."

"The advantages of a niece," I said. "You can treat her like the daughter you never had. But when she gets obnoxious you can say she was raised wrong."

Grand began buttering a Parker House roll. He'd do me next.

He grunted, chewed, stared into the tablecloth, and scowled. He'd had too many catered dinners, too much room service. He needed a hot towel on the pores.

"This one really stinks, Duffy," he offered. "Not even a toss-up. Two guys bidding for a ball club and they get whacked quicker than you can say proxy fight—"

"One guy. We don't know about Ossee," I said.

"Don't matter. What matters is it happened right in front of me, goddammit. Couldn't have been more of a spectacle than if it'd been at Cooperstown. Hell, I'm a *witness*. I'll have to talk to the cops! Some bastard has the guts to goose me while I'm sitting in the front row eating peanuts like a mope."

"Hey, how do think I feel?" I said. "They were honoring me, for cryin' out loud."

"It's the amoral shit I don't like, Duf. Comes straight from the boardroom. Wall Street. The bottom-line crowd. Dammit, I hate that phrase. Take your Trumps and Millkens and Boeskys; they're all saying 'Greed is good.' Like it's the same as 'Take one and hit to right.' Common thieves, if you ask me, Duffy. Like Veeck used to say, 'All the stealing comes from the guys with the pencils.' Or something like that."

"How much do you know about the franchise mess?" I asked.

"I got a file full of reports, but you can bet that's all obsolete now. My pipeline is full of leaks. That's why I want you to tear into this. Haunt every bastard who's making a run for the club. Find out where his money's coming from. You were always good at the front-office beat."

"Because nobody else on the sports page was paying any attention to it," I said.

"Well, they are now. Work your sources, Duf. It frosts my ass to think that one of these jagoffs decided to get rid of the competition."

He tore another roll apart.

"Find out how desperate Patsy Dougherty is," he said.

"Aw, don't even suggest that, Grand," I said, and too quickly.

"Have to," he said. "She's one of four women owners—I'd call 'em ladies, Duf, being from the old school—but these ain't no ladies. I know Patsy—hell, she eats me alive in the league meetings. She plays hardball, Duf, don't think she doesn't."

I swallowed.

"She may be tough, Grand," I said, "but that doesn't make her ruthless."

Chambliss grunted. By this time he was faced with the exquisite pastry of a beef Wellington. He cut into it and the meat shone with a perfect shade of rare. The aroma made you want to buy land in Montana. I toyed with sea scallops rinsed with a sauce of dill. They were good—the Atlantic waters seldom fail—but my palate wasn't in them. I coveted the red meat.

"It's the cutthroat kind of thinking that's come right through the turnstiles, Duf," Chambliss went on. "Front offices are salted with guys who think a gentleman's agreement doesn't rule out a dagger in the back. Anything goes. Buy low, sell high, or kill the sonuvabitch who's in your way.

"Commissioner of baseball, right? My job's reduced to dealing with the men in the gray flannel suits. And all their 'of counsels.' They're my bosses. Hell, what I'd give to have Veeck and Finley and Calvin Griffith and all those whirlybirds back in the cockpits. They were a lot more of the genuine article than the franchisers we've got around now."

I couldn't add to that or argue with it. Chambliss had said it all while ravaging his entrée. And I think the words ruined the taste. He ignored the baby carrots.

"Two guys want to buy a ball club and somebody laces the chewing tobacco with rat poison," he mumbled. "So get 'im, Duffy. Get the bastards."

Wherever Petey had gone that night, it didn't bring her back in time to join us. Grand and I sat too long and let the waiter talk us into far too many brandies.

"People don't drink anymore," Chambliss said, and then contradicted himself.

I stayed even with him, something I shouldn't have done. When it came time to pry my fingers off the snifter, bid adieu, and get up to the room, I staggered. The elevator buttons were heat-sensitive, and my fumes set them off.

Petey roused me early the next morning and we set off for the ballpark to get caught up. From a block away we could see the fuss. News crews, reporters, and people with nothing better to do had converged on Fenway. You couldn't step off a curb without tripping over a cable. Surly guys swung cameras so close to the back of your head that your hair stood up from the breeze. Or they just out-and-out ran into you without so much as a grunt. I never did like the equipment jockeys—the roustabouts of journalism—and I liked them even less now.

But Chambliss had me in the middle of it, among hundreds of reporters and newsreaders lurching and darting like a dizzy school of fish. It soon became obvious to me that none of them was getting much more than the plain-as-the-ripe-tomato-in-your-face story that had one, maybe two guys dead of poison. And nobody officially knew the details, the source of the toxin or the method of delivery. I certainly didn't.

If my niece and partner, Petrinella, felt similarly empty, she gave no sign. She was glad to hop into the subway and go from scratch. Petey is one of those self-starters, a young woman with more perk than a rabbit and gifted with the same speed. If she knew depression, it wasn't on a first-name basis. She was, in the words of reviewers, almost too good to be true. And I wasn't about to tamper with her chemistry.

Still, her zeal at the thump of a body in an alley irked my chops a little. It made me downright queasy to see the stomach she had for this thing, the glee, her eyes widening with anticipation of a murder probe when the bodies had yet to release their final shudders. Not that Petey was jumping out of character, for she had similarly thrived on the Wrigley Field homicide; and she had dug into the Dodger Stadium mess like a terrier in a rat hole.

But there was not much to be gained outside the ballpark that morning. Red Sox officials equivocated into the cluster of microphones and said nothing. I suggested we retreat back to the hotel. Petey, however, wanted to hover around the news conference and pick up what she could. When she disappeared into the pack, I left the area and wandered. I went left when I should have gone right, cracked a few doors, and before I knew it I was in the open space of an empty Fenway. I walked in and sat down in a blue seat just behind third base.

Like every visitor to Fenway Park, I gazed out to my left at the famous Green Monster, the Wall. There is nothing like the silence of the Wall in the morning. Brooding like a medieval redan over a shallow left field. It is a seamless expanse, lightly pocked, a flat ocean, a broad-backed target. And the screen above, its tip sixty feet and six inches from the earth, sways like a temptress in the breeze. Even to the hiss of Mass Pike traffic just yards away beneath Brookline Avenue, the wall is a barrier. Silence.

The sun over the right-field roof was warming the grandstands, those bays of navy and red seats that feel as old as the game itself. Seats? No, pews, for I was sitting in the chapel called Fenway, the sacred cathedral of the profane Red Sox. Scattered among the seats, I noticed, were several other supplicants and soreheads partaking of the communion of clubhouse coffee and chaws of Red Man.

They were sitting hodgepodge in the seats behind the Sox dugout along first base, staring out over the empty park and into the yaw of the Wall, seeing drives they'd lifted themselves, some caroming, some carrying over the big partition. They chattered and quipped and groused among themselves, telling exaggerated stories of Pinky and Cronin, Flaggy, Dom and Spoke. Hundreds of games, countless innings, careers.

Their reverie was occasionally interrupted by the sod crew tending the playing surface, crosscutting the rich, tight grass, hosing and raking the clay. But for now the boys sat in the morning light in their navy windbreakers and caps, rubbing gnarled knuckles and liver spots. They were old men who needed no passes to get in. You play for the Red Sox, for the late Mr. Yawkey, and you don't need no stinking passes.

Now, Boston has the Garden, that elegant barn of parquet, the rafters hung with Celtic-green banners. And who can deny Red Auerbach's victory cigar, the black-sneakered grace of Cousy, Russell, Havlicek, Bird? Then pull the floor in favor of ice, and they've got the memory of Bobby Orr, a pucksman as good as any. Add their Marathon, I suppose, the run that gives this city a name for a day, like the race cars do Indianapolis, and while I doubt there are two Americans walking side by side on a given afternoon who can come up with a winner's name, it's a hell of a jog. Then there are the Harvard scullers cutting the Charles. One time their coach made the cover of *Sports Illustrated,* and wake me when *that* happens again.

Which is to signify that if you root in Boston, Hub City of New England, seedbed of the Revolution, you've felt the glow of victory fires, chirped, pranced, and gloated over those sweet but fleeting triumphs that made your Beantown boys the best in the land. And the bells of St. Stephen's pealed.

Yet the true glory and triumph on the playing fields of Boston is shrouded by Fenway.

Fenway.

This Back Bay bandbox. Baseball's oyster. The well of prose and poem for the Harvard scriveners. Open for heartbreak in 1912, which would have been a notable debut if the S.S. *Titanic* had not sunk nearer my God to thee on the same day. Creaky, columned, patched—why, it had fires in the grandstands—a park

where Babe Ruth once wore Red Sox colors. Babe: the kid southpaw with no equal. Not the waddling Babe of the home run, but
the gnarly, muscled kid pitcher, six-two and one hundred ninety-
five pounds, an Adonis of nineteen when he broke in here.

In five full seasons after that, the young Ruth won eighty-
nine games with a Red Sox uniform on his back. Then Harry
Frazee, a New York guy, struck an iceberg and sold young Ruth
for a sum equivalent, in the minds of Hub fans, to thirty pieces
of silver. And in the ensuing years, Fenway has been a cruel
temple. Cursed. For in no other house of baseball since 1918 has
a single team striven so desperately and failed so often, won so
many sixth games, gotten so close to the winner's roses and pulled
out thorns.

"Not so, Boston" reads forward and backward, as Mr. Angell
sadly devised. The Cardinals, the Indians, the Reds, the Mets—
it has not mattered who sat in the visitors' dugout. For somehow
the opponent has stolen, stitched, leaked, or squeezed out enough
sap from the Red Sox, usually from one immortal goat who hesitated or booted or misjudged, at *the* crucial moment and snatched
the cup. Every New England fan knows the details as well as he
knows the words to "Paul Revere's Ride." One if by Pesky, two if
by Buckner . . .

Fenway. A Boston ballyard named not after a beer baron but
a fancy swamp. A *fen.* Now that's a word you don't hear much
nowadays. The English coined it for the marshland, which they
have in certain parts of their country. So when the Brahmins of
Boston, being partial to the Brits before the Massacre and Tea
Party business changed their minds, were laying out some park-
land off the Charles River Basin in an area of town called Back
Bay, they dubbed the parks "Emerald Necklace" and named the
centerpiece the Fens. They made it as pretty an area of ponds
and park as you will find in any city. The road around it is called
the Fenway. Naturally, when Red Sox owner John Taylor built a
new ballyard there in 1912, he said it should be called Fenway
Park.

Now, if you're not fond of that Jersey Street brick pile, then
the Old North Church and *Old Ironsides* don't do much for you
either. Me? I'm partial to Fenway for a few reasons, not the least
of which is that it is one of those scrap-iron parks built in the
middle of a quirky city full of fickle streets running every which
way. Throw in the pinch and squeeze of the rail yards and the

meander of the Charles River, and you end up with a ballyard shaped like no other.

But everybody knows that. Just as everybody knows of the Green Monster, that wall only 315 feet away in left field. Did I say wall? That's no wall. That's a temptress, sucker's bait, a heavyweight's unprotected chin just waiting for a hard right. It's also a myth, something Homer would have cooked up in the *Odyssey* if he'd played in our league instead of the Aegean circuit.

But there I go again, calling in metaphors like a poet, an Updike, an Angell—those Ivy League birds who have strung more pretty words together on Fenway and the Red Sox than Melville did on whales. They're good, I won't deny that, even if they wrote in the comfort of a woodburning fireplace instead of the rush of a deadline. And the Red Sox supplied them with enough tears to sop the prose and enough sorrow to summon the invective of Jonathan Edwards. Hub fans, indeed, have long languished in the hands of an angry God.

Much of my affection for Fenway goes way back to a humiliating day in my Chicago boyhood. I was playing a match of wall ball, one of those homemade competitions devised for the crowded, claustrophobic brick and concrete alleys of my old West Side Chicago neighborhood. This game was stickball without a stick. We bounced a rubber ball off the walls and pavement and translated the bounces and caroms into scores. There were about eight of us, including a kid named Billy O'Connell, who was a hard guy and who went after a catch and knocked me on my butt.

"On yer duff!" O'Connell hooted, and everybody got a big horse laugh out of it. And I was tagged Duffy House from then on. To hell with them. I could live with it then, and I have ever since.

Yet I soon came to savor the tag with the discovery of something in faroff Fenway Park called Duffy's Cliff. I read about it in the sports pages, the holy writ of my youth. Duffy's Cliff was what they called the ten-foot grassy incline in Fenway's left field that led up to the wall. It was named for a peach of an outfielder named Duffy Lewis who negotiated the slope like a mountain goat. From 1910 to 1917 he played alongside Tris Speaker and Harry Hooper in the Fenway pastures, and there wasn't a fleeter trio of outfielders in either league. Duffy Lewis's job was made much more difficult by the cliff and the wall, and he made a science out of it. Others, particularly fielders for visiting squads such as the White Sox, were no match. Fat Fothergill, who, with his 230 pounds, put in only a single season in Fenway, once tripped and rolled down it like a runaway barrel.

I mightily enjoyed the idea of a piece of big-league turf with my name on it, even if it lasted only until 1934, when some genius leveled it. To this day I cannot look at left field in Fenway Park without considering my cliff.

If you look over to right, you see the big red retired numbers hung on the roof's facade—9 4 1 8—the digits made immortal by Williams, Cronin, Doerr, and Yastrzemski. The crybabies of Fenway like to point out that the numbers can be read to mean September 4, 1918—the day Babe Ruth clinched the last Red Sox pennant to turn into a World Championship. Well, it's a nice thought but it's baked beans. Babe clinched the pennant against Philadelphia on August 31, and he won two games of the World Series against the Cubs on September 5 and 9, not the fourth. But yes, 1918 was the last time Boston hugged a World Championship, an undeniable but overplayed fact you learn almost from the moment you snatch your first breath of Atlantic coast air.

Now I live and pursue my emeritus status in Chicago, home of a team that has not won baseball's grand garland since 1908, so I know a little bit about longsuffering. And while I'll remind them that they are not alone, I will grant Boston fans their travails. After that solid win in 1918, in which the Red Sox beat the Cubs in six games, it was the beginning of the end for the scarlet hose.

Despite the World Championship, owner Harry Frazee was desperate for money. He got it by selling the meat of his roster: Ernie Shore, Duffy Lewis, and Dutch Leonard all went to the Yankees. He kept Ruth, but not for long; in 1920, Frazee sold him for $125,000, an astounding sum in those days, to Jacob Ruppert and the hated New York Yankees. He was so broke that he also begged a $300,000 loan out of Ruppert, using Fenway Park as collateral. Consider this: Had things continued to go bust for Frazee, the Yankees would have owned the House of the Red Sox.

There was not a fellow sitting there with me that morning who did not know all that. Did not ruminate about it from time to time with the dew still on the outfield grass. I looked around and recognized a few of them. Then I spotted one I certainly recognized. It was Pesky, of course, because Fenway *is* Johnny Pesky, né John Paveskovich, sitting just behind the Sox dugout and working on the day's first chaw of Red Man. He was alone and thinking his own thoughts, looking out at shortstop, which was once his.

Others lounged nearby, mostly stadium guys and a few smart kids from the organization who enjoyed the pluck of the geezers and wanted to be within earshot. Might pick up something. Might consider the fact that it didn't all start with them. I knew a few of them, like Don Fitzhue, the clubhouse man, who went back pretty darn far himself. And John Kelly, the club lawyer; Joe Rooney, the groundskeeper. Bring Yawkey down among them, in the flesh instead of the spirit, which never left the place even after he passed on, maybe sneak Megaphone Lolly Hopkins into her seat on the aisle, and you'd have Red Sox sentiment thicker than the smell of sausages on Lansdowne Street.

I could feel it as I sat there, minding my own business, hearing the ticks and sighs of the old brickyard as it warmed in the sun. It was a privilege. And for a brief moment, yesterday's treachery in Fenway dissolved in my reverie.

—— 3 ——
The Widow Dougherty

TAKE THE SALEM WITCH-HUNT—LITTLE ANN PUTNAM AND friends pointing their Puritan fingers at those presumed possessed and bringing a noose down on nineteen necks—and Lizzie Borden; don't forget Sacco and Vanzetti, the Boston Strangler, Albert DeSalvo, Chappaquidick, and then that recent business where the Stuart kid shot his pregnant wife and then jumped off the Harvard Bridge when his game was up. All right, take all that and smother it with some grilled onions and green peppers, add some New England treachery and some Beacon Hill money, the soft grass and sifted clay of the ballyard, and you have the Boston stew that was the Fenway murders.

Now Boston, from that day in 1849 when Professor Webster skulled Dr. Parkman with a piece of kindling, has always been a good murder town. Killings get good press here, almost as good as baseball. Put the two together and the Beantown news dogs have a hell of a bone. The deaths had moved the tabloid *Herald* to blaze three-inch headlines and the grim *Globe* to banner the story on its front page. The deceased had been partners in a hostile franchise bid, and they had died within minutes and yards of each other. You could almost hear the media rubbing their collective palms together.

That Criger and Schreckengost had been murdered, not simply struck down by a bad batch of mayonnaise and too much Red

Man, caused this midsummer story to explode. Reporters and camera crews from all over the nation descended on Boston like cannibals on a thigh.

At the same time, I intended to meet my previous commitments. At three that afternoon I was scheduled to scale high tea with Patsy Dougherty. It was no surprise to me that Petey wanted to come along.

"Beacon Hill . . . I want a taste," she said. Petey always did have a palate for the social plate. Don't get me wrong—she was much too feisty for the Junior League circuit, but she could play at it. Dabble, wear a string of pearls, sip the sherry, get under their well-manicured cuticles.

At midafternoon we were on the busy Boston sidewalks for our visit to Beacon Street. On the way I told Petey what I knew about Mrs. Dougherty and the family fortune. While she was generally identified by her husband's name, Patsy was no chorine who sneaked in the boudoir door. She was an Adams, *that* Adams, as in not only Sam and John but Abigail, the country's first strong and influential first lady. Indeed, Patsy Adams Dougherty's blood was as blue as the sea her ancestors had crossed on the *Mayflower*.

Tom Dougherty, her husband, on the other hand, had inherited an Irish whiskey fortune that went back as far as Shays' Rebellion. By any accounting, he was a gentleman bootlegger not unlike some guy named Joe Kennedy, but nobody seemed to mind that. Not after his booze profits afforded him the Red Sox, a moribund franchise if there ever was one in the late twenties, which he had done a creditable job of rebuilding.

Dougherty's real catch, however, was Patsy Adams, a summa cum laude Smith grad who had forsaken the models' runway and the cover of *Vanity Fair* in favor of a desk at Houghton Mifflin, publishers here in town. She gave instant class to Tom's operation, both personal and professional. She was also a dish, a blonde with Carole Lombard looks, a trophy on Dougherty's elbow. They made a handsome couple and for decades were a fixture in Boston society. As a bonus, their kids were toothy and well-bred, and somehow managed not to embarrass the clan with drug busts or midnight debaucheries on the Cape.

It was Patsy Dougherty's personal style that made it all work.

She was part Eleanor Roosevelt, part Jackie Kennedy, a champion of everything from the public library—she raised $8 million to restock its shelves—to the Public Gardens. She put money and effort into charity, and actually looked as if she enjoyed visiting sick kids and homeless dogs. The lady had unadulterated charm, the pundits said, and a smile that withered curmudgeons. When slings and arrows came her way, however, she recoiled with New England tartness, occasionally penning crisp, pithy replies to her critics in the *Globe*.

Tom, good old Tom, meanwhile, ran the Red Sox for better or worse. He hired good baseball men to oversee the player side of things, and the Red Sox showed well. Didn't win, but showed well. Patsy was visible at Fenway, but she never let it appear as if she were a cog in the front office. "What I know about baseball you could put in a bowl of drawn butter," she once said. Most figured she was fibbing, but they liked the image anyway.

When Dougherty died a few years ago, however, Patsy didn't hesitate a minute. She took over as CEO of the Red Sox and ran the ball club, making the big decisions and delegating the small ones to guys like Ossee Schreckengost. Hers was the proverbial iron fist inside the velvet glove.

Patsy's biggest job, however, was to deal with the onslaught of Red Sox suitors upon her husband's death. Suitors may be the wrong word, for in Patsy Dougherty's eyes, and in those of Bostonians pledged to keep the Red Sox in the family, the would-be buyers were predators. Their advances were possible because Tom had not planned for his death as far as the Internal Revenue Service was concerned and also because the Doughertys, it turned out, did not own the franchise outright. With Tom's demise and Patsy's increasing age, there were factions among minority owners who wanted to entertain bids for the club. It was rumored that Patsy's children also wanted her to sell. But the good widow was having none of it. She did not say "over my dead body," but she came close.

I reprised all that, more or less, in the time it took Petey and me to hoof over to where the widow lived. The Dougherty domicile on Beacon spoke of ancient courtliness and symmetry with finely cut stone, a multicolored tile roof, gargoyles at the downspouts, and pilasters at the corners. Petey and I paused briefly to take in the edifice.

"Holy landed gentry," she said.

We were let in by a pleasant young woman who looked more like a resident than an employee. We gawked at the high ceilings, the jade, and the Persian rugs as we followed the young lady into a study. Its leaded-glass door and rich oak woodwork was outdone by an ebony Steinway grand piano poised in the corner. There was sheet music on it, and I was transported to my Aunt Elsie's home in Evanston, the cultural haven of my youth, and the sound of a Chopin prelude emanating like a dream from the keys.

The creak of an errant floorboard brought me to, and Patsy Dougherty appeared.

"Hello there again!" she sang, and swept in on both of us.

This time she was a two-handed greeter, and her warmth seemed genuine. I flashed back to our brief encounter in the Red Sox clubhouse the day before, and I liked this one better. The lady looked wonderful: tall, remarkably erect for a woman of my vintage, clear-eyed and smiling, with a thick and still very blonde head of hair. It was an expensive tint job, as the promotion went, but she was worth it.

I sustained my hold on her hand as I took in the view, and then in a move uncharacteristic to the point of being out-of-body, I upped her knuckles to my lips and kissed them. It was a wonderful, succulent moment. If my gesture seemed out of the ordinary to Mrs. Dougherty, her expression gave absolutely no indication of it.

She smiled. "Your professional reputation, Mr. House, falls short of the whole story."

My mind raced with the statement, for my reputation as a lady-killer had gone the way of Tristram Speaker, and when Petey chortled—a slovenly display, I might add, and I would talk to her later—I decided Patsy was speaking of my writing.

She wore a short-sleeved, belted linen dress of a crisp ivory hue. A simple gold chain accentuated her long, aristocratic neck. It was the skin of that neck, however, that swayed me, for it was as delicate and textured as that of a girl. I am a sucker for lovely skin, skin sprinkled with a few freckles. Add a whisper of fine, downy hair here and there, at the edge of the lips, near the ear lobes, or the small of the back, and I am reduced to jelly. I long thought that particular feminine allure would fade with my advancing age, that it was a young man's fetish. But that has not been the case, alas, and Patsy Dougherty, a magnificent-looking woman, brought it once again to my surface.

"Uncle Duffy!" Petey was saying, and I snapped my head to her.

I'd apparently been away, and she gave me a look she normally reserves for produce managers who fondle the mangoes.

"Is tea preferred, Uncle Duffy?" Mrs. Dougherty asked.

I nodded. She could have offered me Gatorade and I'd have nodded.

"And do call me Duffy," I said. "Uncle's a formal term I prefer only with those too young to remember Ellis Kinder."

Petey snarled. We followed Mrs. Dougherty's lead and sat down on leather wingback chairs. Mine was situated alongside Patsy's, and we leaned shoulders toward each other like two old-timers in a private club. Petey sat across the way, which is where she belonged.

The room was not large, and it reeked of an opulent and tasteful coziness. There was an oil painting of oyster gatherers in the harbor that I would have hung in my living room in a minute. I half expected James Russell Lowell, and Amy and Robert for that matter, to come through the walls. Patsy crossed her legs above her knees, revealing gams every bit as impressive as the rest of her patrician carriage. I tried not to stare, fearing I would make a fool of myself. Nor did I dare look in Petey's direction, but I felt her stare in the side of my neck like a shrimp fork. There was a regal air about Patsy Dougherty; and genuine ladies, I must admit, have always exerted some unnamed force over this shantytown duffer.

"I said I'm devastated by what happened yesterday. The day was ruined," Patsy said. "It was dreadful."

I simply nodded like a mope. From the cut of her glare, Petey was just about ready to get up and slap me around.

"Ossee collapsed right in front of me," I quickly recovered. "He was in bad shape."

"He'd been eating, hadn't he . . . ?" she said.

"If you remember, we all were eating," I said.

"John Kelly, our lawyer, told me they think Ossee had a massive attack. Maybe a stroke. That does not sound like it came from something he ate," she went on. She was obviously agitated. She rubbed her hands together in her lap. I had the feeling she had gone through this many times before we got here.

"I'm no doctor," I said.

"And Criger had this nicotine poison, whatever that's about," she said. "Why, it looked like he'd been shot—how he went down like that! It was a horrible sight."

"What do the police tell you?" I asked.

"Nothing. They've been very coy."

"It's quite a coincidence, Criger and Schreckengost, if you know what I mean. . . ." I said.

"And *only* a coincidence," she quickly added.

By this time the tea had arrived on a tray that also held a dark bottle.

"Madeira?" she said, her tone of voice suddenly brightening. She poured a touch of the wine into a trio of small glasses. It was a nice touch.

Patsy sighed.

"This on top of all the rumor and innuendo," she said. "The papers were already making a circus out of the whole thing before yesterday even happened. Don't tell me those men weren't trying to take the club away from me, Duffy! And the Red Sox will remain in the Dougherty family, I might add."

"Why is there even a fight for the team?" Petey interjected.

"Because our lawyers handled Tom's affairs badly and we had estate problems," she replied. "And because we have minority ownership. That was Tom's way of rewarding old friends, who now have a lot to gain if the club is sold. And, finally, Miss Biggers, because some people don't think I should be the owner of the Red Sox. Welcome to Boston."

Her tone could have etched glass.

"Do you really *want* to own them?" I asked.

"Why—!" she sputtered. Then she caught herself and actually chuckled. "I'm very comfortable over on Yawkey Way, thank you. Good people work for me and I know how to let them do their jobs."

"Like Ossee Schreckengost?" I asked. I had to ask because I knew the former manager had been a favorite of hers before he aligned himself with Lou Criger.

She uncrossed her legs and reached for a cookie.

"I miss Ossee dearly," she said, as if she she were describing a poodle. "I wish he'd never left us. He was being used, you know.

He worked for me and that made him an invaluable resource to anyone who came after the club. Invaluable."

"Like Criger?" I asked.

"I don't have to tell you. Criger would have done anything to get the Red Sox, so help me," she said. She lowered her cup from her lips. "Anything. People don't realize that. He could taste it, and he was using Ossee and what money Ossee had and anything else he could think of to get at me. I could tell you stories. If I have an exposed nerve, you've touched it."

"But he wasn't the only bidder," I said.

She sniffed.

"He was the worst of the bunch. I know what he'd do with the Red Sox. Knock down Fenway Park, for one thing. Probably sell the label right off the uniform to every fast deal that came down the Turnpike. He was a crass, devious man, Duffy."

She finished off her tea, put down her cup, and looked me right in the eye.

I took pause before I replied.

"Words like that, Mrs. Dougherty, will turn you into a suspect," I said.

"Of course!" she replied. "But I wouldn't have touched Ossee, the dear. I feel so bad for Marilyn."

"Tell me—I'm thinking out loud here—is there anybody in town who disliked Criger as much as you did?"

"Not too many, because I really *loathed* the man," she said. "But who are we kidding? A lot of people don't want to see his group get anywhere near the Red Sox. So is that what it's come to nowadays? People kill each other over a baseball team?"

"Greed and ambition," I offered. "Even Shakespeare appreciated them as motives."

"How about Jack Slattery?" Petey asked.

Patsy made a face. "Jack you have to know to appreciate. He never got over the fact that people stopped cheering for him when he wasn't playing baseball. He can't cope with that. I think he's trying to buy the team because it might give him some satisfaction in life. He doesn't really have any, you know. He sells beer, but he doesn't like the stuff."

I had the feeling she could have gone on for hours. She knew as much about the Red Sox and the fraternity of club owners and would-be owners as anybody we were likely to talk to. She spoke with a deliberate ease, with an almost poetic lilt to her speech.

Here was a lady truly to the manner born—if any Americans are. With my tongue of clipped journalese flapping like a noisy air conditioner, I felt like a piker. Her elegance reminded me of another graceful lady, a woman named Wilma who had given me a measure of civility and spruce for forty years.

". . . You know," Patsy was saying, "as corny as it sounded, Tom always said we didn't really own the Red Sox. Not any more than we could own the Old North Church. We just keep it in trust. He said that a lot."

Her voice softened with that. It was the kind of soft you'd want to go soft on you.

"So," she resumed. "We've talked enough about that. And it's not why I asked you to dawdle over tea."

She turned and brought her knees closer to mine. She smiled, a smile that put all the talk of franchise fights and murder as distant as the cheap seats. For a moment I thought she even winked. No, I'm certain of it.

Petey smiled too, I noticed. She was going to school on Mrs. Dougherty.

"We didn't think we'd be one-dimensional today, did we?" Patsy said. "You see, Duffy, I'm writing my memoirs. I'm actually doing it. Pen to paper, every day just as religiously as P. D. James, whom I love. And what I really covet is your input, Mr. Hall of Fame sportswriter. I've always loved your work, Duffy. I've been moved by it. And it occurred to me how wonderful it would be to apply your sharp eye and your good ear to my ungainly prose. Like a consulting editor? How does that strike you?"

As she said it she dropped her hand on my forearm and looked at me with a pair of suitor's eyes. I could hardly concentrate, hardly consider, hardly entertain a proposal that struck me as so preposterous, so silly, so unworkable. It was as if I had been asked to shape up Harvard's scullers.

"Of course," I blurted.

Petey coughed and nearly lurched out of her chair. Had any tea been in her cup it would have splashed onto the Persian rug. She kept coughing and sputtering, a shabby cover, for what did she expect? Mrs. Patsy Dougherty, the loveliest lady I had encountered in too long a time, a woman with a comic arch to her eyebrows and a neckline as soft as a whisper, had just asked me to be her consort. This would not be the last of my visits to this home. There would be times when I would be called to lean over her shoulder, my cheek inches from hers, and peruse her script. We would talk and linger.

I am not sure, but I think I swooned.

On the way home Petey said, "You could use a cold shower, Unk. I've never seen you like that before."

"It's been a while," I said.

"Hubba, hubba," she said.

—4—
Berkeley Street

Not even a drop-everything, round-the-clock, top-shelf assignment from the commissioner, my only but demanding client, could sway me from my appointed rounds. At noon a Kiwanis bunch in Braintree had a place setting with my name on it, and a chapter of the Baseball Writers of America wanted me to yammer with them at one of their overpriced meetings in a downtown sports bar. I told them I never went near those places, and they told me to come anyway. In my emeritus and celebrated state, my dance card was clogged.

That meant Petey had to fend for herself in the initial stages of this assignment, something she did easily. From the antique writing table in her nobly furnished room in the Parker House—which adjoined mine in a setup fit for Brahmins instead of the Houses—she plied the phone and cajoled her way through the bureaucracy of the police department and the medical examiner's office in order to find out whom she could tap for the skinny on the late Ossee Schreckengost and the later Lou Criger.

She was good at it, a phone mechanic with the ability to spread the clout of the office of the commissioner of baseball around like jam. After the better part of an hour she had a couple of names to seek out.

"I'm off, Unk."

"Where to?"

"Cop H.Q. On Berkeley Street. The morgue's at Boston City Hospital, but I don't think I have to go there. I'll leave the cold cuts for you. I should get what we need from the detectives."

"You got your bearings?"

"No sweat. Boston's a small town, Unk. The cowpaths they turned into streets don't seem to follow sometimes, but the worst that can happen is I'll get lost. Then I'll learn something."

She needed me like a player's agent needs an ego.

"Keep good notes," I said. "Fill me in and don't leave anything out."

"I'm your eyes and ears, Uncle Duffy, your shining emissary in the grubby halls of government."

"Just don't act up and don't fall in love," I said.

I shouldn't have added the latter. Petey, who had a heart, threw a measured look back at me.

"What are your instincts on this?" I asked.

"Murder for hire, Unk. Probably the nastiest we've run up against. A pro with a contract."

"In the ballpark, Pete? What with access problems for one thing, and all the witnesses? You couldn't move without a thousand eyes on you out there yesterday."

"That's the point. So many people running around, nobody pays attention to anything. Take a look at the pass list. Six pages long, according to the P.R. office. They let every Tom, Dick and Dan Rather in from Bangor, Maine, to cover this thing. And the shooter—"

"The shooter?"

"Okay, the *lacer* knows that. He cons an I.D. and gets right up close to these guys without either one of them suspecting anything. Think about it: It's a lot easier than ambushing them on a dark street or putting a charge in the Mercedes."

"How soon can we see the pass list?"

"I'm counting on you for that," she said. "But who knows that the guy didn't get in with the grounds crew or the vendors? Maybe slipped security a double sawbuck. It doesn't take much if you got the balls, Unk."

"Listen to you . . ."

"I'm serious. Say all you will about security nowadays but you still get gate-crashers all the time. You get kooks sipping champagne at the Inaugural Ball or sitting next to Dustin Hoffman at the Oscars. Look at Morganna with her knockers and her hair from hell and still she gets in the box seats and gives Clemens a kiss on the mound in the first inning. Security never touches her.

"Shoot, Uncle Duffy, I knew a kid in college who made a bet with his frat-rat friends that he'd get on national TV during the Kentucky Derby. The Derby, right? So what does he do but hop the fence the night before and hide in the bushes around the final turn, and when the horses head for the wire, out he jumps and moons America."

"You made that one up."

"I swear every word is true. And you know I'm right. You know how many times you look around the infield or in the press box and you say, 'Who in the hell is *that* guy?' So I say, whacking these guys during an exhibition game that's pretty loosy-goosy in the first place is perfect. It's inspired. We may be dealing with genius here, Unk. We should be flattered."

With that she was up and stuffing her things into an oversized purse. Her red hair was pulled back for less wind resistance, and she wore a look that bordered on theft by deception. I trusted Petey implicitly. She was blood, the finest fruit of my sister's loins, and a good kid. Add to that the fact that she had saved my neck in recent capers, and there wasn't much she couldn't get away with around me. And she knew that, dammit. Dressed in snug, bleached blue jeans and a pair of unconscionably expensive running shoes, a cotton top with a splash of silk-screened color on the front, her neck ringed with a thread of gold, she slid out the door.

"Catch you later," she said.

Petey had no trouble finding the fine old stone building on Berkeley that is the cog of Boston's police department. As she was to relate to me that night, dozens of other reporters and legmen were ahead of her, clamoring in the dim light and marble of the lobby like extras in a disaster movie. Which did not count the ones who were dogging cops at old Station Six in South Boston or at the D.A.'s office on Court Street or out at District Four, the Back Bay Station. Where there was a flatfoot, there was a newsie looking for a crumb.

Among the media downtown, each digger said he had an appointment with some honcho upstairs, and each one was shuttled off to the overflowing press room by the uniformed cops at the front desk. The cops all seemed to be named Kelly and lingered a year or two away from a pension and regular pinochle derbies. They smoked Camels and wore I-seen-it-all looks as polished as their badges. No matter if you came from a network or a weekly shopper in Natick, the Kellys replied to your insistent query with a Boston-Irish brogue and the back of their hand.

Petey gauged the hubbub and tried an end run, but a Kelly got her before she could get into an elevator.

"Hold on there, Red," he said. "Nobody goes up."

"I'm here with the blessings of Lieutenant Hughes," she said, invoking the name of the head of homicide.

"Join the crowd," Kelly said.

She moved to her next name on the list.

"Okay, then it's Parent. Detective Parent. He insists that he see me in person."

Kelly looked at her and grinned.

"That's a new one," he said. "He *insists*. And in *person*. How 'bout that."

He hitched his pants and blew smoke, but went to his desktop printout and riffled the pages.

"Little lady says she knows somebody named Parent. That ring a bell with you?" he said to his flanks.

The two other Kellys looked at Petey, looked her up and down and lingered in between. They were pros in the ogle game.

"Now you got me going. Made me curious," the first Kelly continued as he punched the phone. "I know 'em all up there and I don't know no Parent. What's this Parent?"

After several muffled grunts Kelly lifted an eyebrow in Petey's direction.

"And you might be—" he said.

"Biggers. Petrinella Biggers. From the commissioner of baseball's office."

He nodded his head slowly and replaced the phone as if he had just been noodled.

"Well, open sez me," he said, handing her a visitor's badge and motioning toward the bank of elevators. "Your boy's up there. Parent. That's a new one on me and I thought I knew 'em all. So you're golden."

"Thank you, gentlemen," Petey said, throwing a two-finger salute at the three of them as they stood in a row. And she made her way to the elevator.

"Hey, whi' you're at it, relay our highest compliments to Mr.

Baseball Commissioner," the middle Kelly said. "Tell 'im the boys here in Boston like his taste in employees."

Petey turned a hip. "You killers," she said.

Three floors up she was pointed to an open area of library tables set with phones and files. Three cops in summer slacks and short-sleeved shirts, leather holsters sitting high on the belts, stood at the tables, picked up the phones, and shuffled their files. They wore wingtips, Petey noticed, and for a fleeting moment she wondered if it was wise to know men who wore wingtips.

The one in the middle, a tall, slim guy with his back to her, took her first glance. He had a full head of hair and a nice butt, went maybe a hundred eighty-five pounds, and was no more than thirty-five. That should be Parent, she thought. Though she was only twenty-four, she had discovered sometime after high school that most men needed about ten years on her just to be in the running. Long enough for the beer commercials to wear off.

And the man in the middle *was* Detective Sergeant Fred Parent—he turned when she inquired—a cop in his thirties who was lean and grew a good scalp. But upon a full frontal view, Petey realized with her practiced and discriminating eye, a peeper occasionally blurred by tawdry, superficial considerations such as sinew, that Parent was a male specimen as homely as she had ever seen. He was an out-and-out frog.

She thought this not hastily, uncharitably, or out of any attempt to be callous or aloof. Detective Parent was simply, Petey understood in a brief moment that gave her pause, a hound dog of a guy, a visage that presented the world with a nose too large and a chin too small, fish eyes, hollow cheeks with folds of pasty skin, and a head, despite the healthy hair, that was too small for its shoulders.

And yet he smiled at her like a collie. The smile had possibilities. His companions, two older guys with thin hair and paunches, paid her little if any attention.

"You found me," Parent said.

He offered his hand and Petey shook it. She realized hers was bigger.

"You musta pushed some buttons," he went on. "We're not talking to anybody."

One of the detectives threw a pained look at him.

"This is Detective Sergeant Pickens and this is Kane," Parent said. "There's gotta be, oh, two dozen guys on this thing, but us three coordinate everything right here for the lieutenant, okay? What's on the street comes up here. He taps any one of us and he knows exactly what we got. Like a task force, okay?"

He was as friendly as a beer vendor.

"Baseball commissioner, huh? He sends a dolly of your speed in on this?" Detective Pickens asked. He was a head shorter than Parent, with a part just above his ear and a decade more on the job.

"Maybe you should ask him, Detective. If you can get through," Petey said matter-of-factly, and reached into her purse for a notebook.

Pickens glared at her before a buzzing phone grabbed his chin. Parent took up the slack.

"Hey, no questions asked as far as I'm concerned, Miss Biggers," he said. "You won't get a fight from me."

Petey smiled at him.

"Not a fighter, eh?" she said.

"No, it's just that—well, I don't cop an attitude about people," he said.

"Too bad," Petey said.

It was Parent's turn to grin, which he did nervously and with a nudge of his hand against Petey's forearm. He was a nice guy, homely but nice, and trying very hard.

"So, can you bring me up to date on this?" she asked, eager to get Detective Parent back down to the pavement.

He turned and faced the expanse of the table, pulling up reports from neatly arranged colored folders.

"Sure can. We've got two subjects. Both ingested substances at Fenway Park. First one, Schreckengost, male Caucasian, age fifty-nine, expired at Mass General. Cause of death was cerebral hemorrhage, possibly brought about by drug interaction."

"What drugs?" Petey said.

"Still waiting for that," Parent said. "Tox says it looks like some kind of antidepressant. Here, give me the report and I'll try to tell you how it was explained to us. I'm no doctor and I don't play one on TV, so bear with me. This is a little complicated.

"When this guy played ball he got a lot of spike injuries on his legs. Damaged his veins and made him prone to blood clots. Happened enough so he was taking a pill every day to keep his blood thin. Where is it?—here, called warfarin. Daily dose.

"But that's not all. According to his doctor, Schreckengost also was on something called Parnate. That's the antidepressant. Bein' a Red Sox manager is enough to make anybody depressed. But the stuff reacts real bad with other medications. And that's what we think happened here."

"So he was definitely poisoned?" Petey said.

"We're leaning that way because of the second guy. We're waiting to know for sure. But the doc says the victim ate something—he thinks it was a simple decongestant—that interacted with the antidepressant to blow his blood pressure sky high. Blew out the arteries in his brain. That's where the blood-thinning medicine comes in—you still with me?—because the thin blood made the bleeding in his brain fatal. Probably dead as soon as he hit the floor."

He scanned the preliminary toxicology report as he spoke.

"Wow," Petey said.

"Well put," said Parent.

"So we're going on the premise that it was no accident, if that's what you're after. It'll help when we know exactly what it was that killed him. Lab says by tonight maybe."

"And Criger?"

"Second subject, male Caucasian, age fifty-two, DOA, Boston City Hospital. That's the morgue. Death due to massive respiratory muscle arrest brought about by nicotine overdose. But here's where it gets real different from Schreckengost, okay? Stomach contents showed that this subject didn't eat at the stadium. He didn't take a single bite from the buffet table."

"Papers had him eating right alongside Schreckengost," said Petey. "From the table in the clubhouse."

"Nope. He was there, but he didn't eat. Stomach bears that out. Right here, let's see, 'Juice and oat bran.' And plenty of tobacco juice, too. He was chewing a big plug like the old guys liked to do. They found it in his shirt and had the good sense not to dump it. It's been spiked with enough nicotine to kill a buffalo. Ever heard of nicotine poisoning?"

Petey made a face. "With ballplayers? Never."

"I just got off the horn with a lab guy who says it's definite. This guy had a patch too, you know. One of those arm patches people wear to quit smoking. Puts nicotine directly into the system."

"Along with the chew?"

"Yup. Couldn't resist a plug in his cheek once he got in the ballpark. A lot of the old guys did, but he was the only one who went down."

Petey stepped back and lowered her notebook.

"This is really weird," she said.

Parent nodded his head and ran a free hand through his hair. Petey's thoughts were locked on to what he had just said, her mind's eye seeing Lou Criger taking a dive as he rounded first base.

"So the causes of death aren't the same—not even close," Petey said, trying not to sound like an incredulous rookie. "But this isn't out yet, right? As far as the public is concerned, both guys ate poisoned food."

Parent grabbed a nagging phone. Pickens and Kane, who'd been answering phones right along, were scowling at him, and at Petey.

"Right. That's where we're at on this," Parent said, his left hand covering the receiver.

He turned to converse and left Petey to herself. She went back to her notebook, scribbling as fast as she could, looking closely at a lab report Parent had read from.

She went from that to other field reports. One included a complete list of credentials issued by the Red Sox as well as a roster of Old-Timers and guests. It was crammed with names.

"Can I copy this?" she said.

"No," said Detective Pickens.

She looked at Parent, who nodded at her.

Petey continued to peruse the files, keeping her head down and her pen busy, but not failing to notice the unbridled glares Kane and Pickens were casting her way.

"Cover for us, Freddy," Kane said to Parent. "We're gonna get a smoke," and shooting Petey one last look, the two of them walked off.

"Those jerks," Parent said, putting his hands on his hips. He reached over to the file containing the Fenway pass list and gave it to Petey.

"Use the copier over there. What else do you need, Miss Biggers?"

"You can call me Petey," Petey said, wondering if she should have. "And I could use some suspects, or even a motive. Or is it too early in the game for that?"

"It never is," Parent said. "Our guys are turning things inside out as far as the subjects are concerned. That's this pile right here. The victims were trying to buy the team, so that jumps right out at you. Not much else. The older guy—Schreckengost—was a real sweetheart. Everybody's pal. The other guy had his enemies, but all from back when he played. You a fan? Criger was no Mr. Congeniality behind the plate. Both of 'em made a lot of money out of baseball. All legit. Otherwise, everybody on the field's a suspect, so what we got is a lot of blue-sky work. As soon as we know more about the poisons we'll go after that. In the meantime, we're waiting for the phone call that cracks something open.

"Look, have at anything you want here. Stay as long as you want, so help me, and come back anytime you want," he said to Petey. "Here's my card. Call me anytime."

She smiled and waved him to the phones, which all started to ring at once. He reached for one with his left hand and held his card out with his right. Petey glanced at his card. On it he'd printed, "Off at six."

Oh, my, she thought. It was good to have a friend in the Boston police department, but maybe not *that* good a friend. She went over to the copy machine and made her duplicates.

About ten minutes later, Petey decided she had gotten about all there was to get for now. She gathered her things and nudged Parent's elbow as she passed behind him. He turned and mouthed a bye-bye, smiled, and Petey noticed a piece of fuzz in his ear.

——5——
Under the Lights

THOUGH OSSEE AND LOU LAY ON THE FRIGID SLABS, NEVER again to recite the glory of their times, life in Boston went swiftly on. Winter still turned to Summer Street. Out-of-town drivers still drove in circles trying to get out of downtown and onto the Mass Turnpike and they blasphemed the souls who laid out the city's streets each time they missed it.

For visitors and gawkers, the Fenway murders were a grand diversion. When their dogs were tired from slogging down the Freedom Trail, they lingered with a *Globe* or a *Herald* from a corner box and reveled in the headlines and the sidebars. Tourists and townies sat side by side in the summer sunshine of the Common and read all about it.

Down the street in Copley Plaza, the murders tied things up. The lines at the Marriott's reservation desk were queued three deep with unhappy claimants, most of them yesterday's Old-Timers. Until the cops could sort out who was who and who was where around the time Schreckengost and Criger last swallowed, nobody who'd gamboled in Fenway was allowed to leave. And that had the boys fuming.

I looked around the lobby and thought I was in Fenway's infield. Alums from as far back as the good Williams-Pesky-Dom DiMaggio teams of the forties were biding their time. Jowly and

white-haired, they sat right alongside the Yaz-Petrocelli squads of
the sixties.

There were plenty of familiar faces. You couldn't step out to
take a leak without bumping into a Mel Parnell or a Catfish Met-
kovich. Fish reminded everybody within earshot that he got the
name not for catching them but for stepping on one and injuring
his foot. There was Willie Tasby, Frank Malzone, Faye Throne-
berry, Vern Stephens and Gene Stephens, and more.

Detectives were fingering everybody for the interview routine, and taking their sweet time about it. With an inside job—
and they were convinced it had to be—they don't want their per-
petrators running outside. There were no exceptions. You could
have driven in from Framingham, or flown in from Maine, and
you still had to stay put until Homicide Lieutenant Hughes's dicks
ran you through their wringer.

To their credit, the detectives rented a pair of second-floor
meeting rooms, which meant their interviewees didn't have to go
far. On the other hand, the meeting rooms were those airless
refrigerated dens big enough for a wedding party or a kangaroo
court, and with all the comfort of the latter. Until you were lucky
enough to spend an hour under the lights with them, you had to
sit around and twiddle.

I too was numbered among the witnesses, which explained
my presence in the hotel on Huntington Avenue. I was not thrilled
about it myself, but it was the price I paid for having cuddled up
too close to celebrityhood. On the other hand, the old Sox howled.
They were former major leaguers, never forget, alumni of the
most pampered and elite group of individuals this side of a sheik's
kid. Right out of high school these guys have their eggs ready for
them, their bags brought up to the room, and they still expect it.

Have a chat sometime with any team's traveling secretary.
He's the faceless guy who is the true Job of a franchise. His duty
is to move the whole team and its belongings from away date to
away date. The only thing the players have to do is tip the clubhouse attendants, something most of them do very badly, and
make sure they get to the bus on time. That is a struggle; once
they're off the field, ballplayers, even retired ballplayers, don't
move very fast. They do not like to wait in line, buy tickets, or
show identification. They cope atrociously with detours and de-
lays. As they were doing today, even if the reason happened to
be a couple of murders.

So the Old-Timers lingered and drank and got grumpier by the minute. Which was fine by me. The sorer their asses got, the more I wanted to be around them. Once the we-are-all-Red-Sox mantra left their lips, I'd hear the snarls, the bitching. Even in retirement, the scabs were still there, and if I waited long enough they'd start picking at them. If a jamoke got lucky, he might even hear about some feelings hard enough to move a guy to poison an old teammate.

And do it shrewdly. Two separate poisons, for crying out loud, two completely different methods. Which meant, it seemed to me, two very definite targets. These were no random mickeys slipped into the baked-bean crock, no cyanide salted in a dozen Tylenol capsules and put back on a drugstore shelf. They were specific, calculated, and well executed. Like a hit-and-run. A suicide squeeze. Just eyeing the dozen or so former players waiting around the lobby in their street clothes, drinking too much, fidgeting, trying to snow the waitresses, I considered the talent here. These were guys who'd made careers out of being able to execute.

Finally it came my turn to talk to Homicide. It's usually the other way around. I try to leach off the department's murder detectives whenever I can. They're better than I am at the shamus business, because they go at it like research librarians. They keep better notes. They get fingerprints and hair samples and DNA tests from the lab like a sportswriter gets statistics from the home team. The word *dogged* hangs on them like a cheap suit. Most of them are young guys, but colorless sifters possessing a noticeable lack of passion.

They have hairless fingers and Twist-O-Flex watchbands. They flip through eight by tens of the crime scene—photos that cause jurors to retch—as if they were looking at the side of a box of macaroni and cheese. Oh, they say certain cases affect them, get to them, but when I look into their sallow clerks' faces, I wonder. And I say that without an ounce of deprecation. They are bloodhounds, and if I ever murder, they'll nail me.

So when the young lady with a Boston P.D. name tag made contact with me in the hotel's lobby, I followed her into the breach. I entered their makeshift office with my notebook out. There were three of them, all young suit coats with Irish names I didn't remember. They'd arranged a wooden table in the middle of the room, put a fat cardboard file box on it, and pulled a few padded chairs around. The lights were too bright and the air had a taste to it; the place had the charm of an IRS hearing room. It was only midmorning, yet the detectives looked tired.

I took a seat at the end of the table and waited for a good knife to cut the turkey.

"First thing you're gonna say is make yourself at home, right?" I ventured.

They looked at each other. Levity wasn't on the menu.

"You're good at baseball, we know that," one said. "We've read all about you. Us being in local homicide—you know, little murders—this ballpark stuff is new to us."

"Okay, fellas," I said, smelling a turf problem from sixty feet six inches. "Throw the hard stuff."

"You were in the clubhouse. Anybody there seem a little too interested in Schreckengost?" asked another.

"Maybe a dozen guys with notebooks and recorders," I said. "And Lou Criger."

"And Mrs. Dougherty, of course."

"Mrs. Dougherty, sure."

"Didn't she stand out?"

"Like a woman in a men's room, I guess. Then again, she owns the place."

"And one of the guys trying to buy her out drops dead right in front of her."

"Well, fortunately, looks don't kill. . . ." I said, and stopped myself before I became too profound.

"Was Schreckengost eating when she arrived?"

The question came from my left. I abandoned any notion of keeping my three interrogators straight.

"He was eating all the time, from what I could tell. But then, most of us were. There was a real feed bag going on in the clubhouse."

"Was she near the food?"

"Was the food poisoned?" I asked.

"The potato salad, we think. From what we can figure, Schreckengost had three helpings. It was full of phenylpropanolamine—"

"That's a mouthful," I said.

"A decongestant," the same fellow said. "Over-the-counter drug. Fairly harmless unless you have the subject's condition. He was taking other prescription drugs and he had a real severe reaction to the stuff. And somebody obviously knew that he would."

"Hell, I ate some potato salad myself," I said.

"What we were told," he continued, "is that anybody who had some potato salad maybe got a little jolt that cleared their noses. But it gave our subject a hell of a blood-pressure attack."

"Somebody knew his chemistry. Anybody else get a headache?" I asked.

"Not that we know of. Just Schreckengost, and just in that span of time when he was in the clubhouse. As were you, Mr. House."

"Yeah, but I was heavy on the baked beans."

One of them exhaled. My words were going into a tape recorder from which they would leak into the ears of some poor transcriber. None of these guys would ever read the hard copy, I was sure of it.

"How difficult can it be to narrow down the traffic around Ossee's plate?" I asked.

"Difficult."

"And that doesn't help you with Criger, does it?"

"Not a bit. Right now they're two separate cases. But there's no particular wisdom in that," said the detective sitting to my left.

"And Criger? My niece tells me he didn't eat anything."

"He didn't."

"We know what killed Criger," detective number two said. "Nicotine overdose in his chewing tobacco—"

"That's right—Lou was a spitter," I observed.

"Yeah, well, this time he shoulda given it a pass."

"What amazes me," I said, "is that somebody saved his cud and put it under a microscope."

"We look at stranger things than that," the detective said.

"My hat's off to you," I said.

"Do what we can," he said. "Seems the stuff Criger was chewing had been doused with some kind of nicotine syrup. Plus he was wearing one of those nicotine patches. You lay that much of the stuff in your system and it'll kill you."

"Jesus H. Christ," I said. "*Another* chemistry lesson. Somebody who knew their beans really wanted Lou Criger dead."

"They got what they wanted."

"Why? The franchise fight?" I asked.

"That's one possibility."

"That's my bailiwick . . . and I wish I knew more to help you on that," I said.

"Well," detective number three said, getting up and looking at his watch like a parole officer, "you have been very helpful, Mr. House."

On their own, my eyebrows sank.

"No, I haven't," I said.

—6—
Knights of the Keyboard

AFTER THAT, I NEEDED THE CANDOR OF SOMETHING ON THE rocks. I looked out over the lobby of palms and the giant vases stuffed with dried flowers, and I spotted a few faces I recognized, a few I knew, and a few I could even waste a little time with. I tilted toward the pink and burgundy mezzanine bar, knowing it would exact a fin for a bottle of beer and inflate from there, but I needed a drink nevertheless.

A bark, a tinny voice coming over my shoulder like a heckle, stopped me.

"House!" it rasped. "The writer, for godsakes. The only goddamn one that's worth a shit."

Such a dubious compliment could only have come from Buck Freeman. The former fly catcher and flier over the cuckoo's nest was loose in the lobby, obviously with time and demons on his hands, and I had fallen within his grasp. Freeman was certifiably unstable, had been hospitalized during his career—a few stays in Westborough State Hospital—and in retirement had had a couple of breakdowns or firestorms or whatever he was calling them. Right now his jaw was twitching, the heat of his stare made my skin itch. His psychoses curled my hair.

"Tell me, Buck, why should I waste my time with somebody who hates my profession?" I said.

" 'Cuz you know I'm fulla crap, but I give it to ya straight," he said, and grinned like Mother Goose. "And who else you gonna find as fascinating as me?"

"That kid changing the sand in the ashtrays."

"Nobody smokes anymore," he said. "Fuckin' habit police in this country."

"Habit police?"

"You like that? I just made it up."

"You okay, Buck? You feel all right?"

"You, House, you're all right, and thanks for askin'," he went on. "You did a job over there in Chicago. Wrote the game, not the personal shit. Didn't get on no fuckin' white horse—nooooo way. Never told me how to play. Not like the pricks around here. These Boston dipshits. I grew up with 'em. I read 'em when I was a kid and I couldn't stand 'em then. When I was playin' I'd spit in their eye if they came near me. Just get *out!*"

"Still taking your pills, Buck?" I inquired.

He cackled. Then laid into me.

"I'd *kill* anybody else who said that," he yelled.

As I was rooting for his daily dose of lithium to tether him, he grabbed the sides of my head and kissed me flat on the forehead.

"Mmmmmmmmuh!" he grunted.

No man had kissed me—on the forehead or anywhere else—since my father welcomed me, pink and fuzzy, home from the pediatric ward.

"Cripes, Freeman!"

"Hey, I ever tell you about when I did that to Higgins? Ol' Pinky and I were going at it and he said, 'Freeman, you can kiss my ass!' So I kissed him on the forehead."

I let him go on that one, and when he settled down I motioned him toward the bar. He nodded me toward the door.

"There's a couple of guys across the street," he said. "Mitchell and Lewis are there. Slattery's around, that prick. We go over and see if they'll buy."

I followed, and he orated all the way, turning his head back and forth in my direction as he jawed. He had on a pair of soft loafers and a tight pair of lemon-yellow slacks.

"You ever play, Duf? Huh? You probably could. Trouble with most writers is that they never played. Just look at 'em. Look at how they dress—shit, I seen one wearin' sandals behind the screen one day. These sandals were made out of old tires. Had treads on 'em, I swear. Sandals the hippies wore at Wood-fuckin'-stock. So I'm takin' my cuts—four and out—and I see this guy with 'em on. And I think to myself, *He's* gonna write about me. My career, I mean, how I play the game, is in his hands and he's wearin' Goodyear radial sandals. Gimme a break! I told him, I said, 'Pal, don't you *ever* come into Fenway Park with those things on again. Never! Ever! Or I'll hit you with a bat.' He looks at me like I'm nuts. Which I was. Very effective thing, Duf, bein' crazy. I mean, people gotta be careful about what they say about me. If I don't like it, I'll punch their lights out, then plead temporary insanity. I know all about that, boy. People are just scared as shit that I'll wig out. Like this kid by the screen, Jeezus. And this asshole's got the right to write about me in the paper? That's what we had here. I don't like writers. The writing profession, I think, is *shit.*"

By this time Buck had spit bubbling in the corners of his mouth, he was breathing hard, and he had a point. Boston was always a great baseball writers' town. Eyeshade, bottle-in-the-drawer, wet cigar and wet pants writers who fed the sports-reading goat and damn near strangled the thing at the same time. The papers were competitive as hell, and each one of them assigned a busload of writers to cover the prized and luckless Red Sox. Ted Williams complained in spring training once that the writers ought to have numbers on their backs. They competed like dogs with each other, and because they left no red sock untossed, the players fairly despised them. You could feel the rancor; the suspicion between the two of them ran thick. The words were tart, the needles long, the raspberries wet.

Not even the splendid but dour Williams was immune. He brought untold umbrage upon himself in '41 when he refused to doff his hat to the crowd and made bold to spit on them instead.

The *Record*'s Dave Egan, dubbed Dave "Ego" by some, wrote of Williams when the Red Sox scheduled a special day for him prior to his leaving for Korea in 1952, "Why are we having a day for *this* guy?"

Williams, in turn, singled out the press upon his retirement: "In spite of some of the terrible things written about me by the knights of the keyboard up there," he said, "and they *were* terrible things—I'd like to forget them but I can't."

They were not all killers in the Boston papers. There were aces on the beat. Harold Kaese was one. Moe Berg, he of the brilliant mind and good hands who backstopped for the Red Sox in the thirties, once told me that if he had to read anybody about a big game, he'd read Harold. Then again, Bob Cunningham was first-rate. And Joe Cashman had been around since the days of Duffy's Cliff.

But for the most part, the Beantown scribes were corner fighters, and unless you ate the worm at the bottom of the bottle, you would not have wanted to get involved in their spats. I tried to avoid them, usually not knowing whether or not to take sides or lift my pant legs. I was never a shill or a homer or a soft touch, and if I got played by some sharpie I kicked myself for a week and vowed revenge. But I was never a knocker, either. Prose spitballs are too easy to wad and easier to fling, especially in sports where failure goes with the territory. Better to find the fiber, expose character, enjoy a foible, quote a feathery thought or two.

"If you weren't crazy, Freeman, I'd take everything you say about my peers and me, and then I'd deck ya," I said.

He liked that.

On the corner of Huntington and Exeter we swung inside a tavern of the variety I usually avoid. It was called the Original Sports Saloon and was one of those joints where sports is religion and the decorating is pennants and team shots and magazine covers instead of stained-glass windows. If you were a fan—and Boston has boatloads of them—then you worshiped the gods in the shape of Bruins, Celtics, and Red Sox. Famous photographs—and if you don't think the shot of Fisk waving his homer fair in the Sixth Game was here, well, the barkeep should close your tab—hung like icons. The holy water was sweat. If your tastes ran to ballet or chess, to politics, geography, or quilting, just about every priceless artifact in this Original Sports Saloon, including the papier mâché sculpture of Ted Williams bursting through the wall like a rabid landlord, was wasted on you. Cheers.

And this was where Buck Freeman had led me. Two of his old roster mates were already stapled to chairs in Celtic Corner. At least that's what I called it.

One of the current pair of sitters was Ted Lewis, former shepherd of Fenway's left field, bona fide star, and a very African-American individual who, despite having drawn millions from the Red Sox over the years, never thought they treated him very well. Sweetheart that he was, he refused a day in his honor when he hung things up and would have no part in something as convivial

as an Old-Timers' Day. He certainly hadn't been there yesterday.
I wondered what he was doing here now.

To his right was Fred Mitchell, a white guy who could jump,
as amiable a fellow as Lewis was a stinker. Of course they were
friends, had been roommates, I think, which is one of those social
mysteries I'll never figure out. Mitchell was better known for the
fact that for a couple of years he played both pro baseball and
pro basketball. That was back in the days of Gene Conley, when
pale, lanky birds could play forward in the NBA even if they did
embarrass themselves against the likes of Oscar Robertson, when
the NBA did not want those rosters too Negroid.

"If it ain't salt and pepper, ebony and ivory, Sacco and Vanzetti," Buck Freeman announced as he swung into a chair.

Lewis snarled; Mitchell grinned. They were both big guys,
ex-jocks with chiseled torsos tucked into pastel-green and rose-
colored golf shirts, the uniform of the retired player. Sweat on
Lewis's forehead made him look like a Celtic at the free-throw
line. A quartet of Sam Adams beer bottles was harmonizing at
their elbows.

Two more figures were hunched in chairs nearby, just off
Fred Mitchell's left elbow but close enough to look like they belonged. They were aged, lumpy guys whose semibald heads barely
shone over the cubes in their tumblers. When they saw Buck, I
swear the two of them seemed to well up behind the booze, like
cats turning sideways and arching their backs to look tough. When
they saw me, however, they relaxed.

"Duffy! Still in town. Now we're talkin'," one of them said.

It was Hobe Ferris, all rumpled, jowly, seventy years old and
looking older. He stood up and pumped my hand a little too hard.
I'd seen Ferris at the game the day before but he had never
stepped my way. At the moment you would have thought I was
his pension-fund manager. His partner was Chick Stahl, another
emeritus scribe whom I had talked to at the park.

"Aw, shit," Buck Freeman said, as he scraped a chair in place.
"Hobe Fuckin' Ferris and Chick Fuckin' Stahl."

So much for Buck's opinion of their writing style. They were
both gravelly guys who'd spent eight years covering Freeman
among their three decades of covering the Red Sox for the defunct
but not much missed *Record*. True to Boston's rag sheets, Stahl
and Ferris used to rip these guys new rectums almost every week.
I always liked them in person, but on the page they were different

guys. Knockers, churls, writers who spread their bile around like discount margarine. And spared no one. You never wanted to be the first to leave when Stahl or Ferris was in the room.

And here they were, no more mellow in old age than slices of blue cheese left too long in the icebox, sitting with Ted Lewis, a moody black guy; Fred Mitchell, an amiable white guy; and now Buck Freeman, a lead act in the Titticut Follies who was looking to mooch drinks. I, the interloper, figured to be lucky if I got away from the group without getting my jaw broken.

Freeman started it.

"It's bad enough *I* brought a writer," he said. "You guys already got a couple. That makes three members of the so-called writing profession where there shouldn't be none—and with you I use the term *loosely*, Hobe."

"Well put, Buck. *You* should be a writer," I said.

"No, he doesn't get pencils. No sharp objects allowed in the ward," Chick Stahl put in.

"With you guys it's worse'n bein' bugged," Buck went on. "Every word we say to you cocksuckers will turn up in the paper sooner or later."

"Don't flatter yourself. You stopped being good copy twenty years ago," Stahl snapped. Then he coughed and tried to clear his throat of a phlegm lozenge that must have been the size of Cape Cod. It was a wretched sound and an awful sight.

"Hey, hey," said Fred Mitchell, slamming his palm on the table. "Let's have some suds and stop the rag-ass."

A waitress with a brush cut and three gold picks in her left ear was on the spot with fresh coasters, napkins, and peanuts. The old ballplayers rented beer, the old columnists massaged beakers of clear, neutral spirits. Chick Stahl recovered enough to signal for a refill, but he still didn't look real well.

"A silent toast to the departed," I ventured, raising my glass. The others joined me.

"Ain't that a crock of shit," said Freeman, never one to offer much in the way of silence. "Whackin' those guys right on the premises."

"Food was always bad, but not *that* bad," said Ted Lewis.

"Patsy Dougherty's idea of home cooking," said Ferris.

Were he still a byline, you knew that line would lead a column.

"Are we convinced they were poisoned? Do we know this for sure?" Mitchell asked.

"We know," I said. Then I caught myself. I was not sure I wanted to share the details with these guys.

"*Globe* said Ossee was on medication for depression," Ferris said.

"No shit?" Freeman said. "Explains why the cocksucker managed the way he did. He wasn't dumb, he was depressed."

"What about Lou?" asked Fred Mitchell.

"Lou was chewing on a wad of Red Man with enough nicotine in it to kill an elephant," Ferris said.

"No shit?" Freeman repeated. "That means Don Zimmer should be dead twenty years ago."

Mitchell loudly exhaled. "Since when did trying to buy a ball club put you in the morgue—?" he began.

"Hey, who said they got it for that?" Freeman cut in. "Those two should have been shot a long time ago. Criger drops his pop fly and Ossee jerks his best reliever too quick and we lose two World Series. That's enough for me."

"Got a point there, Buck," Hobe Ferris said, then made a face.

Freeman did have a point. Everyone knew of Criger's boner, but Schreckengost had boo-booed big once, too. It happened during the only Series he managed. He had ridden on the back of his ace reliever until the seventh game, when, inexplicably, he pulled him for a pinch hitter with the score tied in the eighth inning. The rookie he sent in got pummeled in the ninth, and the visitors ended up jumping all over themselves in the infield while the Red Sox and their stalwarts wept. That lapse hung with Schreckengost. It was mentioned whenever another franchise had an open manager's slot, and whenever Red Sox fans rued the team's fate.

"What in hell is going on, Duffy?" Mitchell said, interrupting my musing. "You're from Chicago; you know all about this stuff."

"Forget it," I said. "I'm a suspect like all the rest of you."

Ted Lewis raised his massive, two-toned hand. "Not me. Wasn't in the park. For once the African didn't do it."

That got a laugh, but not from him. He drained his bottle. He had been a magnificent dead pull hitter in his day.

"But I thought about it every time I walked through Fenway's doors," he went on. "Thought about murder."

He said the word like a pit bull growls.

"Ouch," said Freeman.

"Yeah, fuck your 'ouch,' Bucky boy," Lewis snapped. "You ain't lookin' at no Pumpsie Green here. I put a career in for that family in that park of theirs. You wouldn't know it from them."

"What? They pay you in scrip?" said Chick Stahl.

"Scrip? Who's scrip?" said Freeman.

Mitchell belched a laugh.

"Forget it," said Stahl.

"Look," I cut in, "I don't mean to be a Dag Hammarskjöld here, but can't we talk some? Cut the fishhooks?"

"Wouldn't be Boston without a little pepper," said Ferris. "Goes good with the chowder."

"Okay, try this: Takin' the club away from the Dougherty clan is chancy business," Mitchell started in. "Schreck and Criger got in up to their necks, pulled some wrong money in with 'em, and push came to shove. Takin' the Red Sox away from Patsy is askin' for trouble."

"She was in the clubhouse when Ossee kicked," said Freeman. "You know what they say about a woman's place bein' in the kitchen. And that's my unsolicited opinion."

"Indict her ass!" Stahl chuckled. "Any jury will eat up that line of thinking, Buck, once they stop laughing."

"Hey, Chick. What say we quit screwin' around and I just kill ya, you prick," Freeman replied.

"Shut up, Buck," I said, raising my voice. Our table was making more noise than any other in the joint. People were staring at us, but nobody seemed to mind. Buck Freeman considered it an insult if people didn't stare.

"It's been a mess ever since Mr. Dougherty died," said Fred Mitchell.

"It was a mess before that," said Ferris once again.

"Come on," I said. "I've been around a lot of franchise fights. I used to watch Charlie Finley up close. You got lawyers and proxies, estates, trusts, and family feuds. But not murder. I can't see Patsy Dougherty as a murderer."

"Read an eye chart lately, Duffy?" said Stahl.

I wanted to punch the guy myself.

"Ain't nobody had any use for Criger's ass," said Ted Lewis.

"Well, *you* didn't," said Mitchell.

"Tell me when anybody had any use for anybody on that team," said Stahl. "That's why they played like they did."

Buck Freeman leaned his head over the table and stapled a leer at Stahl.

"Here we go again, boys," I said. "Ted, why don't you take Freeman into the lavatory and stick his head in the water closet. Hobe, you and Chick go buy some sunflower seeds and stick 'em in your nose. Mitch and I will sit here like adults and talk homicide."

They chewed on that, and so did I. Right here in this little hokey sports museum was the curse of that Back Bay ball club—in all its rancorous glory. The waitress brought over another round.

"You know," said Fred Mitchell in a tone I liked, "there was no team I'd rather been on than the Red Sox. Up from Pawtucket that first year, God, I was living a New England kid's dream. Put on that uniform. Red letters across the front. Fenway Park. There's nothing like it . . ."

"Cue the violins," said Ferris.

"I'm warnin' you, Hobe," I said.

". . . and I remember thinking early on," Mitchell continued, "that with the Wall and right field—remember, there ain't no field any tougher to play than right field in Fenway—and those fans, and I remember thinking, *What a home field advantage.* Think of it. Teams had to come in here and play. Like fighting the Vietcong in their own rice paddies. And then I go into the clubhouse, and it's all different in there. Real different. The team. Coaches. The press. It was like a buzz saw. Everybody had it in for each other and nobody ever let up. It was like, this is Boston and we're supposed to make life miserable. Self-destruct. Even with the teams we had, the talent—why, we had Williams—and still we're killin' ourselves. We always did. Take that home-field advantage— the famous Green goddamn Monster—and we *still* never won the big one!"

"Amen," said Ted Lewis.

"I couldn't have said it better, Fred," said Ferris.

"You couldn't write it better either," said Freeman.

"Had that coming, Hobe," I said, and pulled out a double sawbuck to feed the kitty. "And now they take two bodies out of the place," I added.

"What a deal," said Ferris. "Criger and Schreckengost died for our sins."

"They got off lucky," said Ted Lewis. "Some of us are still dyin' 'cuz a that place."

I winced. Fred Mitchell, however, yawned loudly.

"I'm in with the cops in an hour," he said.

"They gonna use the lie box in there?" Freeman said. "Bring it on. I'll break the damn machine! I was great in shock treatment, Duffy. It was those fuckin' headaches afterward that killed me."

At that moment Hobe Ferris lifted his glass and nodded in the direction of someone making an entrance just over my shoulder.

"The big boy," he said. "Slattery."

Freeman wheeled in his chair. The rest of the table followed.

"Kiss-ass time!" Buck said.

Ambling into the Bruins section of the Original Sports Saloon was Jack Slattery, the Red Sox highlight film for two decades after Williams. Apart from Teddy Ballgame, there was no more famous member of the Red Sox than Jack Slattery. And he knew it. Now in his mid-fifties, but with good teeth and Ronald Reagan's hair dye, he looked a lot like he did when he was lacing doubles into the right-field corner. In the years since he'd quit, he'd distributed beer. A lot of beer. Nobody in New England, including Fenway Park itself, could not buy volume beer from Jack Slattery. He was a rich man. He lived on Martha's Vineyard; he owned Boston. And of course, like just about every other rich man in Boston, he wanted to own the Red Sox. He was the front man and loud partner of yet another syndicate in the hunt for the franchise. Which is why he came into the saloon like a Kennedy and signed autographs. Top of his form.

Slattery spotted our table and made a friendly face, like a Shriner mugging at his cohorts on the Fourth of July. Which was new to me, because I'd never known Jack Slattery as Mr. Cordial. Of course, I'd known him when he was trying to loot the coffers of the Red Sox, not operate them.

"Why, look at these bums," he said, standing over the table. "And Duffy House from Chicago. They were spreadin' it pretty thick about you yesterday," he said, and with that he extended me his big mitt. I had voted him into Cooperstown on the first ballot with nary a second thought.

At that Freeman yelped. "Don't shake with me. Nooooo. Just because I covered your ass in the outfield for eight years."

Lewis and Mitchell said nothing.

"If I coulda brought ya in the Hall with me, Buck, I woulda," Slattery said.

My rectum constricted; I imagined that Freeman's closed up altogether.

"What you gonna tell the coppers, Jack? Two less bidders for the franchise?" Ferris asked.

"I'll let you in on it first, Hobe," he said with a serrated smile. "You know that."

He glanced at Mitchell and Lewis. "Fred . . . Ted," he said.

Then he swung back at Ferris.

"Take a look at their financing," he said. "There wasn't much there, Hobe."

Ferris raised his eyebrows.

"What if *you* get us? We got a chance at a pennant? You gonna part with a buck?" Chick Stahl asked.

Slattery exhaled, then reached down and looked at the label on a bottle on the table. It wasn't one of his. Ted Lewis, who'd ordered it, broke a grin as bright as a beacon.

"Whattaya mean, 'us,' Chick?" Slattery said without a trace of charm in his voice. "You ever play? I don't remember. Help me out, Buck. He ever play? Maybe manage? Huh?"

"Go get him, Jack," Freeman said. "Shove the barrel up his ass. Pull the trigger."

Stahl buried his mug in his glass.

"Just get somebody who can hit with two out and a man on third," Ferris snapped; then he too retreated into his beaker.

Slattery glowered at him. He'd left some famous runners stranded in his day.

"Keep it up, boys," he finally said. "We buy the club and you make sure you call me direct for your passes."

He moved for the door. "Mitch. Ted. Duffy," he said, and he was gone.

"There you fuckin' have it," said Buck Freeman.

And there we did.

—7—

Mace Cuppy

Feeling like i needed a shower and maybe even acupuncture after that group broke up, I looked to employ a cab for the short trip back to the Parker House. Before I got one, however, I watched as Hobe Ferris and Chick Stahl helped each other limp out of the saloon and teeter toward the Marriott.

"Hobe, can I pick your brain soon?" I called to him.

"Easy pickin's," he said. "How 'bout tomorrow?"

He paused and pulled out a card from his suitcoat pocket. It was his old *Herald* card with his home number penciled over the office phone. Then he stepped off the curb. Stahl was coughing again, walking unsteadily, and looking worse on his feet than he did off them. The two of them could have passed for the Sunshine Boys, old cronies on Collins Avenue in Miami Beach, and as I checked the skies for buzzards I told myself I had to stop hanging around with old people. I saw a cab and wheezed a yell.

It was getting late and about time I checked Petey's doings. We might even compare notes. I always feel a little uneasy with her along in a strange town. I'm still her uncle and protector, if a pensioner can be that to a twenty-four-year-old college graduate with pierced ears and a cash card. On the other hand, I'm also her partner, her associate in the shamus business, and therein she has no leash. I usually compromise and remind her as often as possible that she's not bulletproof. She is not convinced.

The Parker House was busy and the elevators were full, but
Petey was not to be found and had not stuck a note under my
door. I got to my room as the beers I had quaffed with the boys
kicked in and I landed on my bed. I slept like a drunk and awoke
sometime into the next day to the growl of a garbage truck and
the glare of the red digits on the clock radio. I didn't want to
know the hour. I only wanted the tile of the bathroom floor to
cool off my feet and clear my head.

Before I got there, however, I spotted a folded sheet of hotel
stationery that had been slipped under the door along with the
Globe.

"Dear Unk," it read in a handwritten scrawl. It was Petey's
printing hand, a frenzy of capital letters that ran across the page.

> Are you dead? Oops. Take that back. Your phone
> doesn't pick up. Marjorie of Grand's office called. Mace
> Cuppy's got food poisoning and he may be a goner. I
> rented a car to get to him if I can. Lives in Hartford,
> Conn. Call ya when I get there.
>
> Petey

Cripes, I said. Then I felt my head, mistook it for a canta-
loupe, tasted steel wool in my mouth, and sought steam.

Petey, meanwhile, embarked on an odyssey she was to describe to me in detail sometime later. She had been unable to get
to me or Grand Chambliss to talk about Cuppy, and she didn't
want to wait for us. She signed her future over to a car-rental
agency dubiously named Alamo. They leased her a Plymouth, and
with a glimpse of a map and a heavy foot, she was on the Massachusetts Turnpike heading west out of Boston at an hour when
most were heading in, passing the scene of the crime, or Fenway
Park, as it had once been known.

A pair of tollway booths later, Petey was in the far suburbs
of Boston, then into the handsome Massachusetts countryside.
The air was clear, the sun high. The landscape looked like it had
jumped off a Wyeth palette, and Petey wondered why any young
men ever went west. She drove effortlessly, her radio tuned to
noise, the road map open on the seat beside her. The drive would
take her a couple of hours.

By mid-morning she neared Hartford. She played with the radio search until she'd beamed in a local station, getting a good signal and bad news: Cuppy had died in the early morning hours. "Third Red Sox Old-Timer," the newscaster said, and went on from there. Petey uttered an expletive most foul.

Debating whether she should return to Boston or pursue Mace Cuppy's demise, she wound through Hartford and past the Connecticut state legislative buildings. The city was nothing but stone to her now. By this time she was onto the limits of West Hartford and she took the next exit onto Main Street, site of the Noah Webster Museum and quaint as all get out if you were in the mood for it. She was not. She found a telephone instead.

"He's dead, Unk," she said.

"I just heard."

She'd caught me after a pot of coffee had put me back together again.

"What's your strategy now?" I asked.

"Check in with the local cops," she said. "See what they got, or what they'll give me. Check the coroner. If there's nothing here, I'll be back by dinner."

"Make a pest of yourself," I added.

"Always do," she finished.

She started at the local gendarme shop. Dressed in blue jeans, a sprite from the perch of her sunglasses in her red hair to the squeak of her shoes on the tile, she nonetheless got nowhere. She had no badge and no way to verify her clout with the commissioner's office, and that meant no entrance to the West Hartford clubhouse, at least not as far as the local sergeant was concerned. Petey fumed. In Boston she walked into the eye of its homicide corps; in West Hartford she got shut out. Where was Detective Parent when she needed him?

On her way out of the building she spotted a woman with a briefcase and a name tag who was about to step into a clay-colored car so plain it had to belong to the city. Petey took a chance.

"Excuse me a minute," Petey said.

The woman, who had loose blond hair, a good tan, and the secrets of someone over thirty, paused in front of her open car door. She smiled, and Petey went for the look.

"I need some help here in West Hartford," she began, trying not to squint at the print on the name tag. The woman was a Det.

L. Horwitz, West Hartford Police, and her laminated photo didn't do her justice.

"We all do," Detective Horwitz said. It was a good answer. The detective was secure in her station.

"I'm in from Boston," Petey said. "From the commissioner of baseball's office. Came here to talk to the player who was poisoned . . ."

"Mace Cuppy," the detective said.

"That's him."

"He's going to be hard to talk to," Horwitz said.

"So I heard."

"You better stick with Boston. Their guys will hog all over that thing. This is a minor-league town, you know."

"Has there been an autopsy?"

"Probably doing it right now. At UConn, in Farmington. Not far away."

Petey worked over that data. Detective Horwitz threw her purse into the car and seemed eager to get going.

"Are you on the case, if I may ask?" Petey said.

"We're not even sure there is a case."

"Huh?"

"We got a death. We don't know if we got a homicide," the detective said. She was a pretty woman camouflaged in a blue business suit. "The medical examiner's the most popular guy in town right now."

"I should get over there," Petey said, thinking out loud. "May I use your name?"

Detective Horwitz paused on that, ran a fine hand through her hair. Finally she said, "Baseball commissioner's office . . . that's a new one."

"Granville Chambliss," Petey said.

"Can you get me into Fenway for the Blue Jays?"

"Ouch," Petey said.

Horwitz sniffed. "Go ahead, use my name. The L stands for Lisa. The medical examiner's a guy named Wackerman. He's okay. When you're done there, check out the Casa Loma. Little Italian joint in Hartford where Cuppy expired. They'll like you over there. How's that for cooperation from the West Hartford PD?"

Petey hustled for a pen. "Wackerman?"

"Bob. Or Robert, depends on his mood."

"Casa Loma in Hartford?"

"Check."

"And the Blue Jays? Weekend game okay?"

"Here's my card," Detective Horwitz said.

It was embossed, and Petey absently ran a finger over it. A female detective in a gentrified New England town. There was a story in there someplace.

"Have you always been a cop?" Petey asked, not sure she'd get an answer.

Horwitz shook her head. "Used to be a librarian," she said. With that she was off, the thick tires of her police car plowing into the wilds of West Hartford.

Petey tucked away her notes, then went back inside the police station and used a public phone to call the medical examiner's office. Passing herself off as a reporter for the Boston *Herald,* she learned that Mace Cuppy's autopsy wouldn't be completed until midafternoon at the earliest. That left a few hours for Italian food.

Back in the Plymouth, which was a metallic blue that actually looked okay next to her green jersey, Petey pulled her sunglasses out of their perch in her coppery nest of hair and retraced her freeway miles until she caught I-91 cutting through Hartford. The old city was full of spires and a hodgepodge of architectural styles. While the government buildings looked medieval, a structure off to her right looked like a futuristic glass ark. And then there was the old Colt .45 factory, home of those famous gats, a building crowned with an onion-shaped dome that could have been lifted from the Kremlin.

As soon as Petey got off the highway onto Airport Road, she liked South Hartford. It was gray and grainy, cracked at the edges. Beset with years of grit and character, pocked with real neighborhoods and neighborhood joints, most of them Italian, South Hartford gave Petey a feel. It was as far away from West Hartford as Tony Conigliaro was from Jim Lonborg, and Petey looked forward to the visit.

One story, brick, with a meandering addition, an asphalt parking lot on one side, a gas station on the other, Casa Loma was an overgrown local tavern. If you felt comfortable in South Hartford, this place drew you like the smell of a good pesto sauce. Petey was drawn, pausing at the door where a sign read FLAG BURNERS BEWARE! YOU MUST HAVE POSITIVE I.D. SO WE CAN NOTIFY NEXT OF KIN.

Because it was approaching noon, the place was filling up with a mixed lunch crowd of men and women, some in suits and some in windbreakers. Most went to the dining room off to the right; Petey hung left into the tavern area. An old, elbow-buffed mahogany bar stretched nearly the length of the room. A few sitters hugged stools and eyed the soap opera on a corner set. Wooden booths with blue Naugahyde cushions and blue-checkered tablecloths lined the wall across from the bar. They were populated by a handful of loungers and tipplers, most of whom remembered when Eddie Collins signed Ted Williams for a thousand-dollar bonus.

When Petey walked in, she lifted heads like an infield fly. Casa Loma's boards were trod by females, but most of them were fetching Italian girls with coal-lined eyes and thigh-gripping jeans worn above three-inch heels. Petey's jeans were snug enough, to be sure, but her green eyes and burnt-orange hair, the cocky nose and busy lips, made her anything but a *paesan*. And she wore heels only to funerals and fugues.

Conscious of the customers' stares, she kept moving, walking to the rear of the place where a waitress with hair the color of margarine was loading a tray. Petey glanced at the wall of photos behind her, the usual restaurant gallery of glossies that made bedfellows of Shecky Green and Arturo Toscanini. She spotted Tommy LaSorda, which was never difficult, and then fixated on a splendid photo of Babe Ruth posing with a guy she did not recognize.

"That's Willie Pepp. Used to run with the Babe," came a voice behind her. "Willie still comes in."

"Hung out with Ruth? And he's still around to tell about it?" Petey said, and turned to face a muscled, black-haired guy at the tail end of his thirties. Half a head shorter than she, he had hard arms coming from a red golf shirt open to a hairy collarbone. If he wasn't Italian, then Rico Petrocelli was Dutch.

"Alive as me. Tony LaRosa. No relation to Julius. I own this place," he said, offering his hand and trying to get a read on Petey.

"Julius LaRosa . . ." Petey wondered.

"*Arthur Godfrey Show*," LaRosa said. "Before you wore diapers."

Petey smiled. LaRosa still had not let go of her hand. He was close enough to promote his aftershave and his dental work.

"You a reporter?" LaRosa said.

"Sort of," Petey said.

"Got a name?"

"Biggers. Petey Biggers."

"What's the P.D. stand for?"

Petey laughed. Then she extricated her hand from LaRosa's and clopped him on the shoulder.

"I need a beer, Tony," she said, and leaned on a stool.

LaRosa grinned and bobbed his head. He wasn't used to red-haired women with quick laughs. The bartender, who had been listening in, drew a glass of Elm City from the tap and set it in front of Petey. She drained half of it, then turned to the proprietor.

"Petey, as in Runnells," she said. "I work for the commissioner of baseball. Granville Chambliss. I came to Hartford to talk to Mace Cuppy, but I was too late. I was told to come here. Said you had great pictures on the wall and that Cuppy hung around here. That's my brief."

LaRosa liked that.

"You hungry? Plate of calamari? Maybe the chicken Casa Loma. It's primo. Sautéed in garlic and fresh chile peppers. My kid'll make it perfect for ya."

"If I said no, would I get out of here alive?" Petey asked.

LaRosa liked that too.

"Boy, you're a broad. Where you come from?"

"Chicago."

"Yeah? I know Chicago. Gotta cousin lives there. Well, what can we do for you?"

LaRosa nodded at the photo wall and went on.

"See that picture in the middle? Guy in the suit with Di-Maggio, that's Bob Steele. Most popular announcer in New England. WTIC. Lotta people don't know it, but he's a Chicago White Sox fan, Steele is. Howdaya like that?"

Petey nodded. She didn't want to interrupt. Finally she ventured, "Was I right? Was Cuppy here?"

"What do I get if I tell ya?" LaRosa said.

"A gum ball," Petey said.

By now the bar was filling up and none of the regulars paid any attention to LaRosa and his new friend.

"All right, Mr. LaRosa. I'll give you the commissioner's number in New York if you want to check me out. But I'm here because Mace Cuppy is dead and he was at the Old-Timers' Game at Fenway Saturday where two guys were murdered. Poisoned, from the looks of it. And now Cuppy dies after eating in here. So that's my story. You don't have to help me out if you don't want to, but judging from all the ballplayers you got hanging on your walls, maybe you'd want to. Maybe?"

Petey stopped when a heavy china plate full of chicken was plunked down in front of her.

LaRosa stared at her, then leaned back on his stool, slapped the bar, and bellowed a laugh.

"Hey, Ronnie," he called to the barkeep. "You oughta hear this babe. You oughta hear."

Just then another margarine-haired waitress appeared and complained to LaRosa about something in the kitchen. LaRosa grumbled into his coffee.

"So, alright, things are starting to degenerate around here and they need Mr. T. to fix it. So here's the story. Mace was family here, understand? On the wall over there, there's five, six shots of him. With Pesky, Williams, all them. Take a look yourself. He'd be sitting in that booth right now. He knew my Dad real good. Only thing different was him being here that time a night. He was usually home with the ol' lady. But with the Old-Timers thing, it was a special night for him. We made a little party out of it. Lotta old faces. He sits at the tables over there with his buddies and people were coming around like always. Everybody loved Macey."

He slurped the last of his coffee and scowled as if he'd gotten a mouthful of grounds.

"Then he was down," LaRosa said.

He pushed the coffee cup away.

"First thing I seen he's on the floor over there and people are shouting for nine-one-one. Gino said he was chokin' but it wasn't anything he ate. Macey eats big but he don't order at night, he eats early. He'd come in right about now and have a plate, not at suppertime. Beer and coffee's all. And that's all he was having that night. Then we got a wagon here and he was over to Hart

General and next thing we know he's gone. We don't believe it. We sat here 'til two in the morning cryin' like a buncha little kids. And that's how it happened. You can ask the boys over there. I'll tell 'em who you are."

Petey finished with her chicken. She'd consumed enough garlic to keep legions away, but it was wonderful. She left most of the pasta on the plate, licked her fingers, and used up every bit of a paper napkin.

"Did you see him yourself? Was he choking?"

"Yeah. I got over to him. But he was already down. Not moving much, far as I could see. If you want my opinion, it looked like he caught the big one. Heart attack. It happens here, believe me. People who like to eat ain't always in the best shape."

"The other two were poisoned."

"Hey c'mon! Don't say that word in here. I gotta business to run. Somebody gonna mickey somebody in my place? *C'mon.*"

"Just thought I'd ask," Petey said.

"Yeah, well, you can put a cork in that."

Petey reconsidered.

"You see anybody strange? Anybody new?"

"Hey, it was a big night. I know everybody in here one time or other. But on a Saturday night you can't always keep up."

"Those guys would know?" she asked.

"Maybe yeah, maybe no. Go ask 'em yourself. I'll take you over. But ease off on that poison stuff."

With that he swiveled off the stool and headed for a booth of gray old men.

"Gentlemen, this lady's named Biggers," LaRosa began. "She's a piece of work from Chicago. Works for the commissioner of baseball. Get a load a that. Wants to know about Mace."

As he spoke he laid his hand on the small of Petey's back and lightly got a grip. She felt it. He was good.

"You come back, Pee-dee. You and me, we'll talk," LaRosa said, and lowered an eyebrow when he said it. When the time came that Italian guys didn't come on to her, Petey thought, she'd get embalmed.

"Hello, fellas," she said.

There were three of them, all pensioners but still thick in the chops, heavy guys in thin jackets who looked like they'd been cornermen for Jake LaMotta. They sat like bricks, smoke curling from cigarettes planted in their fists.

"That's some red hair," said one. "My niece got hair like that."

Petey straddled a chair. Three sets of baggy, dry eyes told her they weren't interested in eulogies. If they were in mourning, it was a muted variety.

"What happened to Mr. Cuppy?" she said.

"Expired."

"Right there where you are, young lady."

Petey fidgeted. "How did it happen?"

No response.

"Did he say he felt ill?"

Still nothing.

"Was he choking or gagging?" she asked.

"Was he choking or gagging?" said the guy in the middle. He swiveled his head toward his two bookends.

That and nothing more, one with a hand the size of a Thanksgiving yam gripping a glass. They sat like slugs. Petey felt like a probation officer.

"You ever seen anybody die?" the left one finally said.

"No," Petey said.

"They do a lotta chokin' and gaggin'. And they crap their pants. How 'bout that?"

"Was he poisoned?" she said, thinking what the hell.

She got nothing with it. An iceberg of silence passed.

"Okay, men, try this. Did any stranger buy Mace Cuppy a drink?" she asked.

"Mace couldn't buy hisself a drink," said the left end. "People wouldn't let him take money out of his pocket."

"Hmmmm," Petey said. "So, okay, I won't bother you anymore."

She rose from the chair.

"I was sittin' with him," said the guy in the middle. "He sits on the end so he can get up and go to the head. Up and down. Had prostrate. He was still hopped up about the ball game. People came over. Bought him rounds. Mace was pop'lar with everybody."

"Strangers?" Petey asked.

"Some. Some not. You don't know everybody now'days," said the guy to her left.

"Next thing you knew he said he had a bellyache," added the fellow on her right. "And the next thing you knew he was down."

"Then what?" Petey asked. "Did he clutch his heart? His throat? His stomach?"

"Sure, that's what he did" came the reply.

That was all. Eyewitness accounts. She wasn't sure she would get any more out of these guys.

"He was dead 'fore he hit the floor," said the middle man, and added, "Now'days, that's the best way to go."

"*Salute*," said the other two, and raised their beers.

"Thanks, fellas," Petey said.

She turned to the bar and asked for her check.

"There's no check," the barkeep said.

"Yes, there is," she said, and laid a twenty on the bar. Casa Loma was a tough club to crack but worth it. It had more atmosphere than all of West Hartford put together. The Chicken Casa Loma was every bit as primo as Tony LaRosa, proprietor and spokesman, had promised. But it was not a place in which she should leave any chits.

Backtracking through Hartford on the way to the coroner's office in Farmington, Petey smelled cigarette smoke in her clothes and thought of Mace Cuppy on the floor of the Casa Loma. Now she had to find out what killed him. Who would have the chutzpah to poison Cuppy while he sat with those three blocks of granite back there?

She easily found the medical center where Cuppy's remains lay. The building was one of those tastefully bland, modern stone designs that try to blend in with the landscape despite an asphalt parking lot the size of a soccer field. It had an atrium, a big metal sculpture, and easy access. It looked great for a bonehouse, but as far as Petey was concerned, it was still a bonehouse.

Inside, she was given a copy of a two-page press release printed on the stationery of the Hartford County medical examiner. It had been date-stamped an hour earlier and said that the primary cause of Mace Cuppy's demise was a massive coronary attack. What she was really interested in—toxicology—was still in the works, the release said. That must have been good enough for the newsies, because she did not see any reporters or TV crews. They had either beaten her to the punch or weren't interested.

"Is the medical examiner available?" she asked a receptionist.

"Oh my, I don't think so," she said. "He left when the television people did."

"How can I reach him? I'm from the commissioner of base-ball's office."

"Oh my," the woman said, and looked at her phone in dismay.

"George Winter to the rescue," came a voice behind her. It was attached to a young, lumpy guy in a lab coat. Winter clearly spent more time with formaldehyde than barbells.

"Assistant Hartford County medical examiner," he continued. "Personally in on the cut. Come into my laboratory."

He was cute in a cocker spaniel kind of way, Petey decided, maybe twenty-eight, a little short and decidedly intense, but just the ticket for what she needed now. Petey followed him down the hall and a set of stairs, and into an overlit office. He jabbered the whole time. Said this was a hot case, full of surprises, full of intrigue.

"Coronary as big as a rocket," he said. "For starters."

"I'd love to see the autopsy report," Petey said.

George Winter turned and fixed a scan on her, then shook his head from side to side, smiling the whole time. He was as happy as a joy buzzer at a Shriners' convention.

"No way. No can do. Boss'd nail me. But how 'bout twenty questions?"

"Start with the coronary," Petey said.

"Definite. Massive. DOA, Hart General."

"Cause?"

"Convulsions. Respiratory arrest. Arrhythmia. Fibrillation."

"What's the last two?"

"Rapid, irregular heartbeat. Old guy's pump went to the races. If I didn't know better, I'd think he got into some good coke."

"But Mace Cuppy didn't do coke," she said. "So now what?"

"Who knows? He had a history of high blood pressure, we're told. He was on Inderal. That's a beta blocker. His arteries were so-so . . . heart was so-so, a little large. Smoker. Liked the juice. He wasn't a kid anymore."

"So, help me out. What happened to him?" Petey asked.

"On or off the record? You really with the commissioner's office? Good gig. Tell me some secrets. You get in on the Boggs-Margo thing? *Wow.* Tell the kid."

Winter was hard into a character, Petey knew, working like crazy at a Ken Kesey/Jack Nicholson bit. Tics, blinks, quirks. Somewhere he'd read that women like quirky; or he was just quirky.

Petey didn't mind the patter, except that she didn't know her part.

"Missed Boggs. A little weak on Rose," she said. "For now we're off the record, trust me. I wanna know if Cuppy was ripped."

"You and the restaurant cats. South Hartford spaghetti mob . . . they been all over this. Bad publicity for the joint."

"Just came from there. Had the garlic chicken."

"Feel okay?"

"Don't change the subject."

"Where was I? Okay. You and me. Hey, what's your name?"

At that, Petey burst out laughing. She introduced herself, and added a few particulars about law school, Wrigley Field, her relationship with Chambliss and me.

"No shit," Winter gushed. "No shit."

His eyes wide, his little hands kneading one another, he was clearly excited. He had been in West Hartford too long.

"Look, I got a confession to make," he said. "I was born in Chicago. Canaryville on the South Side. Played Little League in Armour Park. And I know your uncle. Man, do I. I read him in the *Daily News*. He tried to get Nellie Fox into Cooperstown, God love him. Nellie ever gets in, you know there's a God."

Petey's eyes widened. "You couldn't've made *that* up."

"No way," Winter said. "In these veins flows White Sox blood."

"The world's small," Petey said.

Winter nodded his head and grinned.

"Okay, cover my ass and I'll give you everything you need on this," he said. "I can feed you shit nobody else gets."

Petey waited.

"Okay? I'll take a chance," he went on. "You're looking for a third victim, right? Well, you got one. I'm betting caffeine. Heavy dose. People Cuppy's age don't tolerate it. Throw in a little booze, and zip-zap! Didn't know what hit him. We won't know specifics for a while. But I'm usually good on tox."

"Caffeine?" Petey said. "That's my drug of choice."

"Sure. Mine too. But you get this guy's age and get a straight shot and it throws you into a theophylline convulsion—that's where everything blows—and bye-bye. Somebody knew his chemistry and what he was taking. Gave the old guy a speedball. His system went apeshit."

"How soon will you know for sure?"

"Can't say, and that's the truth. Soon as I do, I'm on you. In the biblical sense, of course. Where you at? How we doing?"

"Calm down," Petey said.

Then she said it again, for assistant sawbones George Winter was looking back at her with the rabidity of a certain Boston homicide detective. Winter was panting like a puppy, pledging to be her inside man in Hartford, an expert on all deadly doses, a well-placed source. With Detective Parent, that made two. Casewise, Petey was elated. But oh, she sighed, the possible strings attached.

To Winter, however, she did not let on.

"Hit away, George," she said.

Petey had all she could do to tap-dance around an invitation to dinner, slow dancing, a tour of the Hartford metropolitan area, and a look at George Winter's home video library. The lab rat was as persistent as a virus, talking faster than a disc jockey on ether, but Petey wanted to get back to Boston.

By the time she had finished her conversation with Winter, she could not sidestep the fact that it was his quitting time. He urged her to join him for coffee at a health-food delicatessen in the village, and she decided it was unwise to turn him down. For two hours, as she surreptitiously checked her watch, Winter regaled her with memories of Chicago and mysteries of the medical examiner's office. A little of Winter went a long way, Petey rued, but she hung in there. She would no more hurt the feelings of a valuable source than she would step on a clue.

Finally, with the sun set and darkness creeping over the trees, with Winter's direct office and home numbers in her possession, Petey got back on the road. He had reluctantly advised her on how to find the interstate—as opposed to his place—and she followed his directions. Even in the early evening light, this was pretty and rugged country, pocked here and there by overdesigned pieces of real estate. Petey gawked at the spreads, and as she did, she forgot Winter's directions. She drove deeper and deeper into the Connecticut countryside. She had not seen a sign to the expressway in a long time.

She peered far ahead for signs of an intersection, a turnoff, or just some hint of where she was. Drivers who are lost generally fall into a herky-jerky, impatient routine, and Petey was no exception. She sped up, then wondered if she should turn around, then pounded the steering wheel in frustration. Nothing looked right, and the road signs she could read told her nothing.

In her confusion she tried to ignore the traffic around her, the drivers who scooted close to her rear end and impatiently passed her at first chance, and those who simply hung on her tail. One in particular, however, she could not ignore.

The headlights were in her rearview mirror. Headlights pitched slightly upward so the reflection seared into her like a flashbulb. Headlights that would not relent. She cursed, then jerked the steering wheel when she suddenly saw she'd strayed over the median. She looked for a side road, a driveway, anything to pull away from this moron and his headlights and let him pass. She slowed, and the headlights slowed; she sped ahead and the headlights sped with her.

Asshole, she fumed, and punctuated it by suddenly wrenching the wheel hard to the right and barreling down an unmarked road that seemed even more aimless than the one she'd left. To her surprise the headlights stayed with her, a little ways back now and giving her a moment's glimpse of a long, low, dark-colored car, navy-blue maybe, a muscle car right out of greaserland, a TransAm, a Camaro perhaps. This one growled behind her, close once again, and she punched the accelerator.

The road narrowed; there were no houses or road signs to be seen. Petey felt herself perspiring. Up ahead she saw an overpass and she prayed it was the expressway. It was, but this road passed beneath it with no entrance in either direction. The lights behind her bored into her rearview mirror.

Her breath came in short bursts; she looked frantically for a haven, a drive, a service shed, some evidence of civilization that might be enough to rid her of the steel monster on her tail. Just then she spotted a sign for a community college, yet she saw no buildings of any kind. She gunned the engine and shot ahead, now speeding at close to seventy miles an hour on a drag built for half that rate. Her pursuer stayed with her, his headlights brighter than ever. This wasn't a game anymore.

Suddenly the road veered left into a tight area of trees and brush. Petey groaned, then shuddered. Her hands strangled the steering wheel and she ached with the strain of trying to keep the car on the asphalt road. The pavement suddenly dipped, and she yelped as her head bobbed, scared out of her mind. This was madness. He was trying to kill her, and she decided then and there that she would fight him. The chase had been his idea, and now hers was to end it, to stand on the brake and see how much he valued his front end.

She never got the chance, because just then she felt a great nudge, a bump strong enough to jar her, the whiplash punching her head back into the top of the seat, and suddenly she was off the road and careening inexorably over a decline of thick grass and infant pines. All of it was against her will, for the steering wheel did nothing for her and the brake did less. The car was hurtling, skidding, and circling, limbs and trees slapping against the sides and the windows. Petey screamed and kicked out her legs against the floor; then she was tossed and flipped like a rag doll in a laundry chute, and she screamed and screamed again.

Just when she could bear no more of it, she felt the world come up in her face. The car was airborne, having slid sideways into a ravine and flipped over like a penny on a sidewalk. As it did, Petey's door popped open and she flew out of it. Nothing restrained her. She was vaguely aware of space and dust, of whirling and stinging, of carnival lights, the smell of firecrackers, and Bernie Carbo. Then black grass, and a body slam harder than she had ever thought possible.

—8—
Injured Reserve

I CAN PULL A PANIC WITH THE BEST OF THEM, AND WHEN Petey was a no-show that night, I started kicking the water cooler. Problem was, I couldn't do much about it. I had no contacts in Hartford, no numbers, no friends. My telephone poll of the police placed Petey in and out of the station sometime in the afternoon. But then the trail went as cold as Williams in the '48 Series. And as the clock slouched toward midnight, I sat in the quaint luxury of the Parker House sucking my thumb.

My nerves were settled by a cop, a Boston homicide detective of all people. His name was Parent and at that late hour he called the room and told me about Petey's accident. Somebody at the Hartford Hospital with a head for these things found his name in Petey's purse and phoned him. And he got to me. Sometimes life is fair, even considerate.

Parent also convinced me of the stupidity of hightailing it to Hartford at that time of night. Petey, he said, was in fair condition at Hartford General, having suffered a concussion, a broken nose, and multiple bruises and abrasions. But from what Parent could perceive from hospital insiders, she was okay. Bandaged and tucked in for the night. We'd get to her in the morning—Parent said he would consider it part of his Fenway Park investigation—first thing.

*   *

She said it seemed like a vast, endless quiet. Then there were lights, a sensation of being lifted and jostled, and once again more of that quiet—a heavy, drugged quiet as gray as week-old bean soup and peopled with nobody. Her lids were heavy now, but open, aware of voices and light. Her head still seemed mired in that bean soup along with aliens and wars fought between clouds, and a sense of being nowhere for years.

"Hey, Unk," she said.

She said it like a prizefighter on the mat. And regardless of what the emergency-room scullions had said, she looked worse. Patients with concussions get awakened every half hour, and Petey looked it. But I didn't let on. I smiled as I stood over her bed, squeezed her hand, and felt damn happy to see her alive.

"I tried to score standing up," she said, her words shussing through swollen lips. "Should have slid."

"Somebody really tagged you," Fred Parent said.

Petey's eyes banked left and met the wide peepers of the detective. She sighed, or groaned, or did something in between. Parent didn't seem to notice. He grinned and bobbed his head.

In his beige police-fleet car, we'd driven from downtown Boston straight through to Hartford. Parent was a likable guy, redolent of aftershave and still moist from the shower, but a decent, even blithe companion. He talked a lot too; in fact, he was the glibbest homicide dick I'd ever run in to. Mostly about baseball instead of murder. If his homicide peers had mined any nuggets in the Criger-Schreckengost probe, Parent was sharing few of them with me.

"We got two men looking into the Patsy Dougherty end of it, but that's touchy," he had said, almost in passing. "Kid gloves when you get up on Beacon Hill, you know. Between you, me, and the wall, Duffy, she's no angel. The ones with all the diamonds never are. But that's as far as we can take it."

"I've met the lady—"

"I know—that's why I brought it u,," he said.

But not without a knock, I noticed, something that seemed to be accompanying every mention of Mrs. Dougherty thrown my way.

Our first stop was the Hartford P.D., where I waited as Parent disappeared into a back office with one of his smaller-town peers. A few minutes later he emerged with a sheaf of reports and an amazed look on his face.

"Take a peek at this," he said.

It was a Polaroid of a light-blue Plymouth that looked like Dick Radatz had used it for target practice. It was dented and muddy. Its roof was caved in and its windows were smashed. The driver's side door was open and pinned against the left front fender.

"Your niece's car," said Parent.

"Good Lord," I said.

"Said they found it out in the middle of nowhere. Birdseye Road, or something like that. Flipped over twice," he added. "She must have been moving."

"How'd she—I mean, how could *any*one survive that?"

"They found her in the weeds. Looks like her door opened and she sailed out."

"Good Lord," I repeated, shaking my head, whistling between my teeth, and making those sounds and twitches you do when the magician pulls the ball out from behind your ear.

A short time later Parent's badge had got us into Petey's room before visiting hours. And we were standing beside her now. What a sight she was! Ordinarily Petey is all together, as fresh as a bean sprout, clean and fixed up. Her healthy good looks and gleaming rust-colored hair seem effortless, as perfect over morning eggs as at evening hors d'oeuvres. Right now she was a mess. She looked worse than an old bat bag. Terrible. Her face—the part of it not scraped and raw—was dead white and innocent of any makeup. Her wonderful freckles stood out like coffee grounds on clean linen. Her nose was broken, and a purplish sunset was beginning to creep from its bridge to the hollows of her eyes. Her lips were swollen. And her hair, that brilliant haul of protein, was stringy and unwashed, having been pulled back by medics working on her face, and it hung behind her ears as limp as seaweed at low tide.

Biased as I am about my favorite niece and her beauty, I had to admit that she was a sight only a lonely homicide dick could love. And when I looked over at Parent, he was doing just that. Petey, even in her diminished, gamey state, wasn't savoring the attention.

"What time is it?" she asked, trying to sit up. "I'm hungry. I've got a headache. What happened to my nose?"

"It's broken," I said. "You also got a slight concussion. So let us ask the questions. We're pros at it."

"How you doing, Miss Biggers?" Parent said.

Petey frowned.

"Always a cop around when you don't need one," she said.

We chuckled at that one, happy to hear evidence of her spunk.

"Call room service," she said. "I wanna milk shake."

That made Parent nod even harder, the smile on his face running from left to right field. He looked like a Cuban batboy.

"I'll grease the caterer, Pete," I said. "You tell us what happened."

"You tell me," she replied.

Parent showed her the photo instead. It widened her puffy eyes, and she took a while to respond.

"Now I feel worse," she finally said.

"You were lucky. Thrown clear. You remember?" Parent asked.

She shook her head. "So much for seat belts," she said.

"Oh, aren't you cute," I harrumphed. "One case in a million where not wearing your seat belt saves your life. Maybe you can make a commercial."

"Mr. Cheerbeam," Petey said.

"Sorry," I replied. "It's just, well, you're pretty banged up, Petey. Coulda been killed. And that scares the hell out of me."

"Me too," she said, and squeezed my wrist.

Over an omelet and toast she told us what she remembered. She had been lost, she said, stopping and going, maybe driving too slowly for the locals.

"Then this guy's headlights were on me. That's one thing I remember for sure," she said.

"For how long? How long was he behind you?" Parent asked.

"I don't know," she said.

"You remember him following you down the frontage road?" he added.

"Where's that?" she said.

"Where they found you," he said.

"Yeah, okay. I turned off and he did too. I tried to ditch him. And then the fat lady sang."

We let her finish eating. A nurse and a doctor came in, tinkered some, then left. Petey seemed tired and, despite her usual quick tongue, somewhat groggy.

"Do you think this is connected to the poisonings?" she said to Parent, turning to him for the first time.

"Hard to say," he said. "Who knew about you? Who knew you were coming to Hartford? Or driving down that road? It's all pretty coincidental, if you ask me. Right now I'm leaning toward a cowboy in a pickup truck who didn't like your driving."

"It was a hot rod," she said, "not a pickup. A greaser's car. And blue. It was dark blue."

"Do tell," I said.

"I think," she added.

We nodded. She was exhausted, filled with painkillers, and due for some solitude. A hospital is a bum place to get any rest, and we weren't helping any.

"We'll be close by, so don't run away," I said, and reaped a smile that brightened her inelegant face.

In the hall we met a Hartford detective, and we exchanged notes. They'd gotten very little from the scene. Nobody had seen anything. The other vehicle had not left any outstanding marks on the rental car. All in all, Petey caught the brunt of it, and almost got her eternal waivers. I shuddered at the thought of it, the dour sight of my abraded and fractured niece just now getting to me. My stomach didn't feel so well. And I knew I'd have to tell her mother about it all.

"You don't think Petey's flip is in Mace Cuppy's ballpark?" I said to Parent. The Hartford cop paid attention.

"Good question. How would anyone know that she was sniffing around out here?" he said.

"We don't even know the status of Cuppy's case yet," the Hartford cop said.

"Let's go to work on that," Parent said. "You comin', Duf?"

I went, and for the rest of the morning, as it turned out, we retraced Petey's steps: the medical examiner and Winter, his assistant, the restaurant, even a chat with the widow. With Petey's concussion, her contusions, and the possibility of internal injuries, the docs wanted her to stay on Hartford General's books for at least another day. You could have called that one. Hospitals are like ball clubs nowadays: higher ticket prices, no doubleheaders, and bleed that fanny in the seat. But Petey was best right where she was, and I promised her I'd pry her out in twenty-four hours. Before we left, we told her just that.

"You're on the disabled list, kid," I said, taking her right hand in mine. "Enjoy it. Eat ice cream. Get a rubdown. Don't give any interviews."

As I spoke, a male nurse was maneuvering around, adjusting her bed, patting and tucking.

"We'll beat the bushes while you're down," said Parent, taking her left hand.

He was an affectionate cuss, and Petey's eyes skated briefly his way. I did not know what to make of it, if anything. She was too whipped even to whimper, though a slight smile crossed her swollen lips. With a nice touch of drama, and superb timing, she sank into a drug-induced sleep. How about it: two grown men holding her hands, and others hovering nearby. Even beyond the fringes of consciousness, Petey had the situation under control.

We didn't say much on the way back to Boston. I kept wondering whether or not I should have stayed there with Petey.

"If somebody went after her, we're making a big mistake by leaving her alone," I said.

"If . . . if," said Parent "If ifs and buts were candy and nuts, we'd all be happy at Christmas."

"Huh?" I mumbled, wondering if I should take the wheel.

Parent grinned. "I don't like how this Cuppy guy went. Suspicious causes. Too close to the Fenway homicides. I don't like that. I'll see what I can do to put a Hartford copper by her room. Least till you get there tomorrow."

"Day after next," I said. "I lied. She shouldn't go anywhere for at least a couple of days, and I'm not getting her released."

"Good man. We should all have uncles like you, Duffy," Parent said, and drove on.

"Sheesh," I thought.

Back in town I touched base with Hobe Ferris, and the old sportswriter said he had plenty of time to huddle. What else did he have to do? We made a date at a Cambridge Street deli for the next morning.

There was another call I wanted to make, and this one was to John Kelly, the Red Sox longtime lawyer. Nobody knew the franchise and the Doughertys better than Kelly; I wanted his take on Patsy's legal standing in all of this. He had been candid with me in the past, and right now I was looking for candor.

"Whattaya mean, 'What's my take on this?' I'm up to my eyebrows in crap over here, that's my take," Kelly began.

He was in no mood.

"You got your eyeshade on now, House? Or you working for Chambliss? Maybe like the sonuvabitch called me yesterday wantin' to know if we'd murdered our competition. Now you—"

"Take it easy, John. Mrs. Dougherty and I have our own working arrangement. I'm not coming at you cold on this."

"Good. Then ask her. Hell, read the papers. They're experts. Experts! Know more about the ball club's finances than I do, the lovely bastards."

"So how are the books, John?" I asked. "Can Patsy hold on to the club?"

I detected an indelicate utterance on his end, a cross between a grunt and an expectoration.

"I'd be a blathering moron if I told you. Not to mention, it's none of your goddamn business," he spit.

And that was that.

With Kelly's rancor fresh in my ear, I turned to the matter of the wrecked rental car. I was prepared for the worst. Here the car was sitting in an out-of-state police tow lot, bumped, battered, and bent to the point where it was fit only for a chop shop in Chelsea. My contract showed that I'd initialed the right insurance box, so there'd be no skin off my nose. I felt like the only house standing in a tornado alley.

And yet nothing of the kind happened. The clerk at the rental agency acted as if I'd spilled nachos on the front seat and nothing more.

"You wouldn't believe what happens to these cahs," she said.

In no time she'd leased me a new one. Unscratched. Ready for flipping.

The Parker House was close enough so I didn't need the car to get to the Metro Deli the next morning. It was raining, a fine, pissing drizzle that fools you into not packing an umbrella and then soaks you like a waffle. From the hotel I walked the few city blocks past City Hall and the Government Center until I found the delicatessen. I liked it right off. One of those storefront, steamy-window joints, the Metro was two rooms of long tables, plastic trays, and no time limits. You could get a bowl of macaroni and cheese or liver and onions, or you could just gum the eggs and hash.

A motley crowd was doing just that. Loners, students, philosophers, and statisticians, they all fit in. People who read newspapers. Some who read and talked to newspapers. An Arab at the grill cooked hamburger steak for $4.75. Or pancakes, an omelet, steak tips. Or you could just nurse a bowl of chocolate pudding. Sit there long enough and one of the counter boys came around with a piece of fruit—an apple, maybe a banana—at no charge. The table was more than likely sticky with juice from the apple pie. At no charge.

Hobe was there before me. He'd put money down for the coffee, and I took his lead. It was just after nine. I'd slept like a middle reliever the night before, and I was hungry for some eggs and salami. We—Hobe in a plaid shirt that looked like something you'd wear to shovel snow—sat next to the window, and life in overcast Boston passed us by.

"Damn sad about Mace," Hobe said. There wasn't much sentiment in it.

I filled him in on Hartford and what had befallen Petey. It was all news to him and he gave me an ear.

"Cuppy doesn't fit in with Criger and Schreckengost, if that's what you're asking next," he said.

"That's what I'm asking," I said.

"Well, Cuppy wasn't in on it. Which is sayin' something. Since Dougherty died, just about everybody from Mike Dukakis to The New Kids on the Block has tried to buy the Sox."

Ferris was off and running. I plowed into my eggs and listened. He had pipes rubbed raw from a lifetime of Chesterfields, so his words came out like a growl. Kind of thing that scares grandkids right off your lap.

"Thing is with Mrs. Dougherty, she being a widow and no candidate for the chorus line at the Old Howard even if there still was such a thing, she says she don't wanna sell the club. Hah! She'll sell to the *right* people. Then again, maybe she'll sell a chunk of it and hang on to some points so she can keep her table in the Six-hundred Club. New paragraph, you with me?"

He went on without prodding.

"The franchise fight is a can of worms, Duf. Criger and Schreckengost had funny money, if you ask me. Somebody silent with a big bankroll and a bad personality. I got a few hunches but nothing I'd bet the house on. Patsy said those two'd get the club over her dead body. You shoulda seen how she took after Schreckengost when she found out about his group. Painted him a turncoat and a traitor. See, Ossee used to be her manager, for Pete's sake. He was her water boy. Her front-office lap dog. Got chapped lips kissin' her ass. And she turns and calls him a snake in the grass for wanting to buy the club. Shit. Ossee was a lot of things, but not a snake. He didn't have the shape for it."

Ferris was limbering up. He plainly enjoyed going on like this. Without a column where he could hold court, I was the next best thing. My eggs were good, so I kept busy, and the waiters wouldn't let Hobe see the bottom of his coffee cup.

"Then there's Slattery and his bunch. They're players, you can bank on that. Jack's personally worth a fortune, and he can tap plenty more if he needs it. Patsy just doesn't like him, that's all. Never did. You could freeze over the Common when the two of them get together. And there's a dozen other rumors about DeBartolo coming in or another pizza mogul or some shopping-center guy from Edmonton—you know all the guff. Next thing you know Victor Kiam'll go on TV and say he liked the Red Sox so much he bought the company."

He liked that one. Not a column lead, but it definitely would have made the first turn.

"Any other drama?" I asked. "Isn't there an idiot son or a brother-in-law around somewhere to complicate things?"

"Well, try this one. You probably don't know this story. 'Member Tommy Dowd? Was head groundskeeper for years. Not that he was out there rolling the turf or liming up the batter's boxes, but he was the boss. Big guy, big mouth. Thick arms like Culberson, and he always wore a T-shirt to show 'em off. Dowd was a pal of Slattery. Two of 'em used to cat around together. Slattery gave him a piece of his Series money in '67.

"So when Slattery leaves the club, boom! Dowd gets the ax. Out the door so fast it missed his considerable ass when it slammed shut. He was no kid, but there wasn't a good reason for it. He was a drunk, but hell, there's enough red schnozzes around Fenway to light up a Christmas tree. Slattery was hot about it. Hit the second deck. Wasn't more'n a couple years later that Dowd's dead of a heart attack. Press played that one up big. Died of a broken heart, all that bullshit.

"But here's the angle, Duf. Dowd has a kid. Tommy junior. He's on the payroll too. Natch. A professional sprinkler head, ya know what I mean? But when the ol' man tanks, Dowd's kid, who ain't all there in the first place, he breaks in the goddamn ballpark in the middle of the night. He's got his old man's ashes in a Maxwell House can and he's gonna make a big thing about spreading 'em all over the infield. You wanna bad hop, how 'bout one that skips off Tommy Dowd's elbow? The kid tipped off the press before he went in, of course, so we had that donkey show in the papers for a week.

"Thing is, most people don't know who sent Tommy Dowd to the showers. Well, it was Ossee Schreckengost. He was Patsy Dougherty's guy, and he did it. I know 'cuz he told me he did it. And he told me Dowd's kid threatened to kill him because of it. Right in the ballpark. And you better believe the kid was there for the Old-Timers' Game. He's still on the grounds crew. Club didn't dare get rid of him.

"So, Duffy, Mr. Chief Investigator. You want somebody in Fenway that day who can get around without nobody paying any attention, well, you got him."

I looked at Ferris, then out across Cambridge Street and the glistening drizzle.

"You know the Dowd kid?"

"Seen him around."

"Got any brains?"

"How much brains does it take to poison the potato salad?"

"Okay, all right. Cops talked to him?"

"I don't know," said Ferris. "And here's another one for ya. Guess who gave Buck Freeman his release?"

"C'mon."

"It's true. Good ol' Ossee again. He did it for all the right reasons, believe me, but it was because Patsy told him to. She got sick of Buck. Sick of his bullshit, plain and simple. And you probably remember how Buck blew a cork over it. In fact, he's hated Schreckengost ever since. Said Ossee took away the best job he ever had in baseball. Cried like a goddamn baby over it."

We were interrupted by a waiter who gave us each a banana. I peeled mine like a pro, and had at it. Bananas are okay.

"So, Hobe, suddenly here I got jolly Ossee with more enemies than piles," I said. "The lady owner thinks he's betrayed her. The kid grasscutter thinks he killed his old man. And the nut-case ex-outfielder thinks Ossee drove him out of Boston."

"Whatta you think, Duf? Enough leads to write a novel."

"I'm surprised Ossee showed up without a bodyguard," I said.

"That was Criger," Hobe said.

I considered that, then pushed my seat back and stretched. I thought Hobe was done at the calorie trough. His banana lay unpeeled on the table like a bad idea. Without an announcement he got up from his chair and returned a few minutes later with a plate heaped with strawberry shortcake. Enough whipped cream on it to give you an insulin attack. His fork tore into it.

"Holy cow, Hobe," I said, and was ignored.

"You were havin' a nice time at the game before all this happened. Quite an honor for a guy from Chicago," he said.

I was not sure how far to take his compliment. I don't think the Red Sox ever honored Hobe Ferris.

"Nice to be back," I said.

He nodded and chewed.

" 'Member the old clubhouse?" he said. "Back when both teams dressed on the first-base side with just a wall separatin' them? Back when we had Dom DiMaggio and the Yanks had Joe. And you had to walk past the visitors' lockers after the game. I remember how Dom would walk down the corridor and stop at the doorway and look in where Joe was sitting. He'd just look at him there, then walk by without a word. Yeah. I saw that more than once, Duffy."

I let him have that scene. It was a nice one.

"So I have some more people to see," I resumed, sticking with business.

He nodded, and talked with his mouth full.

"Look up Patsy—"

"I already have," I said.

"I know. So go back and don't let her finesse you," he said, not hiding a smirk. "Don't think she's above the muck just because of her address."

I frowned. A lot of people seemed to think it necessary to educate me on the character of Patsy Adams Dougherty. Was I being that obtuse, that callow? Did I appear that smitten?

Ferris's fork paused. The shortcake took a breather. He looked up at me.

"By the way," he said, "Chick Stahl lives right around the corner on Joy Street. Number sixty-seven. Drop in on him. He'll be flattered."

"He didn't look so good the other day."

"Chick's dying," Hobe said. "Lung cancer. They cut his left one out last year and now the right one's shot."

"Ah, shit," I said. Life was not being good to my old press-box mates.

—9—
Chick Stahl

I LIKE CITY STREETS LIKE JOY STREET. THEY ARE NARROW, with brick and stone row houses three, four, sometimes five stories up and built right to the red-brick sidewalks. A touch of England, if you will, from the wrought-iron gates to the gas-lamp–style streetlights, and you look up and see a lady fussing over her flower box. On sunny days she lofts a good-morning smile back at yours. Both of you smell the buds of the Aolanthus, the stink weed grown amok into considerable and messy shade trees.

From Cambridge Street, Joy rises steeply on its way to Beacon, so you have to trudge to get up to number 67. Old people with white hair and young people with wild hair pass by, and you feel like it's a good mix.

Charles "Chick" Stahl lived in a third-floor walk-up, 3A, and when I knocked on the varnished door I got a growl. It did not come from the customary apartment pooch, the poodle or cocker, but from something more considerable. Maybe a leopard. The growl stomped and bumped behind the door until I heard foot-steps and Chick Stahl rasp something like "Bernie!"

Then, "Who knocks?"

"House," I said. "Noted sports columnist."

The door cracked and Stahl stood there in a bathrobe stolen from Ralph Cramden. Stahl was seventy-three—I'd asked—and looked ninety-three. Old newspaper rats don't preserve too well, and Chick was no exception. Next to him was the growler, an old German shepherd with the chest cavity of a lion and a coat that looked like it came from the same bolt of cloth as Stahl's bathrobe. He saw me shake Chick's mottled hand and trotted off heavily across the room, fetched a rancid squeeze toy, returned, and dropped it at my feet.

"Takes right to you. Knows a columnist when he smells one," Stahl said.

The dog flopped onto his side and lolled his tongue.

"Get up, Fergie. You're making a fool of yourself."

"Fergie?" I inquired.

"After Ferguson Jenkins. Fergie didn't pitch here long, but he got in Zimmer's doghouse first thing. Endeared himself to me."

As he talked, Stahl withdrew into the apartment, and I followed. The place looked like a flat lived in by a dying old man and his bored old dog. If Stahl ever had a wife, she'd taken the vacuum cleaner with her when she left. Stacks of newspapers, magazines, books and mail, insurance forms, prescriptions, matchbooks and rolls of candy and bottles of Maalox covered every available surface. Wide-slat Venetian blinds hung in front of windows dull with residual smoke. There were empty, lime-encrusted saucepans on the radiators. In the middle of it all was a portable TV stand and a set fixed with rabbit ears that would poke your eyes out. The whole place smelled like a janitor's sock.

"Fergie Jenkins was one of the 'Buffalo Heads.' You remember them, Duffy? He and Carbo, Bill Lee, and Jim Willoughby, I think. Jenkins said buffaloes were the ugliest animals alive, and that's what Zimmer reminded him of."

"A bit of Red Sox history that passed me by, Chick," I said, and nudged past the dog.

"How you feeling?" I added.

"Like shit," he hissed. "Prostate's the size of a punching bag. Lungs are shot. Shot, hell, they're almost gone. I'm the legacy of the Marlboro Man, Duffy."

He wasn't kidding. Before I sat down on a dining-room chair, I spotted half a dozen oversized ashtrays the size of catcher's mitts scattered around the place. And every one of them had caught something: cigar stubs, wrappers, pipes, cigarette butts, ashes, fresh tobacco, matches. Stahl was a walking soot factory.

He padded into the kitchen and returned with a pair of beakers and a bottle of cognac. He splashed the insides of the glasses with a surprisingly steady hand.

"To *your* health, Duffy. Mine ain't worth it," he said.

We both took a belt, and it liberated a phlegmy rattle from somewhere deep in Stahl's throat. He pulled a box of panatelas from the windowsill and offered me one. I hadn't smoked a stogie for years, but it seemed like the appropriate thing to do. Might as well get my smoke firsthand. I stripped off the cellophane and stoked it off Stahl's match. The two of us were soon engulfed in white, coke-oven smoke, savoring the instruments of Chick's imminent demise without an ounce of remorse. It was a great country.

"Good booze . . . good tobacco. Go down with the best, I always say," Stahl declared, then hacked again.

Of the cynics ensconced in Fenway's press box, Chick had held his own. He was an ample cheek in the red-ass contingent that ranted about the Sox. Only now he seemed more of a stoic than a cynic; a spent man aware of the ledger.

"You've had a good run, Chick," I offered. "Summers at the ballyard. Winters at the hot stove. Every February and March in Winter Haven. The works."

"Know the year I was born? 1920," he said, sinking into a ratty, overstuffed chair. "January the twentieth. The very day Frazee sold Babe to the Yanks."

"Come on . . ." I said. I sat on a footstool.

"On the nut. Born to lose, I always said. 'Course my daddy was the real fan. He was thirteen years old when the Boston Puritans started up. That made him a charter member of the Red Sox fan club. Saw Cy Young. Smoky Joe Wood. The team that beat the White Sox in '18, and my daddy always said the White Sox of '18 was the greatest team that ever was. And young Babe beat 'em. Yowza."

"Then you came into the world and Frazee sold Ruth, is that how you see it?"

"Almost, Duffy. Almost."

"That's enough to make you a Braves fan."

The dog rolled over and, I'm almost certain of it, belched.

"Hah, let's not go off half-cocked," Chick said. "You live in New England and you're predestined to go with the Red Sox. My daddy died in '49. The Sox dropped that last game of the season to the Yanks and he couldn't take it anymore. The team killed him. And they're killing me." He refilled his glass.

"Tobacco industry'll be glad to hear that," I said.

He sniffed, and as he did he rubbed blotchy fingers that were chafed and cracked at the webs. Eczema. A bad case. He absently picked at it, raising peels of skin from angry red blotches. Stahl's rash probably went back fifty years. He'd had it ever since I'd known him. His casket would be lined with skin flakes like fallen snow.

"Until I was twenty we were in the toilet," he went on. "Came in last six years in a row from '25 to '30, for godsakes. Then we get Foxx and Williams and we come up with nothing but second. Somebody always beat us. Damn Pesky. And then we're up and down. Win it in '67 but drop the Series. You know the rest. We get close. Slam. Door shuts."

"Whattaya mean 'we,' Chick? We, we, we. I wrote about the Cubs and White Sox for forty years and I don't think I ever used the first person plural."

"Too bad for ya then. In Boston, it's 'we,'" he said.

The phone rang and Chick got up to answer it. I heard his voice through the cigar smoke. I'd burned a half inch off my stogie and I clearly remembered why I never took up the habit. I wondered if Castro could have hit big-league pitching.

"Jake's coming over. My kid," Chick said when he returned. "That was him. He wants to meet ya. He's gonna try to get you on that damn radio program of his. Lives a few blocks away. Just close enough to intrude on me."

"That bad?"

"Ah, whattaya gonna do? He buys me my booze and picks up my pills. Takes care of my finances, which means he grabs a buck for every two he deposits."

I shrugged. "What are children for if they can't sponge off parents?" I said, wondering where that came from.

"Least your son's in the business," I added.

"Sort of. Radio guy, like I said. Not play-by-play, but he'd like to be. Covers the beat with a tape recorder. Knows everything. Knows the wives. Knows if a guy orders his onions fried or raw. Knows who has a charley horse and who has a hangnail and what he's takin' for it. Smells the liniment, for godsakes. He should. I took him to the park with me since he was a kid and he never missed a thing. Kid could barely pass math in school but he could figure batting averages on the spot. So what did he do with it? Radio. He's got this telephone call-in show on Sunday night that goes for three hours and bores the piss outta me. But he knows everybody—all the old Red Sox—and they all know him. Mutual ass-kissing society. People like that kind of thing.

"But don't get me started, Duffy. The thing about radio and TV is that none of those jokers ever has to put any form to anything. None of 'em can write a line. My kid sure as hell can't. Not like we used to do, I mean, *compose* something, make it sing. They just aim a camera or a peewee tape recorder at some dumbass, get a few dumbass remarks, and call it a story. So forgive me if I haven't got the highest respect for the so-called electronic media."

I chuckled. "You sound like me," I said.

I was just about to ask Chick to show me his lavatory when I heard a commotion in the kitchen. It was son Jake entering from the back way. Fergie, the German shepherd, didn't even give him so much as a grumble.

"Dad. And Mr. Duffy House. I'm honored," he said.

Jake Stahl was as formidable as his dad was frail. About thirty-five, maybe six five with a great nose and a head of black hair slicked back with enough brilliantine to dam the Charles. Or maybe it was just wet. Young Stahl wasn't tight around the middle, but his broadness kept going up into shoulders fit for a linebacker. He shook my hand the way Jimmy Foxx used to grip a bat; then he looked at his mitt.

"Someday I can tell my grandchildren that I shook your hand," he said, and gave out a laugh.

Dressed in a black shirt open to the sternum with orange poppies all over it, and a pair of white summer slacks, he was handsome and hairy. From what I could see, a black mat of hair covered everything except his palms and his forehead. Reminded you of Conigliaro when he was strong and breaking hearts. On top of that, Jake Stahl had the resonance of a radio man.

"You're embarrassing me, Jake," I said.

"Me too," said Chick, who talked over his cigar. "And how much you want this time, Jake?"

Jake waved him off and went into the front room where Fergie sidled up to him with the spit toy. Jake stooped and bopped the dog's snout.

"Don't give me that fucking snow job! You ain't no police dog," he said, and jabbed at the mutt's ears.

Fergie growled and put some wag into his tail. It was a routine between these two, I decided, and I watched as the old dog hopped a bit. Jake went off into a bedroom.

"How long you gonna be around, Duffy?" he called. His voice was stereophonic.

"Long as the commissioner covers my daily fee," I said.

"Fenway's a mess, dammit. God, can you believe something like this would happen in your lifetime?" he said, reappearing and shoving what looked like his wallet into his back pocket.

"The city's lousy with outside media. Talking heads from everywhere and none of 'em know shit. Gets so you don't even want to get near Fenway. Hey, you wanna come on my show? Sunday night. Take some calls? Give us the real inside edition on this thing? Boy, we'd love to have you."

"Don't waste your time," said Chick, billowing a cloud. "Bunch of insomniacs and incompetents. Howdy Doodys talking to Buffalo Bob."

Jake put on a wounded face. "Dad, you gotta quit smoking those things. They'll kill ya."

I cringed at that one, and Jake turned to me.

"Which reminds me, who was that redhead with you at the game, Duffy?"

"My niece. Petrinella. Came with me from Chicago."

"I thought that was her. Word gets around. A *very* stunning lady. Bordering on Final Four, stone fox, if I may be so bold to say so."

"That's how he talks on the radio," Chick said.

"She's not so pretty now," I said. "Had an accident in Hartford. Put her in the hospital."

"Bad? She hurt bad?" Jake said. He seemed concerned.

"Scraped and cut up. Pretty good head knock. But she'll be okay," I said.

"Let me know if I can provide hands-on sympathy," he said.

"You'll have to take a number," I replied, feeling like a father whose daughter is about to date Wilt Chamberlain.

"All right, I'm outta here," he said. "Where's your lodging, good buddy? I'll call you and we can compare notes. I *really* want to hear where you're comin' from on this whole murder thing."

I gave him my room number at the Parker House; he gave

me a clop on the shoulder and went for the door. Before he left he threw Fergie's toy at the soporific shepherd and it bounced off the top of his head. Buffalo head.

We were left in a cloud of smoke, Chick's of course.

"Dumbass," he grumbled, as only a father can.

After a few nods and some idle chatter, I left the withered old scribe to the solitude of his dog-eared apartment and the bite of his vices.

As I walked back to the Parker House, I was starting to feel downright comfortable in Boston, the way you can when somebody else is paying your room rent and your cab fare. On Cambridge, skirting the sterile strip of granite and stone known as Government Center, my reverie went back some thirty years to when it was still Scollay Square, that rowdy, bustling bazaar of merchants, bookstalls, and tattoo parlors. That was for starters, for Scollay Square's real allure was pig bladders, tassels, and ribald fantasies. It had offered a bump and grind by Sally Rand and other famous strippers. They had been Boston's wild side, its tweak of the blue noses.

More Harvard eyes were opened in those glorious and naughty vaudeville houses of the Old Howard and Casino hotels than in all freshman orientations combined. And yours truly sat among them from time to time, admiring the contours, laughing at jokes on and off color.

Only a plaque still marks the spot. I miss old Scollay, have a taste for a hot dog from Joe & Nemo's, and long to see tassels spin in opposite directions just one more time before I'm sent to the showers for good.

My messages at the Parker House were three. One I expected, for I had not returned to Hartford to bail Petey out of the hospital, and I could almost feel her kicking down her room's door. Oh, she was mad, Petey was. Just spitting and fuming, her voice cracking into the receiver. But I was adamant: She had to lie there and do nothing but recuperate. Scab over. Let her concussed head mend. Still, she barked at me over the phone.

"Put a lid on it, Pete," I said to her long distance. "You're lucky to be alive, kid. Lie there and contemplate that for a day or so. Do you good."

"I've never felt better," she protested.

I'd see her first thing the next morning, no earlier, I promised. In the meantime, no murder suspects would be collared. If she was lucky.

A second message was from Fred Parent, and it had something to do with how soon Petey was going to kick down *his* door, and could he help? It was the third note that jumped at me. It was from Patsy, and it left a number.

I called it, and the lady of the house came on the line immediately.

"How *dare* you quiz my attorney," she fumed. "Nibbling like a nosy reporter. Behind my back—"

"Wait a minute. Time out. I made a routine—"

"Routine what! It was nothing of the sort. You asked John about my finances. How routine is that?"

"Routine as in it's what I do, Patsy. I've been covering franchise battles for forty years."

"I thought our relationship was above that, Duffy," she said.

She painted me with that one, and I felt like a cheat.

"If you want to know something about me, you should ask *me*," she said.

It sounded so easy, so honest, so guileless. I searched for a glib response but had none. She let the air between us remain silent, black.

"Do I interpret your silence as an apology?" she finally asked. "If so, I'd like to talk about it. Just you and me. No lawyers. No niece."

I was pinned on both counts, and murmured an affirmative for the following evening.

The invitation altered things, so I decided to change plans and rescue Petey that evening after all. I called Petey right back and she was excited about the change of plans. It was nice to keep at least one of the women in my life happy. Patsy's rebuke was still on my mind when I pointed the new rental car out of Boston. To ease my discomfort, and even divert me, I did a first in the life of Duffy House. Having not yet succumbed to the electronic age, recognizing television as but a passing fad, abhorring all forms of portable music makers, most particularly those Walkman tape players, and reserving my greatest loathing for the car telephone, I nevertheless went to Kate's Bookshop in Cambridge and, with the greatest of reservations and a feeling I'd normally reserve for a tattoo sitting, paid money for a recorded book. A book on tape, they call it. I don't know what got hold of me, or if I had lost my head, but I purchased a two-hour reading by Jason Robards of Ross Thomas's *Briarpatch.*

So I drove and listened as Robards's cranky baritone pipes read the novel, one of my favorites. And I was taken in, I must admit, captured by Thomas's bleak images, fascinated and baited by the story, the dialogue, wondering as I had when I first read the book, where it actually takes place. It is someplace like Omaha or Wichita, but not either one. And Thomas, while dropping a lot of misleading clues, never says.

The tape evaporated the miles, and soon I was approaching Hartford. Petey was waiting for me, but she did not jump into my arms. She'd washed her hair, and it was pulled back into a rooster tail, but that was the only lively thing about her. She'd styled a hank of hair over her forehead in a futile attempt to cover a zipper of stitches. The painkillers had worn off, no doubt, and the pain of her deep bruises and abrasions was crying out. She looked sore and vulnerable. A strip of tape on the bridge of her nose told of its fracture. The hollows of her eyes were yellowish-purple—despite some uncharacteristic makeup—and looking to darken even more.

"I'm glad you came, Unk," she said with a weary voice.

Even her smile was pained. She put her arm on my shoulder and limped as we walked down the hospital's corridor. With each step I could hear her labored breathing, short exhalations really, no doubt from bruised ribs, and I knew I would no longer have to convince her of how bad an accident she'd had. After filling a prescription and buying a portable pot of coffee, we got back into the car. Petey did not offer to drive. She gingerly reclined in her seat and then did an amazing thing: She fastened her seat belt. I didn't say a thing. Moments after we swung onto the highway she was asleep. I found a station that played Mahler and felt bad for her.

Five hours of driving is enough to subdue a Teamster, much less an old sportswriter with a butt as wide as mine. The Parker House never looked so good. Petey's nap had done her good, and not only was she feeling better but she was ravenous. It was well after nine when we employed room service in my suite, and Petey downed enough chowder and crab legs to bankrupt the commissioner's office. Her bandages and bruises made her look like a prizefighter gorging himself after twelve rounds.

As we ate I gave her a recap of my session with Hobe Ferris—about Mrs. Dougherty and the fight for the franchise, about her boy Schreckengost, about Dowd, the dead groundskeeper, and his kid, the live one.

"The franchise fight is a can of worms," I said. "The Red Sox are the only game in New England, Pete, and they haven't been available for half a century. People would kill to get them."

" 'When in doubt, follow the money.' Who said that?" she asked.

"Charlie Miller. My old editor."

"I thought he said, 'If your mother says she loves you, check it out.' "

"Everybody said that."

"Still, Unk, money never turns me on as a motive," Petey said.

"You've been reading too many whodunits written by women," I said, and wished I hadn't.

"Piggy, piggy," Petey snapped.

"Ah, forget it. How long did they say it'd be before we know for sure what killed Mace Cuppy?"

"My man Winter says soon," she replied. "And he'll let me know; trust me on that."

"Now that you've had a day to stew over it, do you think your rollover had anything to do with it?"

She looked at me and exhaled, clutching her ribs as she did.

"No," she finally said. "It'd be too inside. Who'd know what I was doing? Who'd care?"

She pushed her chair back and reached for the heating pad I'd ordered along with the meal. It was nearly eleven o'clock when we both unhitched our linen napkins and I raised a bottle of B&B.

"This'll take the edge off your bones," I said, and poured her a healthy snort.

"What the hell," she said, and nipped at it.

Thanks to years of practice, I showed her how it was done. I sat back, sloshed the liqueur about the glass, looked at the ceiling, and thought out loud.

"So we're still left with two, maybe three old-timers dead of poisoning. Different poisons. Different methods. We don't know if Cuppy got a dose at Fenway and it just took a little while to down him—is that even possible, Pete? We do know that Ossee and Criger were confederates in a fight that's as nasty as you can get. And everybody's been going out of their way to inform me that Patsy Dougherty is as iron-fisted as she is gilt-edged.

"So there's plenty of motive there even though you don't think it's jazzy enough. And there's plenty of bad blood between the players, which is par for the course with the Red Sox, except that it hasn't worn off over the years. Ted Lewis still sounds like he wants to kill somebody with his bare hands. Buck Freeman is as loony as ever and has harbored a major-league grudge against Ossee Schreckengost. And everybody hates Jack Slattery, who is still trying to buy the club.

"So you got your principals. The only thing we really know for sure is the killer had to be in the ballpark for two out of three. That makes the Dowd kid worth a look. And all the old-timers too, for that matter. Except that in my mind it's a pretty big leap from locker-room grudges and pissing contests to out-and-out murder. Have I left anything out?"

"No," Petey said, her lids getting heavy. "And no offense, Unk, but we don't know squat yet."

I didn't argue with her. Her nose grazed the rim of her glass as she sniffed the fumes of the B&B. If we didn't watch out, we'd both fall asleep where we sat.

Just then the phone jangled, and kicked us both upright. The voice on the other end sounded like Edward R. Murrow reporting from London. It was really Fred Parent from his squad car.

"Your nutcake friend Buck Freeman broke into Fenway," he said. "He's up in the stands threatening to jump and yelling his frigging head off."

"Whattaya mean, 'my friend'?" I said. "Let him jump."

"He's ranting about the murders," Parent said. "I think you should be there. Both of you. How's Petey? She okay?"

"She's okay, Fred. Limps like Bill Buckner, but she'll make it."

"Be out front in five. Both of you," he said. "Buck Freeman's show waits for no man."

—10—
Swan Dive

Parent picked us up in three, jumping out and opening the door for Petey like an overeager bellhop. His goofy face beamed like a kid spotting Roger Clemens at his local McDonald's. She smiled back at him and overplayed her hurts. I thought Parent was going to give her a peck on the cheek. Wouldn't Petey have loved that? For a cop, a homicide dick in a tough eastern big city, he was as mushy as a fig.

In traffic, however, he was a bully, and we barreled through Boston's nighttime traffic, down Tremont and over to Commonwealth. We blitzed through Kenmore Square like a Bolshevik tank, and in moments we were among the brigade of marked and unmarked cop cars wedged together on Yawkey Way. The park was dark, to be sure, for not even Buck Freeman could move management to switch on the floods and bring traffic to a stop on Mass Pike.

Behind Parent's badge, we entered at the main office door just off Lansdowne, and moved through the concourse behind third base and into the expanse of the lower grandstand. The starless night sky, lit by the aura of city lights and the glare of beer billboards, opened to us. It would have been a pretty sight had we any pause to enjoy it. Instead, our attention was quickly taken by the drama behind home plate.

Scattered around the lower box seats and on the field itself were about a dozen Boston coppers. Some were talking into portable radios, others crouched and waited. All of them were peering above the rooftop suite just to the first-base side of the press box. There stood Buck Freeman, a baseball in his right hand, a glinting, chrome-plated gun in his left hand, a two-toned Red Sox hat on his head, and a look of beatific, sheer madness on his face. His eyes glowed like a sacred cat.

"Somebody break for second!" he shouted. "I'll cut yer ass down."

With that he heaved the ball on a line down toward second base. It was a great peg. The ball bounced once on the clay and rolled harmlessly onto the outfield grass.

"Yeah!" Freeman whooped. "I'll tell you another thing: That Tony Perkins threw like a girl! Threw like a goddamn girl!"

"A film critic too," one of the cops said.

"But he's right," I said, recalling that as hard as Hollywood tried in *Fear Strikes Out,* the late Perkins looked about as right as a Red Sox outfielder as Liberace would as a stevedore.

Another cop offered a few rational words, but they bounced off Freeman's psyche like water on a hot skillet. Freeman laughed, cackled really, waved his pistol, and revealed another baseball. It looked like he had a bag of them up there, which, given the strength of his arm, might keep him busy and us here all night.

Behind Parent we proceeded slowly down an aisle, then joined a knot of coppers on the playing field at the edge of the visitors' dugout. It was a good place to be, because we could always duck inside for cover should Buck aim his missiles our way. Parent took some glances from his peers as he squired Petey and me into the area. They were mostly cops in sport coats. The guys who had gone through hostage and standoff school were up front doing all the talking. In the shadows of the press box, which, after Fenway's last renovation, was perched higher than Freeman's spot above the rooftop suites, I spotted a few crouched forms. Yet apart from Freeman's brandished firearm, I saw no weapons. No ultrapowered SWAT teams or snipers with night-scoped rifles on tripods. Not yet, anyway.

"We're just trying to keep him from hurting himself," said one officer.

Parent turned to us and made a face. "Wait till this starts getting boring," he said. "Then they won't be so generous."

"Is there such a thing as a tranquilizer gun for humans?" Petey asked.

"We call it tear gas," Parent said.

Another cop turned to Petey. "Buck's probably so doped up a tranquilizer would be an aspirin to him," he said.

With that another baseball came zipping down, this one thrown at the Red Sox dugout along first base. It bounced off its roof like a stone.

"Wake up in there! We got a ball game going on!" Freeman whooped.

That got a muted laugh from his audience. Another ball came in our direction and slapped off the sand near third base.

"Damn Boudreau tried to make me play fuckin' third base! 'Member that, boys?" he screamed.

Most of the coppers did.

"Turn on the scoreboard! Let's see some video!" he screamed.

The negotiator said something bland.

"Fuck you! Turn it on!" Freeman screamed back at him. And with that he leveled his gun at center field and fired off a round. The report cracked through the park like the snap of a nun's ruler on a desk top, and everybody winced. A family of pigeons flapped off wildly from somewhere under the Jimmy Fund sign in right field.

"Jesus!" cried Parent, and herded Petey into the dugout. He left me standing there like a sitting duck, if that's possible. Freeman certainly had everybody's attention.

"What's the plan, Glenn?" Parent said to another officer.

"No plan. You wait these guys out," he said.

Freeman interrupted him. "Welcome to fuckin' Fenway! The house that Harry Frazee built! Now there's a crazy fucker for ya! Next to Frazee, I'm Albert Einstein!"

I joined Petey and Parent in the dugout. Freeman might spot me and decide I was on his shit list too.

"How long has this been going on, Fred?"

"We got the call about eleven. Buck bullshitted his way past the front desk and the next thing they knew he was up there yelling and throwing baseballs. When they saw the gun they called us in."

". . . So tell me *this*, Captain Asshole, if the fuckin' Green Monster is such a big fuckin' advantage, how come we ain't never won a fuckin' thing?!" Freeman shouted.

His voice carried beautifully. Another baseball came through the air, this one aimed toward the Monster in left but falling far short. Even Buck couldn't launch one that far. Dewey Evans maybe, but not Buck.

One of the cops near home plate said something to Buck about calling it quits so we could all go home.

"No way, Fearless Fosdick! The ghosts of turkeys past are comin' home to roost tonight! This is for Criger, that poor slob!"— and he flung a baseball at the Red Sox dugout—"and this one's for Ossee, that prick!"—and he whipped another one.

"Who's next, Buck?" yelled a cop, deciding to play along.

"You, pal!" he shouted, and a fusillade of baseballs came at the cops standing near home plate.

"Now he's playing with trouble," the detective said.

The radios around him scratched as the cops threw the proceedings onto a new level. I could see more movement in the press box. A window opened—the glint of the video screen reflecting off it—and a gray-headed cop leaned out. He said something to Freeman, though we couldn't make it out from where we stood. Only Buck's voice carried worth a damn. Freeman responded by pointing his gun up at the window as if he were going to pick off a bottle on a fence. It was then that I spotted the first of several rifles in the ballpark.

"If he fires that thing again, he's dead," said Parent.

"Dammit, Buck," I breathed. "This isn't funny anymore."

Just then we heard rapid footsteps in the stands behind us, and we saw what looked to be a handful of reporters hopping down the concrete steps toward the action.

"Hey, newsies! Hey! Hey! Welcome to the freak show!" Buck screamed, and lowered his weapon as he did.

"Shit, shit . . . shit!" hissed Parent. "Somebody let the press in."

"I'm still go-o-o-o-d fuckin' copy!" Buck howled, his voice jitterbugging around the stadium.

In moments the newcomers—three young men and a woman in blue jeans—joined us in the dugout. They were breathing heavily, all obviously in the kind of stellar shape so common to the sporting press through the ages.

Another baseball whizzed through the air and landed near third base, only a few yards from us.

"Jesus! The Bucko's in form," said one of the new arrivals.

I turned slightly and felt someone at my elbow.

"Mr. House? Hello."

It was the young woman, a lean, wide-faced brunette with spikey hair and a light-blue oversized construction shirt tucked into her jeans. For some reason she looked familiar.

"I'm Nora Gibson of the *Globe*," she said, and she extended a ringless hand.

Gibson. Gibson, I thought, and tried to place her.

"I'm Petey Biggers," my niece cut in. She was obviously interested in the introduction.

Then it came to me. Nora Gibson was the reporter who had raised a stink a few years back after a bunch of naked hockey players had exposed themselves in front of her in the locker room. The ensuing flap had got a lot of people in hot water, including the waggers and the owner of the club, and had made Miss Gibson a sports page *cause célèbre*. Even in the dim light of Fenway, there was no mistaking her.

Buck Freeman interrupted the conversation when he squeezed off another shot. This one was aimed at the light tower to his left, and once again the shot rattled everybody.

"That one's for Macey!" he screamed. "A sweetheart of a man, goddammit! A one-gun salute, Mace! God love ya!"

"Buck loved Cuppy—he really did," said Nora Gibson.

"Is that why he's up there?" asked Petey.

"Maybe, 'cept Freeman never needed a reason to put on a show."

It was then that I saw a pair of coppers appear on Freeman's level, far to his right. They were proceeding slowly in his direction.

"Crunch time. You guys stay put," said Parent, and he trotted off to join the officers at home plate.

"I swear, this place is getting terminally weird," said Nora Gibson.

"Fenway never was dull," I said.

"First the Old-Timers. Now this," she said.

"Like the Dowd thing," said a reporter standing behind her.

"Huh?" I said.

"Tommy Dowd's kid, the groundskeeper," Gibson explained. "He broke into the park last year and spread his ol' man's ashes on the infield."

She spoke with a clipped, peppery delivery, a sort of Beantown Walter Winchell without the fedora.

"Hey, what's to that?" I asked, remembering Dowd from
Hobe Ferris's mention. "Dowd senior and junior, I mean."

"Where do I start?" Gibson said. "Tommy senior kept the
grounds in this place for centuries. He was a big buddy of Slattery's. Then Slattery retired and Dowd got bounced."

"By Schreckengost, right?" Petey said. "He fired him for Mrs.
Dougherty. At least that's the way we heard it."

"That's right," Gibson said, "but it was Cuppy who went after
him, you know. Mace was field manager then. Lot of people forget
that he actually managed for a few months. He always said Dowd
did a shit job, and when he got the chance he went to Patsy and
had him canned. Probably the only kick-ass thing Mace Cuppy
ever did."

"Cuppy complains. Schreckengost fires. Both of them die on
the same weekend. Is there a pattern here somewhere?" Petey
asked.

"Did Oswald shoot Kennedy?" Gibson said, and followed it
with a tight, bulldog smile. Nora Gibson seemed like a tough
cookie, and I wondered how she ever got into that major-league
snit over the peckers.

"What happened to the kid?" Petey asked.

"Nothing," Gibson said. "He's still around. Team was too
embarrassed to do anything. Little Tommy had press and TV all
over the park that night. In fact, his buddy, the radio guy, put
him up to it, if you ask me."

"Who was that?" I asked.

"Guy named Jake Stahl. He's on RKO. Chick's son, you know?
A real hambone."

"I got ya," I said, hearing Jake Stahl's silver tones in my
head.

Just then Buck started shouting again. The two cops on his
level were only twenty yards away from him now, and the officer
in the press box had once again poked his head outside the
window.

"Okay, fellas! How 'bout a conference at home plate?!" Buck
shouted.

As he did he rushed a few steps toward the press box and
the officer there.

"You! Get the fuck outta here!" he howled, and he whipped a baseball in the cop's direction. It missed, but kept flying and smacked into a press-box window on the far side of the structure where it curved toward left field. The window rattled but stayed in one piece. Freeman followed that by heaving a few more baseballs at the cops on the field, including Fred Parent; then he turned and winged a couple at the officers on his right flank. Everybody covered his noggin and ducked and cursed Freeman, his great arm, and his altogether unbalanced head.

At that Freeman climbed up and stood on the railing where it met the top edge of the 600 Club, the private, glassed-in executive gallery. He was a good forty feet in the air, teetering on the railing's edge, steadying himself with his left hand on sky-box glass.

"My God!" Petey said.

Freeman stood there and gave out a whoop.

"Go, Bosox!" he yelped.

Then, like a monkey, he reached around the front of the structure and pulled himself up on a metal catwalk that ran in front of the press box. It was a remarkable, acrobatic feat, for Buck had to heft his entire weight with his arms alone and swing up on the catwalk. And this guy was fifty years old.

"Whooooo! Whooooo!" he yelled from his new perch.

He danced and shimmied along the metal lip like a squirrel on a power line. The gun and the baseballs were nowhere to be seen now. His yellow pants stood out against the drab green of the press box. It was a stage, a platform as sensational as any, and Buck Freeman had had a few in his time.

Directly below the Y on the Fenway Park sign and directly behind home plate, he stopped and faced the field. He stood erect and stretched out his arms like a candidate, like a messiah, like a prophet.

"Photo opportunity!" he screamed.

No one budged.

"Come on, you slugs! Get Kodaks out here! I'm only doing this once!" he shouted.

At that a photographer, maybe a cop, maybe someone from a newspaper, stepped out of the knot of police and snapped off a few shots. The camera's flashes flew into the dark expanse of the stands like tracers.

"Thank you! Now get the hell out!" Buck screamed. " 'Cuz yer all wondering, 'What's crazy ol' Buck gonna do next?' Crazy ol' Buck! Well, goin' nuts was the best fuckin' thing ever happened to me, pal! You bet your ass! . . ."

We all were leaning out on the steps of the dugout and staring up at the guy.

". . . so I say to myself, 'Self! Get those assholes in the ballpark!' So here you all are! Inside Mrs. Dougherty's wonderful Fenway Park! Mrs. Patsy—now there's a *bore* for ya! Just *sell* the fuckin' team, why don't ya! Jees-us! And here's Ossee and Louie Criger, who could play, goddammit, and now Macey! God bless 'em all! . . ."

"Where's he goin' with this?" said Petey.

Nobody answered except Freeman himself.

"So watch your ass, Jack! Jackie Boy! Hey, let's do the Slattery Shift, you guys! Schoendienst! Kurowski! Musial! Slaughter!—get in right and the Great Slattery'll hit it right at ya!!"

"Jackie Ballgame—my *ass!* Fucker never won a thing for us! So he's next! He's gone! Outta here! You heard it from me, boys! Jack! Jack! Ballgame's over for *you,* Jack!"

"The mad prophet," whispered Nora Gibson.

"I hope not . . ." whispered Petey.

Just then one of the officers at home plate stepped up.

"Come on, Buck!" he shouted. "Give it a rest! Come on!"

"Okay! Here I come!" Freeman shouted.

And with that he tipped up, raised his arms high above him like a platform diver, and dove like a swan. In a moment of suspended time that I'll never forget, his body hung in the air for one magnificent moment before it plunged like a rock to the foulball screen below. We gasped—and there is no other word for it—as he plummeted. Then his body slammed into the screen, belly down, bounced once and went rolling head-over-ass down to the backstop.

The police ran to the screen as Buck tumbled. But just as it looked as if he would roll off the net and take a nasty fall down onto them, he caught hold of the screen's edge. He was still Buck Freeman, the guy who had bounced off walls so many times in this park, and he knew the edge when he got to it. His fierce, vise-strong, and bloody hands clamped onto the bar, and he hung there between earth, air, and fire.

And then, as the officers themselves started to clumsily scale the screen and grab at his dangling feet, Buck Freeman let out a keening, anguished cry. Never has Fenway heard anything so sorry, so pained, so sad. Unless it was what followed, which was Buck's sobs. For as he was wrestled down to the grass below, he wept like a crazy man.

—11—
Another Widow

It had to have been three in the morning when I finally hit the pillow. You don't witness a mad escapade like Buck's and then mosey on home to sweet dreams. Petey, Nora Gibson, and I found a doughnut shop on Boylston for a wind-down cup of coffee before we went home. Parent would have come along, but he had work to do with Freeman.

The three of us talked Buck Freeman mostly, and Petey picked Gibson's brain about the whole mess. The more the young lady said, the more impressed I was. She was wired into the investigation as tightly as anyone, including Parent as far as I was concerned, and had a line on every angle. I marveled—to myself, of course, for Nora Gibson would not have brooked any avuncular bemusement—as she ticked off her theories, hunches, and leads. She was a reporter all right, a grinder, somebody who still venerated the scoop. If I dug into her purse I'd probably find a green eyeshade. And she wanted the Fenway murders bad, Pulitzer bad.

I wondered if her zeal was an attempt to make people forget her infamous locker-room encounter. I never wrote about the Gibson brouhaha—and don't get me started on the issue of women in the locker room—but I had a hard time finding real evil in that whole mess. Jerks, yes, morons, overdeveloped exhibitionists, and muscle-headed boys, but not targets for a sexual harassment suit, or whatever piece of litigation Gibson had filed, no doubt under the careful guidance of high-minded lawyers. Cripes, if sexual, verbal, or psychological harassment—or assault and battery charges, for that matter—had been pursued by every reporter in my day who'd had a player's private parts waggled in his face or his butt snapped by a towel or his notebook tossed in the shower or his suit stained by a shower of beer or his neck tattooed by a fist, well, there'd have been no one left to play the games and no one around to report them.

Which is not to say that I didn't feel for Miss Nora Gibson and her initiation by unsheathed members. I don't imagine it did anything for her nerves or her appreciation for the male of the species. But it was not anything that any sports reporter before or after her has not seen as often as a bare ass and a tube of Ben-Gay.

As for the current investigation, Gibson was yards ahead of us on the toxicology end of it. For example, she had gotten her hands on the complete toxicology results and was homing in on who could have known the effects of the drugs.

"It's the kind of stuff a trainer knows," she said. "And the person I can put closest to the trainer is Tommy Dowd."

I glanced at Petey. Neither of us had given the Dowd kid much of a nod. Gibson rattled on about how she was digging even harder into the franchise fight, particularly the Jack Slattery side of it.

The Buck Freeman episode—and his Slattery prophecy—was a new and maybe important dimension, she allowed. Nobody really knew how far Buck would go, or had gone, or if we could take a thing he said seriously. And nobody seemed to know what to make of Mace Cuppy's death. She noticeably keyed on Petey for that, and I wondered if she knew anything of Petey's Hartford mishap.

I don't know how much we helped each other, but Petey and I got a feel for where Gibson and the newspapers were on this thing. We also got the impression that Nora Gibson wanted to stay close and know what we were up to.

"You guys are good," she said. "I've read about you."

Then we called it a night. After Gibson went off, Petey turned to me and said, "Why do I think we haven't seen the last of her?"

*   *   *

The next day Petey finally succumbed. Even youth must pay the piper, and Petey had amassed a big chit. She deserved the day in bed.

Late that afternoon, I made my way over to the Dougherty estate. I dragged my feet. I was not anxious to inhale the dragon's breath considering our last exchange. But there was a reckoning scheduled—"we must talk"—and there were hard questions to be asked.

I thumbed the bell and tried not to look like a rookie returning to the dugout after missing the run-and-hit sign. The door was opened by Patsy herself. She smiled and took my hand, and gently pulled me inside. She was wearing a sleek navy-blue silk dress that hugged her terrain. Her neck was draped with pearls. Her blond hair was swept back and she smelled wonderful. If there were any hard feelings left, they dwelt far beneath her elegant surface.

"My Hall of Famer," she said, and I smiled sheepishly.

Moments later we were sitting in wicker chairs in an atrium on the second floor. There was late sun and vegetation everywhere. I half expected Nero Wolfe to come in and fuss with his orchids. For opening small talk I described Buck Freeman's escapade of the night before.

"Buck Freeman is a sick man," she said. "And getting sicker."

"People used to enjoy him," I said. "I never did."

Champagne was put on a table in front of us. And a silver tray of beluga caviar, egg, onion, and stone-ground crackers. I liked this woman.

"There is a fine line between mental comedy and mental illness," she said. "Tom used to say, 'Poor Buck.' I said, 'What about the rest of us?' Buck always took his fits out on the Red Sox."

I nodded, and tried not to slurp the champagne or wolf the beluga.

"Maybe that's over now. They led him away in handcuffs," I added.

"What next?" she said. "What on earth could happen here next?"

I didn't want to answer that, but I could not resist the opening.

"Don't *you* hold the key?" I said.

She paused at that, and looked at me over the thin lip of her glass.

"Are we going down that avenue again?" she said.

"No," I quickly said. "No," I repeated, "but let's face the facts. Two of your competitors are dead. You're getting smeared in the press by people who don't think you should own the team just because your name is Dougherty. I'd be phoning in my job if I ignored your role in this whole thing."

"My role? Do tell," she retorted. "This is something I never asked for. This fight for our Red Sox. Then Saturday's tragedies. And now I'm portrayed as a cross between Lizzie Borden and Joe Kennedy. You cannot know how hard that is for me to bear, Duffy. There's no decency left."

She leaned forward, clutching her glass with both hands, and fixed a green-eyed stare on me. It was searing and supplicant in the same ray.

"The wolves are circling, Duffy. I didn't want to tell you this, but I've even been threatened."

"Seriously?"

"Seriously," she said.

I waited for the rest. She turned her gaze away, as if to emphasize the distastefulness of it.

"Jack Slattery." Her diction cut every syllable of the superstar's name. "He told me that if I didn't get out of this fight, he'd take me out. I consider that a threat, don't you?"

I shook my head, half in disbelief, half in agreement.

"But I'll *not* sell the team," she said. "I didn't want to in the first place and what's happened now has firmed up my resolve. My name *is* Dougherty. And I own the Boston Red Sox. In light of what's happened, and when I see who might get their grubby little hands on Tom's club, I've decided to fight them. Slattery's a damned tin man. He's not got the mettle to beat me."

She blotted her lips with her own napkin. I did the same, using mine to tidy up my own fingers grubby with caviar.

"What do you think?" she said. "I get suspicious when you don't comment."

"I think there's plenty of ego at the plate," I said. I exhaled and looked at her, this woman of bearing who had been dragged into a boardroom brawl. "Is it worth it, Patsy?"

She sighed. "I could easily settle up. My own people want me to do just that. Then slip off to my charity work and my boards. We women do keep busy, you know. But I won't.

"But, you know," she went on, "*ego* is a macho word. Not one connected with me very often. And I like it."

I did too; the tag became her.

"You could work well with me, Duffy," she suddenly offered. "In the organization, I mean. There could well be something for you."

"I'm an old scribe," I replied quickly, "who knows his limits."

At that she put her hand on my knee. A lovely bracelet of charms lay on the wrist. She smiled slightly and threw me a look that bordered on conspiracy and affection. The latter overwhelmed the former, at least in my senses, and I put my hand on top of hers.

"That's better," she said.

We lingered like that for a few pregnant moments, and I lost my train of thought.

"Come," Patsy finally said. "I must show you what I've been up to."

With that we went to the library, where she pulled out a sheaf of old photos and memorabilia. We pored over those, Patsy reminiscing, and time evaporated. We remained in the elegance of her library: one of the richest, most splendid women of Boston and an old sportswriter, dining on quail at a small coffee table, having escaped from the rough edges of the present to the soft sepia tones of the past.

And then, at some timeless moment in the evening, after turning over the last onionskin page of a love letter from Tom, she turned to me and we embraced. Both of us felt an enormous warmth for the other, a need, and, undeniably, a passion.

We talked much of the night, about what had happened and what was to come. We touched. I broke curfew. Destroyed it.

Little but Patsy consumed my thoughts as I walked back to the Parker House the next morning. I was clearly enamored of the woman, the soft side of her, that is. In the midst of her greenery and wicker, however, she had revealed the flip side, a measure of the iron fist inside that exquisite velvet glove. Was I up to that? The words of Hobe Ferris returned to me. Was I being finessed? Was I thinking straight? I did not know, and the sticky air of Boston did not clear my head. Where was Petey when I needed her?

Petey was recovered and in the blocks. While her bruises were still obvious, she had mended remarkably. To Petey, it seemed a concussion was a bee sting. She was eager to pursue the trail of young Tommy Dowd. I wanted to get to Jack Slattery.

She worked her phone while I worked mine. I ran up against Slattery's flacks while she managed to get Dowd senior's address from Fred Parent, who wished her good luck with the widow. She was a tough old kitchen canary, he said, who didn't give much. Then he arranged to see Petey that night. Petey, favor in hand, could hardly say no. A few minutes later she was out the door with the keys to the rental car and a destination in South Boston. I told her to wear her seat belt.

She was to tell me later that she had no problem finding her way across the Summer Street Bridge and the Fort Point Channel, the site of the first Boston Tea Party—I considered mine with Patsy Dougherty to be on the list—and into South Boston. She went south on A Street until she got to Broadway and the heart of the neighborhood.

Now, you can't sojourn in Boston and read its local news without hearing of South Boston. It's Irish, of course, gritty and bare bones, a spawning ground of cops and pols, micks, muckers, and blacklegs, and all of them degenerate Red Sox fans. They holler and heckle like nobody's business, lofting raspberries from their beery lips like spitballs. I know all this, yet I confess I've never been to the place. It is a gap in my Boston scrapbook, like avoiding Brooklyn in favor of Manhattan, or stiffing Taylor Street in favor of the Loop.

Petey more than made up for my lapse as she swung onto the alphabet of hilly, asphalt streets off West Broadway. She criss-crossed Dorchester Avenue a few times before she got her bearings. The neighborhood was chock-full of three-family frame houses with identical facades and miles of green, yellow, or white aluminum siding. They were packed together so tightly a dog would have trouble getting between them. Houses were built right up to the sidewalks, and the sidewalks were full of milky-faced Irish kids with baseball caps worn backward. Barebacked guys washed parked cars with garden hoses. Every corner had a tavern festooned with shamrocks, and every tavern hung a Guinness sign and the flag of Ireland.

Even beat up a little, Petey fielded stares like Spike Owen gobbled bad hops, and with her red hair and freckles, none of the gawks was suspicious. It was hot, and she drove slowly with her windows open. She looked like somebody's cousin searching for an address, and every pooch on the block hoped it was his. She had pulled her hair back and her sunglasses down and was wearing jeans and a new Red Sox pullover.

"Hey, sweethaht," came the first salvo.

Petey smiled, threw a kiss, and kept going.

Finally she found her address at E and Fifth, a two-story building with a large corner turret above the entrance to a ma-and-pa grocery. Petey wedged the car into an illegal parking space and looked for a doorway to the upper flat. She had come unannounced, risking the possibility that Tommy Dowd's mother would not be home but preferring that to a rejection over the telephone. In person, Petey felt, she could persuade just about anybody to talk to her. And she was usually right.

After getting no answer to the doorbell, she found the widow Dowd, whose name was Emily, in the back of the house, in a cramped garden of tomatoes and beans growing up a mesh of chicken wire. The woman was attending to a great jar of tea steeping in the sun. Small, thin as a string, the slightly stooped woman wore a sleeveless, shapeless blouse and baggy slacks over variety-store sneakers. She looked in Petey's direction with watery eyes, then looked down at her jar of tea.

"Who you with?" she said.

"Alone. I'm alone," Petey said.

"Who are you then, all beat up like this?"

"My name is Petrinella Biggers. I had a car accident."

"Go find Tommy on your own. Tell 'im I done his laundry."

She said it all without making eye contact. She had short, painfully thin hair and bony arms.

"How do you know I'm looking for him?" Petey asked.

That made Mrs. Dowd pause, and she stood up and wiped her hands on her hips.

"Ah then, dearie. Now tell me I won the Irish Sweepstakes. Or that Publisher's Clearing House? I won that too?" she said, not cracking a trace of a smile.

Petey gave her that one. "Okay. I wanna talk to Tommy but I didn't expect to find him. I'd settle for your side of things. I work for the American League."

"Go ask the police. They were here lookin' through Tommy's dresser drawers. Maybe ask that other girl from the paper. I didn't let her in. Didn't like her. You're real late."

"A reporter? Do you know who she was?"

"*Globe.* We don't get the *Globe.* Wore those blue jeans like you. That what you girls wear to work? You can't clean up?"

Petey wanted to duck. Tommy Dowd's mother was a ball-buster, enough to make any kid take off even if he weren't wanted by the cops. Petey also wanted to know if she had been beaten to the punch by Nora Gibson.

"Dark hair? All short? Maybe this tall?"

"You her friend? She said her and Tommy were real buddy-buddy, so here she is in my backyard tryin' to get me to find him for her. Ha-ha. And I was born in County Limerick yesterday."

"Okay, so why's Tommy disappeared?" Petey said.

"Whoo! That's a good one. Where you been?" she said, now satisfied with the tea bottle and putting on a pair of rubber gloves.

Petey changed course. "Look, I'll get out of your hair. I don't think Tommy had anything to do with what happened at the ballpark, but I thought I should come here and talk to you anyway. Your husband was a famous man at Fenway."

"Oh, and was he now? Maybe with Jack Slattery he was, but that didn't keep my Thomas on the job when Jack quit, now did it? Thomas gave his life to that place, dearie. He didn't even sleep in this house but in wintertime. They killed him when they let him go. Did you know that, dearie?"

Her speech was punctuated by the snap of the rubber gloves on her fingers. For the first time Petey heard a bit of brogue and sentiment in her voice.

"And that affected Tommy?" Petey asked. "I mean, when he broke in with the ashes and all?"

"Oh, stop that now!" she said, suddenly revealing her pale front teeth. "There wasn't no ashes! We buried Thomas proper. Ashes! All that was made up for him."

"But he broke into the park—"

"He was put up to that, the fool kid! All the radio and television were right there when he done it, so whose idea you think it was?"

She started in on her garden, her gloved hands slashing through the plants, and Petey was glad she was not a weed. She was tempted to leave it at that, to let the woman be. She looked up and her eyes lingered on pigeons on a nearby roof.

"Is Tommy all right?" she asked instead. "Is he okay?"

Mrs. Dowd looked up at her.

"Not a chance," she said. "I ain't seen 'im since the weekend. When that all happened at the park. He never come home. He's out there like a lost boat on the channel. What's he got for money? He'll do something jackass stupid."

"If I find him I'll send him home," Petey said.

"Oh, will you now?" the widow Dowd said, but she was not looking in Petey's direction anymore.

Petey stood there, strangely moved by the tough old crone. She wanted to say something, wanted to get through.

"Is Tommy like his father?" she finally asked.

The woman stopped her weeding.

"So you're asking that, are ya? You Irish yerself?"

"With this hair you think I'm Italian?" Petey said.

Mrs. Dowd stood up again, her hands at her side.

"So if I tell you answers to your questions, what good does it do? Those ballplayers who died were friends of Thomas's. Nobody writes about that. It'd break his heart to know they were murdered on his field. And now the police from downtown come over here and want to talk to Tommy. Thomas Dowd's son. Now how do you think I feel about all that, young lady? You're Irish by the color of your hair, you said. So how do you think I feel?"

"I'm sorry," Petey said.

"Well, that's a start," Mrs. Dowd said.

Petey smiled.

"There was nothing much between them two until Thomas died, if you want to know. It's always like that. Wait till he's gone before we know him. Always like that."

And she went back to her plants.

Petey considered that. It was as complete a statement as any, and more than Mrs. Dowd had intended to say. Petey raised her hand in a feeble, unrequited wave, and retraced her steps, walking slowly back toward the car. Before she got there she paused in front of a storefront pub, a narrow, dark tavern with just about enough room for a bar and stools. A single window was nearly obscured with paraphernalia, the usual Irish colors and shamrocks and sayings. It held a picture of President Kennedy, yellowed, curled at the edges. A quotation from Daniel Patrick Moynihan, the politician, was taped to the bottom. "I don't think there's any point being Irish if you don't know that the world is going to break your heart eventually."

The sun shown as Petey read. Mrs. Dowd's tea would be sharp.

*   *

When she got to me that night, Petey was not chirping. That was not due to how little she had learned in South Boston, but that someone else had beaten her there.

"Our reporter friend Gibson hides her cards," she said, prying open the lid to her painkillers. She was irked, she added, that Gibson had conveniently not told us that she herself had sought out Tommy Dowd's mother.

"What gripes you more, Petey? Getting zip from the Dowd widow or getting to her second?"

"Gibson's just a *sports* reporter. What's she doing in South Boston?" she said.

"Just a sports reporter—hmmm," I said.

"You know what I mean," she said.

"She should stay on her page, right? Stay away from the biggest story in town?"

Petey sniffed. "She can't be trusted."

"Can we?" I asked.

Just then her room's phone rang, and she went to get it. She left the door open, and when her voice rose in something close to disbelief, I wandered in.

"Holy cuckoo's nest, Uncle Duffy!" she exclaimed. "Buck Freeman escaped from the hospital. That was Freddie P. He said Buck's gone. They're looking all over for him."

——12——
Jack Slattery

Boston, this *NEW* boston, was different. Forget, for a moment, all the lore and musketry, all the piccolo-playing pomp and rocket's-red-glare sentiment from the days when the guys with the three-cornered hats were revolting. Forget Harvard Yard and the Kennedy boys, the Celtics, that little guy Flutie, and poor Dukakis. You could even take Boston's Red Sox, the baseball-with-tears Red Sox, the chronicled, fabled, storied Red Sox, and put them on the shelf. Because none of it seemed to fit this Boston anymore, not this hysterical, suspicious, frazzled Boston.

Now, I did not pay too much attention to the flap here a few years back when that Stuart fellow shot his pregnant wife and himself, blamed it on a street thug, then jumped off the bridge when his scam unraveled. That was a police-blotter story, it seemed to me, until it blew up, the fingers started pointing, and it turned into a bonfire of crime and race and newspaper ethics. Boston did what big cities seem to do all too well nowadays: It seethed and fomented and came apart with blame and loathing. And the press—official scorers, usually—the folks I always thought had the best seat in the house, became partisans, right in there slinging and accusing as if Bill Hearst were still alive. What they had with this guy was a good-looking sharpie who took everybody for a ride, and that should have been the end of it.

So, maybe because of the scars of that episode, Boston had

soured, grown gun-shy or hesitant. It wasn't the classy, confident city exuding style and instinct. It was more like a team the year *after* a good season, like the Red Sox in 1968, the year after their miraculous '67 pennant. In '68 nothing went right. Moves that made manager Dick Williams a genius the year before backfired and made him look like a moron. Frustration fed on itself. The harder players tried, the worse things got.

So it was with the city of Boston after the Stuart thing, and now with the killings in Fenway; fur continued to fly, and matters got messier as the days passed. Boston was trying—there's a lot of ability there—but things were getting worse.

Grand Chambliss called me that morning. He was back in Manhattan, but Boston dominated his desk. We both wondered what else could happen here. He was not surprised at my lack of real progress, and he was not happy about it either.

"You've got to bat a thousand, Duffy," he said. "Only ballplayers can strike out and still get a paycheck."

In the meantime, Petey's contact in Hartford, George Winter, checked in. Her eyes rolled upward when she heard his voice, but Winter confirmed Mace Cuppy's caffeine poisoning. Given Cuppy's physical condition, Winter said, the dosage didn't even have to be that high to be deadly.

Petey and I paced our suites and scribbled notes and conjectured our fannies off with all of the above. Nothing jumped out at us. Nothing made sense. Nothing got better. We were the '68 Red Sox.

And we were not alone. The *Globe* and the *Herald* were ablaze with the story, still playing it on the front page, their reporters running up every alley and running down every tip. Buck Freeman's escape kept him in the headlines. A stark photo of his swan dive into the screen was run nationwide, and it made him more of a suspect than anyone had expected. Until he named Slattery as a potential victim, nobody really considered him lethal. Nor did anyone know where he was. Boston's own Mad Hatter, hiding somewhere.

The papers also relentlessly pulled apart the innards of the franchise fight and they checked on everybody who had access to Criger and Schreckengost in Fenway Park that afternoon. They answered every phone call from every crackpot, and they coaxed leads out of the police detectives.

Their counterparts on the television desks, lacking the necessary reporters and researchers to do their own investigating,
lugged their video cameras and followed a half step behind. But
you couldn't ignore them, for they were louder and more per-
vasive than anybody. Alas, in this age most people get their news
from the tube. And they get very little.

With their two lead figures in the ground, the Criger-
Schreckengost group dropped out of the bidding for the Sox.
And Slattery's syndicate leaped to the forefront. New bids and
counterbids from even more contenders flew like fungoes, without
even pausing for more than a moment of silence for the deceased.
Patsy Dougherty stood fast, trying to keep her minority share-
holders from pulling the franchise out from under her, and being
pressed with new deadlines every day. The maneuvering was te-
dious stuff, plenty of extra innings for lawyers, their meters on
overload, and an inane drama unless your idea of light reading
was a mutual-fund prospectus.

Grand Chambliss wanted me to talk to Jack Slattery; and I
wanted a shot at Jackie Ballgame myself. Without a peanut gallery
or a bar full of sycophants. To my surprise, it was not hard to
find him. Instead of stalking bluefin tuna on Cape Cod Bay, he
was in town waiting for his attorneys as they jousted over the Red
Sox. He hung out at the Park Plaza, which used to be the Sheraton
and lodged visiting teams. For a few years, however, it was better
known as the site of Bachelors Three, the notorious pub where
Derek Sanderson, the one-time Bruins bad boy, appeared without
his hockey pads.

At the same time, Petey connected with Nora Gibson. The
reporter talked her into lunch at a little downtown place called
Cornucopia. It seemed harmless enough to me, and Petey seemed
to think she had a score to settle.

Slattery, with his loud sport coats and open collars and bad
English, a sense of humor borrowed from a Teamster, obviously
still felt at home in the Park Plaza. He was a wealthy man who
did not have to pick up a check in Boston if he didn't want to. In
fact, he wrote checks people never cashed just so they could keep
his autograph.

"I keep a suite here, have for years," he said to me.

It was late morning and we were sitting in a deserted, dimly

lit corner of the Park Plaza's piano bar, which appeared open only
to Slattery and me. He was nipping off a glass of bitter lemon and
I had iced tea.

"This time of year you got too many rich kids with Harvard
crew caps on running the halls, but I like the place, if you know
what I mean. They take care of me real good," Slattery said. "Got
a little workout room, a kitchen can grill fish real good, and a
decent bar. What more can you ask?"

At fifty-five, Slattery looked good, his big shoulders still impressive, his hair slick and dark. Blessed with a swing that was a
lesson in geometry, Slattery had never really worked a day in his
life. For some reason, God crafted sinew and reflex, eyesight and
coordination into a splendid specimen of an athlete. What he put
in his cranium was another matter. Nevertheless, after a moment
in the minor leagues, Slattery spent twenty-two remarkable years
with the Red Sox and became a Boston idol.

And he knew it. He gave you that look, that cheek with a
tongue stuck in it. Ask thirty fans what Slattery look they best
remember, and they'll tell you that smug one he flashed after
doubling into the right-field corner, standing on second without
having slid, pulling off his batting gloves as nonchalantly as pulling
petals from a daisy. He could hit clothesline doubles in his sleep,
and did for two decades.

"The place still has the chrome you're used to," I said, glanc-
ing around the room. "But does anybody remember it anymore?"

"Not a place to get laid for old time's sake, right?" he said.

"Uh, well . . . " I hemmed.

With that he thumped my shoulder. Hard.

"Why, you old tomcat!" he bellowed.

At that moment a waiter placed a magnificent plate of fried
calamari in front of us. Magic, with refills and a bowl of cocktail
sauce that watered your eyes. Nothing less for Jack Slattery.

While Slattery and I sat privately in the closed piano bar,
Petey and Nora Gibson fought a noontime crowd at their nouveau
eatery on West Street. Narrow and crowded, the Cornucopia was
designed to death in bottle green and tasteful stained glass. The
downstairs held half a dozen two-man booths and a small bar with
wooden high-back chairs so stiff and severe they made Frank
Lloyd Wright's stuff look cozy. Between booths were granite ta-
bletops. Each table had a vase that held a single thistle.

A roomier second floor held an array of tables set with white linen, but Petey and Miss Gibson got a first-floor booth. Nora liked the thistle, which matched her hairdo, and she seemed pleased to see Petey.

"This place runs a little too precious for me," Gibson said, "but it's great if you're a vegetarian. Which I am."

"I'm a cannibal," Petey said with a blithe smile. "I wear a fur coat in winter and drive a gas guzzler."

Gibson lifted an eyebrow, then leaned back as a waiter with a ponytail longer than Petey's made friends and gave them each a menu. Gibson looked much as she had the other night. Her blouse was badly pressed and she wore the same pair of blue jeans. If the *Globe* had a dress code, Gibson was trashing it. She ordered a glass of red wine and Petey went with the John Courage on tap.

Petey broke the ice. "I had a tough time with Mrs. Dowd yesterday."

"Oh, sure. She's South Boston. What she knows she won't say. I talked to her; did I tell you that?" Gibson said, not meeting Petey's eyes as she talked.

"No, you didn't," Petey said. "You sent me there cold. Should I be pissed at you or not?"

"Not," Gibson said.

"You picked my uncle and me pretty clean the other night," Petey continued. "I have the feeling we were clocked."

"And vice versa, so don't push it, okay? I see your bruises are fading. And your nose—it was broken, wasn't it?"

Petey absently touched the bridge of her nose. It was healing, and she felt a lot better, but what was Gibson getting at?

"From what I hear," Gibson went on, "you had your car turned over in Connecticut. You were after Mace Cuppy and somebody got into your face. Isn't that right? But you never said a word to me about *that* the other night. So let's don't talk about getting clocked."

Petey exhaled. She decided she did not like her lunch companion.

"So to hell with it—" she started.

"No. Truce. Let's not do a male thing, okay?" Gibson said. "I didn't play it straight with you about Dowd. You held out on me. And if that's the way we're gonna play this game, we'll both be losers. Okay?"

With that she smiled, and held her hand out across the table. Petey shook it. Guardedly, but she shook it nonetheless.

"It's just that I'm not crazy about being used," Petey said. "Especially by somebody who knows the score here better than I do."

"Look," Gibson said, laying down her menu and putting her hands in her lap. "You've got a sweet thing going for yourself. Your uncle's a legend. You're wired into the commissioner's office like nobody I've ever seen. I can't even get my calls returned there. You live off room service at the Parker House and you do your own thing.

"Me. I'm still known as the bitch who ratted on the Cro-Magnons when they exposed themselves in front of me. Of course, that's *my* fault. I became a running punchline on *The Tonight Show*. Try that sometime. Not to mention all the calls from jerks who wanna show me their thing. Do you know I've had to change my phone number six times?

"In the meantime I work with a bunch of groins in the sports department who'd love to blow me out of the water on this thing. My editor wants to sack me or get me in the sack and can't decide which. So I've got a lot to gain by getting this story. My credibility for one, and the satisfaction of sticking it to all the assholes."

Petey fanned herself.

"I think the club's mine, Duffy," Slattery said. "Our bid's golden and the ol' lady's got herself in a box. She's gotta sell. Tom's estate doesn't want to take the chance she'll croak and the ball club will go into probate. Then you got her minority stock-holders—hell, her own kids—they wanna cash out and make some dough. Why shouldn't they? I think we're a lock."

He drained his glass and worked on another one. A second platter of calamari and a new delivery of onion rings appeared in front of us without so much as a word. For a guy in what appeared to be great shape, Slattery's diet stank.

"Then why are your competitors getting bumped off, Jack?" I said.

"Who cares?" he said.

"Hey—" I objected.

"Oh, towel off, chief. I don't mean it like that. Those guys were my teammates, dammit. Ossee, Criger, that sonuvabitch. It's a damn shame. A damn shame. But as far as I'm concerned, it was a maniac loose in the park that day. Hell, he could've got *me* just as easy. It didn't have a damn thing to do with me buying the club. Not a damn thing."

"But now their group is out of the box."

"Woulda been anyway," he said. "Their financing was shit. Wasn't there, Duffy. They had funny money up front and a lot of bad real estate in back and they were kiss-assing the ol' lady in hopes she'd cut 'em a deal. And everybody knew it."

He was downing the fried food like sunflower seeds in extra innings.

"What pisses me off is the whole idea that now I'm a goddamn suspect. Like I had Ossee and Lou bumped off. They're tearing into this deal like you wouldn't believe. Me! Jesus Christ. Like I'm going for a seat on the fuckin' Supreme Court. Every time I turn around I got to defend myself on some horseshit, Duffy."

"If you ask me, Slattery smells worse than the harbor on this thing," Nora Gibson said. "Couple of months ago he didn't have a prayer of getting the Sox and now he's the main force."

The two of them were working on an appetizer of pita chips with basil and garlic. Petey, whose intake catered more to fried potato skins slathered with melted cheese than baby snails stuffed in cherry tomatoes, had no choice but to nibble her way through this lunch.

"Why? He's loaded. Why *wouldn't* he be a contender?" she asked.

"Wealthy, sure. But he hasn't got the mega-bucks it takes to buy a franchise in this market," Gibson went on. "And his backers stink. New Jersey money, if you know what I mean. Plus, Mrs. Dougherty despises him just about as much as he hates her, as far as I'm concerned. I know she hates him; she's just too proper to say it. He's on record saying a woman shouldn't own a baseball team. A real modern slimeball. Forget all the times they pose together on Old-Timers' Day—there's no love lost there. And the rest of the American League owners don't think much of big Jack either.

"Plus, you got him right in the ballpark that day, which is perfect, because he has twenty thousand alibis, okay? But little Tommy Dowd, that's another story. He'd drink Drāno for Slattery on account of his old man, and if somehow he's good enough to poison two guys in one day, I'll betcha Slattery has him on a long paid vacation right about now."

Gibson was rolling now, a reporter plainly enthralled by her own notes.

"And try this," she went on. "The Old-Timers pass list turned up one of Slattery's fishing buddies. This isn't public yet, but the guy just happens to have a record for suspicion of homicide in Florida."

"Since when? What's this all about?" Petey asked.

Gibson smiled. Just then the waiter set a plate of grilled potato salad in front of her. Petey had the corn-bread–crusted crab cakes. It looked good, organically correct, perfectly seasoned, and skimpy. Petey contemplated eating both plates.

"I'm still working on it. I got an old boyfriend on *The Miami Herald*. He owes me one. He owes me *more* than one. Stay tuned."

"Buck—now I don't even wanna talk about Buck Freeman, that loony ass," Slattery said. He'd gone from the bitter lemon to glasses of Sam Adams.

"I thought you didn't like beer," I said.

He looked sideways at me. "Who told you that? I love the stuff."

He confirmed it by draining half the glass.

"Does Buck scare me?" he went on. "Hah! Like drawing a bad fortune cookie. But wait a minute—whoever said Buck wasn't smart enough to kill somebody? Not me. I always thought that crazy shit was lethal. He'd stick one of his pills in your lemonade and next thing you know you're jumping out a window or something. Didn't Ossee get it from the potato salad? That's perfect for Buck. That guy shouldn't be allowed in the ballpark, you ask me.

"And then you got Dowd's kid. You know about him? Give me a *break*. Tommy senior was a close personal friend of mine; that's on the record. But the kid's got a screw loose. Like his ol' lady. I ain't sayin' he's not wacky enough to kill somebody either, but don't give me this shit that he did it for me. This is off the record, Duffy, but I could line up a lot better mechanics than some kid, should I want to. I told Patsy he shouldn't even be on the payroll in the first place. The kid's unstable. I ever tell you how he stole a shaver from me once? He pawned the damn thing! Shit, if I were him, I'd be makin' myself scarce right about now too.

"Hey, Duffy, you want a steak or somethin'? Piece of fish? You gotta eat, how 'bout it?"

"If you keep it in Fenway, just with the people who had access, it really points to Slattery," Nora Gibson repeated. "Hey, he's not a young guy. He knows if he doesn't get the club now it won't be up for sale again in his lifetime. And you got to know him, Petey; I mean, there is no more *arrogant* person walking the earth.

"You know how it was when all those Wall Street guys got nailed. Millken, and those guys. Everybody was saying, 'Hey, why'd they have to cheat? They were making millions anyway.' But it's the arrogance, that macho crotch thing which convinces them they're above it all. Nobody'll touch them. That's our friend Jack. Trust me."

Petey had downed her crab cakes, had another beer, and was still hungry.

"Done anything on Mace Cuppy?" she asked.

"Mace Cuppy? Right now he doesn't fit," Gibson said. "A nice old guy who happened to be at the game and then chose the wrong time to die. He just doesn't do anything for me. Unless something comes up there about who drove you off the road, the whole thing is just lying there flat and cold."

"My guy in the coroner's office says the autopsy turned up the wrong kind of drug in his system," Petey said. "Enough to kill him."

"Really? If it's true, it really screws things up . . . but it just doesn't fit if Cuppy was hit too," Gibson said between bites. The grilled potato salad evidently agreed with her.

"I feel like Custer—too many Indians, too many flanks," Petey said.

"So go with the warm one," Gibson said. "God, it'd be great to find the little Dowd shit. If you even get a whiff, you gotta call me."

"I'll keep at it," Petey said. "Especially now that we're not duplicating efforts."

"Thank you," Gibson said. "*I* sure as hell don't know where Tommy went. I've got feelers out and I'm waiting for the phone call that I'm not getting. Even the cops are cold on him, and they're usually real good at finding the mopes."

She finished up, then scrubbed her plate with the last sour-dough dinner roll. Petey had a feeling she was buying this lunch.

"Only guy I'd love to hear from and I haven't so far is Charlie Hemphill," Gibson resumed.

"The Lunar Module?" Petey said, pulling in the image of one of the Red Sox true eccentrics in her mind.

"The one, the only. The cosmic southpaw."

"Zen in the bullpen," Petey said.

They both laughed. Charlie Hemphill was a latter-day free spirit who spouted the wisdom of Chinese philosophers, a left-hander who carried his own dirt to the mound in a baggie, insisting that it was sacred Indian earth, and talked to the ball like a snake charmer talking to his serpent before he pitched it. He also threw a great screwball. As they've said about screwballers since Carl Hubbell, "It takes one to throw one."

"He's the one guy I'd listen to right now," Gibson said. "He's got just the mind to dope it out. He might even know where Tommy Dowd went. A lot of those ballpark rats used to hang around Hemphill. And he gave 'em tickets, between you and me. Dowd was one of his faithful."

"Where's Hemphill live?"

"The Cape. Lives there year-round. Worships the sun and the tides and talks to the dolphins."

"Would he talk to me?"

"Darling, he'll talk to anybody. Gave more autographs than any player I ever saw. I loved the guy."

"So advised," said Petey.

Neither of them wanted coffee or espresso, and the waiter placed the check between them. Gibson not only made no move toward it, she did not even look at it.

"In the meantime," Gibson said, dipping her hands in her water glass and then seriously wiping them with her napkin, "I'm gonna be all over Slattery like a paternity suit. Him and his fishing buddy up from Florida, his pinky-ring partners, the whole pro-gram. Anything I can dig up on Jackie Ballgame."

"So, Duffy, my boy. Put in a good word with your boss, the wise Mr. Chambliss. Tell him you can't dig up anything but pure driven snow on Jackie Ballgame," Slattery said. Then he belched.

I shook my head and passed on more seafood.

"Tell me, Jack," I said, "why do you want to own a ball club?

All the grief. Paying banjo hitters three million and listening to 'em whine. Why not just sit back, enjoy your money, and go fishing?"

"Duffy, I'm so sick of fishin' I could puke."

"So what can stop you from getting the club?"

"You. The league. This whole mess. My name in the same article with Schreck and Criger so much that people start saying where there's smoke there's fire.

"Tell you the truth, I'm real sick of it. Some crazy asshole poisons people—there's no sense to it—just like that jerk who poisoned the Tylenol bottles a few years ago. We all say, there but for the grace of God. I mean, goddammit, what defense do I got? I tell people there were a lot of characters trying to get close to me that day. Press guys, photographers, you name it, and how am I to know if one of 'em hasn't got a needle full of some shit'll send me to the moon.

"So I say better Ossee and Criger than me, for cryin' out loud. But I don't say it out loud. They'd crucify my ass even worse than they're doin' it now. But that's how it sets. If somebody was gonna get whacked, Duffy, better them than me."

It was my turn to belch.

"One thing," I said, "if you're not saying this out loud, why did you go after Patsy?"

"What?"

"Why did you threaten her, Jack, tell her you were going to take her out of the game?"

His beer stopped in midair.

"Where'd you hear that? That's bullshit."

"Impeccable source."

"Wait a fuckin' minute. Think about it. This is Boston. You don't win any friends in this town by threatening a Dougherty. It's not done. I may look stupid, but the last thing I'd do is throw a knockdown pitch at Patsy. I never did. No way. Your source stinks."

I chewed on that. Slattery was adamant, and what he said made a lot of sense. It also confused things. We talked a little more and finished eating.

"Where's the check?" I said. "It'd look bad to have my lunch bought by a suspect."

And I laughed, quick and hard. Slattery grudgingly bought the chuckle.

"Your money's no good here, House. Never will be."

We got up, the chairs creaking with our bones, and padded out of the lounge.

"The whole game is suffering with this thing," I said as we went out.

"Hell, I say what's done is done," Jack Slattery said. "Find the asshole, but don't stop the clock while you're at it. I got a ball club to buy."

—13—
Fingers

I RUBBED MY HANDS TOGETHER LIKE AN ICE FISHERMAN. I patted my biceps and blew into my palms. It was the only way I could react to the chill I felt upon leaving Jack Slattery. Sure, my stomach was full and the man had treated me cordially, if not with a remarkable amount of deference. That has a way of happening when the commissioner blocks for you, I've learned. Still, I retreated from the Park Plaza with an emptiness so palpable that I took deep breaths and slapped my cheeks just to make sure I wasn't coming down with something.

I'm a privileged person, see, one who has spent a career breaking bread and dodging spit from DiMaggio, Mays, Williams, Aaron, Mantle, and just about every other great ballplayer who's performed since Pearl Harbor. And I always savored their presence, that indescribable vigor, a gift so whimsically packaged in one individual. You can't put any kind of finger on it, but it is there as verifiable as aftershave.

And yet I got little of that from Slattery this day. This was the same man who raised the bat high in the air, his fingers drumming a tattoo on the handle as animatedly as Charlie Parker on the alto sax, and hit a baseball as mercilessly as any man ever has. I felt no trace of that craft, no residue of that sweet precision. No. I got only the hard, calculating press of a businessman, an angling, leveraging financier homing in on the deal.

I reflected on all that as I walked into the hot afternoon sun of Boylston Street. The weather had grown sultry after the day or so of rain, and fungus would grow on my suit coat if I did not dress lighter. Boston's heat was not kind. A cab pulled over to hie me back to the Parker House, but not before I grabbed a *Globe* from a corner box. SLATTERY PARTNER IN GRAND JURY PROBE its headline read. Speak of the devil. I waded into the story, another product of the paper's special investigations unit, as the taxi wound its way through tourist traffic along the Common.

One of Jack's backers had collected a pot of insurance money after a warehouse fire in Hoboken a few years back, the account maintained, and now an informant was telling a New Jersey grand jury that the fire had been set. More woes for Jack.

I stuffed the paper under my arm and collected my messages. Parent had checked in again and said it was time to compare notes with our man in Homicide. Jake Stahl had left his number. I asked myself if I really wanted to go on his radio show. And finally, Patsy had called again. I was immediately reminded of the discrepancy between what she had told me and Slattery's response. Somebody was lying.

My confusion, however, did not dampen my urge to revisit her. I returned her call, and though she was not in, her secretary informed me that I was welcome for dinner that night. I accepted. Perhaps too quickly. How eager should I seem? In this age of false signals, what should I presume? Should I change my shirt? Is mouthwash a tipoff?

In the meantime, I had a few free hours, and maybe it was time to buy a new sport coat. A pair of shoes, maybe loafers. I haven't owned a pair of loafers since the Kennedy Administration. I was on my way out when Petey came in. I told her my plans and she chortled. I paid her no mind.

Not having a fashion nose to guide me, I asked the concierge for direction. He suggested the shops of Newbury Street just off the Public Garden. A cab delivered me there and I did not mosey long before I found a little place called Daniel René. I don't know if it was the Boston economy or my good looks, but a couple of salesmen clamped on me like a newly signed bonus baby. I thought a new seersucker might be nice, and they laughed at that. A crisp striped tie, and they just about howled. Instead I was draped with a copper-and-brown-plaid linen-and-cotton sport coat that was "very subtle," a floral-print silk tie that wasn't, and double-pleated brown slacks and a pair of cocoa-suede loafers. The loafers, I must say, were obscenely expensive and probably the swellest pair of shoes my dogs had ever rented. All in all, it was an *ensemble*, believe me, as slick and alluring as pricey new clothes can be, a superb camouflage for my pouchy body. I liked what the mirror held, felt a little like a dandy, but decided to chance it.

It all cost me more than I paid for my first automobile, and I covered it with a piece of plastic. The salesman, who wore perfume, said I'd made his day, and I did not want to pursue that. I walked out laden with boxes and ready for the lady in Louisburg Square.

"Aren't you a peacock!" Petey exclaimed when I promenaded in front of her.

It was just before five o'clock, and I had a taste for sherry. She gave me a great hug, which I wasn't sure what to do with.

"Does this mean I'm on my own?" she said.

"Room service. Thick novels. Bad TV. Sounds about right," I said, and winked. I was winking a lot nowadays.

The phone rang, and Petey picked up.

"Sure, Fred. He's here," she said, handing me the receiver with a puzzled look on her face.

"Did you meet with Jack Slattery earlier today?" Fred Parent asked. No pleasantries.

"Yeah. Park Plaza Hotel," I said.

"You may be the second to last person who saw him alive," Parent said.

I slumped.

The jam, sadly, was becoming commonplace: Boston police cars, marked and otherwise, crammed into every available space outside an unsuspecting entrance. So it was at the Park Plaza. Only now a crowd, informed or simply drawn by the ruckus, had clogged the Park Square sidewalks along Columbus and Arlington. I know, because pressed against the shoulder of a detective sent over by Fred Parent on one side and the hip of Petey on the other, I had to wedge myself through the gapers. The crush did not benefit my new wardrobe; there had been no time to change before Parent's man picked us up. Well-dressed or otherwise, I was commanded to be on the scene. So much for my tête-à-tête with Patsy. I had called her with the news, and she audibly gasped.

We had driven over in silence. Jack Slattery dead. It was too incredible.

"Was he murdered?" Petey breathed.

"Fred Parent doesn't work on natural deaths," I said, "does he?"

Without the police escort, we could not have gotten anywhere close to the scene. There were cops everywhere. The lobby was more like a border checkpoint, with police clearing every movement on and off the elevators and on every floor. Camera lights from video crews were blinding. The net of security was so tight and uncompromising you would have thought world leaders were convening. Then again, as far as Boston was concerned, Jack Slattery enjoyed royal status. His death, clearly, was a catastrophe to thousands who'd never met him.

The eighth floor was quiet, though no less crowded than the lobby.

"Duffy, Petey, over here," Parent called.

He led us to the suite adjoining Slattery's. The crime scene was restricted, for the time being, to all but evidence teams.

"What happened, Fred?" Petey asked.

"He didn't show up for a meeting with his lawyers. His people couldn't find him and they talked the hotel into opening the room. They found him where he is now. Flat on his back in the middle of the dining room. Strangled, as far as we know now. We'll go see him when they're done in there."

We sat down on padded mahogany chairs around an ornate dining-room table, which was now covered with notepads and clipboards. The suite was luxurious, no doubt getting upwards of eight hundred dollars a night, elegant and understated yet now no more than an overdecorated backdrop to a detectives' convention.

Parent and his peers asked me to recall every detail of my time with Slattery. Every name, every aside, every digression. Did he say he was meeting anyone? Did he mention any calls, any threats? Was he bothered by anything or anybody? Did anyone interrupt us? Did I see anyone or anything strange or odd or even the least bit peculiar before or after the lunch?

I told them everything—and nothing. For there was not a shred of the extraordinary in my conference with one of the greatest Red Sox who ever lived, at least not as far as a homicide detective was concerned. The extensive notes taken by Parent and the others would shed little light on whoever ended Jack Slattery's life. Because of that, I felt responsible in a way, no doubt like anyone who'd been in contact, however random, with a victim just before his demise. Could you have saved the child before he was struck? Could I have said something to Slattery that might have kept him from returning to his room? Indeed, did my appointment with the man make it possible for the killer to perform his deed?

All told, it took less than twenty minutes for me to tell all, and my seat was beginning to grow itchy.

"Do you want to take a look at the body?" Parent asked. "It's fresh. Neat. We should be so lucky to get one like this all the time . . . uh, I mean, as far as corpses are concerned. I mean . . . ah, to hell with it, you know what I mean."

At my nod, we got up, and Parent turned to me. "Keep your hands in your pockets just the same. The crime scene tells you everything. They tell me they're finished, but you never know."

Then we entered Slattery's suite. It was elegant in death. The drapes were open, and the low, late-afternoon light picked up the burgundy hues of the Oriental rugs. A brass chandelier was not lit. A lamp with a Chinese-vaselike base was. Except for a few newspapers, there was no clutter, no real evidence that the suite had been occupied. Certainly not lived in.

Still, there was a smell, a dull, blank smell that I could not describe nor could I forget. Petey noticed it too, and I noticed her lip quiver slightly.

Slattery lay on his back near the sofa, his legs crossed at the ankles, as supine as a short reliever taking sun in the bullpen in the early innings. His eyes were closed and his face was somewhat contorted with the same expression you remembered from when he was miffed about a called third strike. Only his neck spoke to injury with angry raw bruises sustained when his life was choked out of him. I thought of his John Wayne voice, hearing it now only in my memory.

Otherwise, he was the same Slattery, dressed in the same sport coat, the same sport shirt open at the collar, same everything. The crotch of his tan slacks was blotted with a small, dark stain that offered a slight odor of urine. His arms were askew, the right one across his chest, the other flopped on the rug straight out away from the shoulder. I wanted to lift him up, slap him on the back and give him a beer, tell him we were all pretty shook up about this.

I also had the urge to avenge this. I cannot explain it, for I felt no real personal attachment to Slattery, but seeing him there, unconscious, *lifeless,* only hours after talking with him, made me well up inside.

"He's been dead about four hours," Parent said.

That meant he had been killed not long after I had left him.

"It looks like he came into the suite and went to the bathroom. Washed his hands. Soap's damp," Parent said.

"We got a toothpick on the lavatory," said another detective.

"Was he chewin' on one? Did you notice?" Parent said to me.

"Uh, I don't think so," I said. "We were in the piano lounge. Maybe he got one from the bar. I can't be sure."

"We also think he knew the killer," Parent added. "Let him in and maybe the guy waited while Jack was in the john. No robbery. Wallet's untouched. Watch worth a good two Gs still on the wrist. No jimmy marks on the lock at all. Desk gave us nothing on anybody hanging around."

We lingered over the body. It was hard not to stare at it. Nothing around us gave any indication of struggle, or damage, or even disarray when the body hit the carpet. A mahogany butler's tray table had been moved aside, but Parent said technicians did that in searching the floor on their hands and knees. They had found nothing.

"His skin—" I began.

Slattery's skin was splotchy, something, I have learned in my latter-day career in the corpse business, caused by livor mortis. When the heart stops pumping, blood is ruled by gravity. The marks can tell you if the body was handled after death.

"The only real marks are on his neck," Parent replied. "That's nasty, as you can see. Somebody throttled him good."

"He was a strong guy," I said. "I'm amazed anybody could throttle him."

"Got him so quick they didn't even rip his shirt," Parent added. "We got a trace of skin under the nails where he clawed at his killer. But not much. No scratches. No blood. Nothing."

"Except the fingers," said another cop, a paunchy guy who seemed to scowl at Petey when she'd first entered.

"Oh, yeah," Parent said. "Shit, how could I forget? Take a look, Duffy."

"What?" I said.

"They're all broken," said Parent.

"My God," Petey exclaimed.

We got down on one knee for a better look. Indeed, Slattery's thick fingers were mangled, bent and crooked like the tines of cheap forks. Yet none of the fractures had broken through the skin, and there was no blood. Only two rows of oblique, uneven, oddly bent fingers. Parent lifted a finger with his ballpoint pen, and it looked like something Carlton Fisk would bring over to the trainer after a foul tip.

"It's the only statement the killer made," Parent said.

"Huh?" I said, transfixed by the corpse.

"Murderers tell you things," Parent explained. "What they do to a victim, the way they leave the body, or where, or maybe something they take. This guy wanted Slattery's fingers broken and he wanted everybody to know it too."

"Were they broken in the struggle?" Petey asked.

"Maybe one or two. But not the whole bunch. No way. Only the thumbs are whole," Parent said.

We stared.

"No rings," Petey said.

"He never won any," I said, and wished I hadn't.

"It was done postmortem, for what that's worth," Parent cut in. "It's the only thing that doesn't fit."

"How's that?" I asked.

"The guy was in control. Organized. Nothing out of place. Everything planned. Usually we see things right off at a homicide that tell us ninety percent of the time who did it. Most murders are spur of the moment—you know, passion. Not here. This one's cold. Yet he does this to the fingers. Hey, that's a statement, you know? Like the mob putting nickels in a guy's eyes. It took some time and says something. We don't know what yet, but it's there. Real personal, you know? It's all we got. Otherwise, this guy was good."

"Sick fucker," said the first cop.

I nodded absently, and stared at the gnarled hands. Slattery's famous hands.

"Best mitts in the game," I said.

"You can say that again," said the second cop.

There was nothing more. Nothing to gain from viewing a body that was losing temperature as we gawked, nothing to pick up from a bloodless, nearly odorless murder scene. Apart from Jack Slattery's carcass, evidence came in almost microscopic bits, retrieved with tweezers.

"Did we get a decent print in the whole place?" Parent asked no one in particular.

At that, a pair of detectives approached with a black vinyl bag and unraveled it on the floor beside Slattery. We watched. They unzipped the bag and, with one man at Slattery's head and the other at his feet, began to lift and slide the body onto the bag.

"Hold on," said a detective standing off to the side.

He came over and helped raise Slattery's back.

"Take a look," he said, and the others closed in.

Under the body lay a watch. It had a sizable face with a shiny mesh-gold band. On their hands and knees, a trio of detectives crowded around the discovery, checking over every inch of the rug and the back of Slattery's coat, yet not touching the watch. Finally, they rolled the body and propped it on its side. A photographer came in and took a shot of the watch. With pens the cops lightly probed and surveyed the watch and anything around it. They were fastidious, and painfully slow, as if they'd just uncovered a prehistoric relic. Then, once again with a ballpoint pen, one of them lifted the watch in the air and studied it carefully.

"Well, well," he mused, obviously spotting something on the back of the case.

"Whattaya got, Sam?" said Parent.

" 'Boston Red Sox, A.L. Champs, 1967.' Engraved," said the detective. "But listen to this. 'This one's for you, Tommy. J.S.' Also engraved."

Somebody let out a low whistle.

"Hellooooo, Mr. Dowd," Parent said, looking at the watch.

"Senior or junior?" I asked.

"There's only one left," Parent said.

The watch was dropped into a clear plastic Ziploc bag as he said it. Slattery was zipped into his bag and lifted awkwardly by two uniformed Boston cops. In his last trip out of the Park Plaza, Jack Slattery would go the back way.

"Good Lord, look at this," Parent said as we waded into the crowded lobby.

It was alive with media, camera crews, dozens of men and women with notebooks and microphones in their fists. Outside the Park Plaza, on the sidewalks and clogging the streets to where police had set up barricades and rerouted traffic, a milling, murmuring crowd continued to grow. News of Slattery's murder had made Boston a very small town, and everybody in it rushed over to see if what they had heard was true.

"Okay," Parent said after we found our way out onto Arlington Street. He turned and faced us, looking over his shoulder in order to avoid curious ears.

"There's a lot of work to do. We need the wrist that was home to the watch. In the meantime, Duffy—and you too, Petey—watch yourselves. I mean it. Everything tells us this guy, whoever he is, is right behind you both. He's too close. I'll stay in touch as much as I can, and I'll let you know what we get with Dowd, but in the meantime, watch your ass."

He leaned over and gave Petey a buss on the cheek. She didn't seem to mind; in fact, she returned a slight embrace. Parent was getting no prettier, God knows, but in the context of an ugly death, his presence was appreciated. At least to me it was. He was a savvy detective, well-schooled in murder, and we were faced with a killer who was better than all of us by four.

By the time Parent left Petey and me alone in the lingering heat of early evening, it was nearly eight P.M. Their arranged plans for the evening had been killed with Jack Slattery. I felt exhausted, as if I'd just sat through a long, dull doubleheader. My new clothes hung on me like a painter's smock.

"What about your date?" Petey asked.

"I don't know. I've sort of lost the anticipation," I said.

"Why don't you call her?" she said. "She'd probably want to know about what we just saw."

"What about you?"

"I'm edgy as hell," Petey said, rubbing her hands together and shivering. "I'm going to root around. Maybe find Gibson. I don't know."

"Be careful out there," I said.

She smiled and tugged on one of my sleeves.

"Truly great threads, Uncle Duf," she said.

My call was answered. I went right over, and Patsy again opened the door herself. She appeared shaken, her eyes moist. She was the matriarch of the Red Sox, and one of its favorite sons had just been put down. Even though she did not like the man—in fact, he had come to be her arch-antagonist—she was no fool: She had to know what he meant to the club and its fans.

"They're killing us," she said. "They're cutting the heart out of us."

There was no mistaking the plural pronoun. And though I said nothing, I was struck by her attempt to grieve over Jack Slattery. I took her hand, and she pulled me to her. We held each other in her magnificent parlor. She sniffled. I smelled the rich fragrance of her hair and caressed her back. She was pliant in my embrace, not stiff or trembling. Her mourning, like other aspects of her life, was clearly under control.

We parted slightly and she looked at me with a tight, resolved smile.

"It's still our night," she said.

I exhaled.

"Wait a minute," I said. "I just saw the body of Jack Slattery—the life throttled out of him. For cryin' out loud, Patsy, all of his fingers were broken. One of the greatest players in the game and he's murdered like a two-bit thief. Pardon me, but that doesn't put me in the mood."

"I didn't mean it that way," she said.

"What did you mean?" I continued. "You told me the other day that Slattery threatened you. And now he's dead, Patsy."

"I didn't mean—"

"What *did* you mean? Did he threaten you? Or was that a play for my sympathy? Because I knew Jack Slattery—hell, I was with the guy this afternoon—and I ask myself, would he be *that* stupid?"

She turned her back to me.

"What are you saying?" she asked.

"I don't know, Patsy. I don't know what to say. Slattery's dead and I don't want to believe that you lied to me."

She pivoted, her arms crossed over her chest, and did not respond. Her eyes did not meet mine.

"You have no right to accuse me," she said.

I used to think I knew when it was best to say nothing, and I had said too much already. I did not hear the door close behind me as I left. I was sure it did.

——14——
Odell Hale's Carom

ONLY ONCE HAVE I BEEN IN BOSTON ON THE FOURTH OF July, and there is no finer place to be. The masses from Lexington and Braintree and points beyond descend upon the city, crowding along the banks of the Charles and the Hatch Shell like giddy campers. Everybody is an American. John Philip Sousa, who knew his beat, is Mozart. Ants are paralyzed by an endless grid of picnic blankets. And the Boston Pops Orchestra finds its true calling among the percussion of firecrackers. The Fourth here, to be sure, is pure bunting, bright and dedicated, as if Boston, the seat of it all, should sizzle and ping louder and longer than any other city in the land.

The crush of a Boston Fourth came to mind as I witnessed the city's reaction to Jack Slattery's murder. Boston had been kicked in the gut, mugged, stripped of a favorite son as genuine as the Kennedys, and it heaved and writhed and spewed a collective anger that hung in the air like the exhaust of a Roman candle. It was pain and impotence all rolled up in a black vinyl body bag carted unceremoniously from the Park Plaza Hotel. A pair of Old-Timers poisoned in the ballpark was a cruel, disturbing curiosity; the garroting of Jack Slattery was a damned outrage. The bare hands of Boston wanted this killer, this thief of Fenway legacy.

Old-timers said the city had not been riled this much since

the summer of '63, when a roster of women was strangled to death with nylon hosiery in their own apartments. That was three decades back, when Boston was a different city in a different age, yet the paralysis and the anger Boston felt over Slattery's murder were the same. The Boston Strangler left no clues. What was even more troubling, I was reminded, was that the police never really pinched the culprit. Albert DeSalvo, a deluded, wigged-out fellow who snatched his fantasies from television shows, confessed from prison and convinced most everybody that he was the strangler. But DeSalvo was never tried, the public never collected its proverbial pound of flesh, and the little menace lived out his miserable days in Bridgewater State Hospital.

Just as they did back then, Boston's homicide dicks—in this case, Fred Parent and his fellow gumshoes—were feeling the heat. White-hot. From the street and from the brass. Parent's team had gone hitless so far: shut out on the Criger-Schreckengost probe, unable to run down young Tommy Dowd, and stripped of Buck Freeman when he flew the cuckoo's nest only hours after he'd forecast Slattery's demise. Buck, by the very fact that he had the paws strong enough to get and keep a choke hold on Jack Slattery, was now a bona fide suspect. Yet he too was a fugitive. At this rate, Boston cops, one newspaper wag groused, couldn't find Sherm Feller during a home stand.

To deflect the outcry, the mayor, a strong-jawed Irishman from West Roxbury, brayed into a bank of microphones that the Boston P.D. would conduct a dragnet for Slattery's killer like nothing the city had seen since "the scourge of Albert DeSalvo." It did not give the citizens comfort.

For his part, Parent was working twelve-hour shifts with no days off, a full-court press that left him little time to compare notes with us. Little, but due to his well-kindled interest in Petey, not none at all. Early the next morning he called me.

"We got Dowd's car. A dog-shit Camaro. Parked two blocks from the Park Plaza. He left it behind, the pooch. We're taking it apart as I speak. But get this: Its right front fender is pushed in. Like it bumped something real good," Parent said.

"Any paint marks?" I said. "Petey's rental car was light blue."

"We know. And I'm waiting on that now," he said. "We also got a pawnbroker told us Tommy came in and hocked the watch a month ago. Said he was sure of it 'cuz Tommy hocked the same piece two, three times before. The watch—you can't mistake it.

The Red Sox gave 'em out after the '67 season, and Slattery gave his to Dowd's ol' man. Him and Slattery were buddies—we know that. The kid gets the watch when the ol' man kicks and he uses it for a stake in poker games, shit like that. Sweetheart, huh? Pawnbroker said he comes in and buys it back a week ago. Only this time he's flush. Good bundle of bills, the guy said.

"Otherwise we don't get much on the kid," he went on. "He's a goof. Unpredictable. Works Fenway and pounds beer with his townie buddies. Sleeps in his car a lot, they said. Probably 'cuz of his ol' lady. And he's big—you ever seen him? Guys on the grounds crew say he can throw the tarp around like a tablecloth. Big enough to choke Slattery. No pinches. Plays the lottery too much. They put him on at the Garden sometimes in the winter on the crew that picks up the parquet off the ice when the Bruins are in. Lives at home. Least he used to.

"So we go over and see the mother. South Boston, triple-decker, the whole works. Boy, is she a beaut! Lady eats tacks. We got three guys in her living room and she doesn't flinch. Got the balls to tell us the watch was stolen. Said Tommy told her it was. Somebody boosted it out of his locker at the ballpark. Did he file a police report? No way. Insurance claim? No way. So that story smells up the joint. I mean, the ol' lady is goin' to bat for this loser. But whattaya expect? She's his mother and that's what mothers do. I had mothers tell me their kids ain't nowhere around when they're hidin' in the fridge in the kitchen eating ripe olives.

" 'Tween you and me, Duffy, we got eyes on that house round the clock. Tommy comes back for a change of underwear and we got him. Phone's tapped so heavy all she has to do is *think* about the kid and we know about it."

It was all a frustrated ramble on Fred's part. He was as mad as anybody about the fact that they couldn't pick up a simple, screwed-up, South Boston kid.

"Buck we'll get. He's too loopy to stay lost," he said. "Where's your niece? We want her to take a look at the car."

"Probably in Tommy Dowd's back pocket," I said.

Actually, she was in the shower.

"Christ, Duffy, if she even gets a whiff of that peckerhead, she's gotta page me. My career needs it right now."

After promising to bring around all the evidence reports on Slattery, he rang off.

A few minutes later I replayed Parent's call to Petey as she stood in my suite blotting her just-washed hair with a towel and offering to devour a plate of room-service bagels with me. She was wearing an oversized terry-cloth robe, smelling of peaches, and getting off to a late start. Despite my late night, I had been unable to sleep in.

"Fred sounded frazzled," I said.

"Hmmm," Petey responded.

"How was Mrs. Dougherty?" she added. "Bereaved?"

"Not sure. Maybe not bereaved enough."

"Huh?" she said, awaiting an explanation.

I told her of Patsy's behavior the night before, and then of Slattery's alleged threat. I don't like the word *alleged,* but it applied here.

"Maybe you expected too much grief from her, Unk," she said. "She's a strong woman, and they don't slobber easily."

I nodded. Perhaps I had been too hard on Patsy. Perhaps I am impatient with people who do not share my reverence at the demise of great line-drive hitters. Perhaps Patsy deserved a fairer shake from me.

"I say we regroup," I said. "Lay out what we got, look at the roster and the depth chart. Try to figure out what's going on in Boston and Hartford and all points between."

For an hour we did just that. We spread out the morning papers on my table and shut off the television because the local station wasn't offering much more than the headlines anyway. A messenger arrived with Parent's promised police reports—a stack two inches high—and we plowed into them. The cops had interviewed family members, friends, ballpark employees, tipsters, and, of course, other ballplayers. They'd run Tommy Dowd up and down the flagpole, even to the point of talking to his high school wrestling coach. Tommy *was* strong.

The cops had run down Slattery's fishing buddy, a thug named Joe LaChance who originally came from Waterbury but who ran a charter-boat service in Pensacola and had a history of getting arrested for bagging bales of cannabis when the sailfish weren't biting. Like many drug dealers, he was often questioned when other drug dealers disappeared. And he had been in Fenway Park for the Old-Timers' Game. When the Boston coppers finally interviewed him, LaChance was totally uncooperative. They had to grudgingly release him when a clout-heavy Boston defense lawyer appeared in person and made a stink. The lawyer had been retained by Jack Slattery.

Petey and I drew sides in the boardroom fight for the franchise. We indexed the interviews and cross-checked names, something that provided yet another list. Then we tried to make sense out of the lab reports. Petey added the one she had been sent by the Winter kid in West Hartford, who editorialized in favor of a lethal mickey in Mace Cuppy's beer. Winter wanted in on the high jinks, and if we'd asked, he'd probably be right here in the suite. We rechecked the Fenway passes and the press-credentials list from the Old-Timers' game. We set up time lines and scenarios and all kinds of possible M.O.s of known suspects. We blue-skied and imagined and speculated and generally tried to think like the snake who was behind all this.

It was a good skull session, the kind of thing Parent and his buddies did every morning, or the workings of a beat reporter culling through his notes and musings after a seventeen-inning game. And when we were all done we could have written a Sunday feature or passed a pop quiz, but we were not very much further in knowing why four men were dead. The table and sofa were littered with data.

"Is he somewhere in here?" I asked.

Petey looked at me, her brilliant copper hair nicely disheveled, gnawing on a pencil, her good brain skittering about like a waterbug on a rapids.

"No," she said.

And she said it with a look, a glint of certainty or just plain cussedness or some rare intuition.

"Tommy Dowd's running—we've gotta find out why," she went on. "Buck Freeman's disappeared. We gotta find him too. It's no surprise that he bolted and I think he's nuts enough to kill. I really do. Slattery's fishing buddy, what's his name, La-Chance, looks suspicious until you put Slattery's murder into the pie. Then he doesn't fit unless we got a double cross."

And her voice trailed off.

"I want to find Charlie Hemphill," Petey said.

"*The* Charlie Hemphill? Planet Mars? Thrower of the U.F.O.?"

"That's the one," she replied. "Nora Gibson brought him up. Said he used to be a hit with Dowd and his crew. Plus he's probably on Buck Freeman's wavelength."

"It's a stab," I replied.

"Sure is. How 'bout you?"

"Work the phone. Then I'll head out to the ballpark for tonight's game. Look around. Talk to people. See how weepy folks get about Slattery when the black crepe comes out."

"Unk, you're not gonna try to mix the murders with something out of Cooperstown, are you? We been down that route already, you know."

"To hell with you," I said. "I don't appreciate that."

"Sorry . . . don't go ballistic," she said. "It's just that, if you ask me, there's a real sour taste to this whole thing. Like greed, revenge. Or just plain meanness. I don't see it wrapped in horsehide."

"Could be. On the other hand, maybe the whole thing's horsehide," I said.

She sighed and shrugged.

"I'd like to come along with you," she said. "I got a taste for a Fenway frank. But I gotta try to run down Hemphill."

We left our materials where they lay and parted company. On her own, Petey had contracted with a beeping service. She lectured me on how to use it, reminded me that it now cost more than a dime to use a pay phone, and presented me with one of the noisy little buggers.

"Twentieth century, Unk—final decade," she said.

I slipped it into my suit-coat pocket. Which doesn't mean I will give in on synthetic turf or the designated hitter.

From then until midafternoon I pulled out the long-distance card and called some people. Old baseball guys, some reporters, a few hats on the business end of the game. I called them to root around, bump ideas. I don't know how much help it was, but the talk was good. These guys were not in Boston, not consumed by the story or spattered by the hot grease. They suggested that I also step back a bit.

It was after three when I left the Parker House and headed for Fenway. I like that time of the afternoon, so I decided to walk. It was hot, but a breeze was blowing in from the harbor and I tried to catch it. I could thrive in Boston because it's a walker's town. I made my way over to Park Street and the Common, which was still fairly green but trampled. It attracts its share of bums, panhandlers, hustlers, and double-talkers, but no self-respecting city park would seem right without them.

I cut directly west toward Charles Street and crossed into the

Public Gardens. An armada of swan boats was out on the lake. I crossed Arlington near the Ritz and began my long westward trek up Commonwealth toward the ballpark. The avenue is really a boulevard, a busy, deviated main artery running through the Back Bay and reminding me very much of the thoroughfares of Europe. The Charles River rippled a few blocks to my right. I walked briskly to stimulate my pump and bellows.

By the time Kenmore Square came into view, I was sick of walking. It was near four o'clock, still hot, and I needed a beer, a domestic vintage rather than the Canadian suds touted by a billboard high above the square. By the time I turned onto Brookline I could smell the vendors' first batches of sausages and green peppers. I opted for two bags of roasted peanuts for sale on Yawkey Way. The metallic clank of a beer barrel inside Fenway made me salivate. If I were navigating a ship, I'd be aground.

My credentials got me into the nearly empty ballpark. A cup of beer and some peanuts would hold me while I caught the Red Sox romp through hitting and fielding practice. The team, in third place with a bullet, had just come back into town after a brief, midweek road trip. Fenway, even with its flags at half-mast and its portals draped in black and purple mourning colors, glistened in its faded beauty.

As I sat and watched, staying out of sight of the few people I recognized, who would have jabbered my woolly ears off, I shelled peanuts and guzzled the beer too fast and thought about why old ballplayers were dying in Boston. This was the proper place to consider it. And that made the fact all the more unbearable. I might kill to enjoy the game, to witness it, to recount its pleasures, but I'd no more kill one of its participants than I'd shoot a barking seal on a stool. What would be the point?

Those thoughts were occasionally punctuated by the slaps and pops and motions on the field. I didn't know many of the kids out there, but they were only variations and late models of vintage performers. I watched a lanky black kid in left, arms drooping like branches on a willow tree, seemingly uninvolved, with yards of green between him and the infield. My eyes were on him just as a left-handed hitter stung a line drive in his direction, the ball slicing off the bat like an angry rocket, and suddenly the somnolent string bean came alive, moving like a lizard to a bug as soon as the ball was hit, dashing into the corner and snaring the whistling drive just before he and it hit the wall. Then he stopped dead, as still as if he were on a tether, raised himself on tippy toes, hopped, then flipped the ball back into the infield as if it were a bad tomato. He returned back to his spot, and suddenly he was sleepy again, arms hanging, having just made the impossible look routine, thinking nothing of it—indeed, if I know anything about this game, not thinking much of anything at all.

I watched other routines, pitchers jogging, long swats, pivots over second. All of them reminded me of things I'd seen in Fenway just yesterday—or years ago. I never saw it, but I'd surely read enough about Joe Cronin's line drive that bounced off Odell Hale's head and turned into a triple play. Nor did I see the dwarf run out from the stands and play third when Cleveland put on the "Williams' shift." And I had to take my Daddy's word for all the dropped balls—and the one Harry Hooper miraculously caught—in the 1912 Series.

I worked to remember Schreckengost and Criger, Cuppy and Slattery, tried to see them in their Red Sox colors, tried to connect them with some kind of awfulness that might elevate them into targets. With Slattery that was easy: The great ones are never all things to all fans. Ossee and Lou were more elusive. With Cuppy I had not a clue. In every spectator sport there are the scarlet sins, of course, the catastrophic errors that lose crucial games, even championships, that make brazen headlines and notorious video footage—film as oft-played as the burning of the *Hindenburg*. They live in infamy, of course, those painful lapses, throbbing in the memories of fans, especially Red Sox fans, like diamond-shaped migraines. Don't even bring them up.

Yet for every brazen, unforgettable gaffe there are hundreds of others—small misdeeds, perhaps a sin of omission, a missed bunt, a failure to take an extra base—that most of us have long forgotten but which have been frozen in some fan's mind and over the years have grown disproportionately more heinous. They turn into flubs as grave as Buckner's in '86, lapses as painful as Pesky's in '46, misjudgments as costly as Darrell Johnson's in '75. Some were witnessed firsthand, others heard over a radio or watched on television, and all were felt, for they cut like a stiletto and the wounds have never been healed by the scab of history. So that leaves plenty of real and imagined villains who have yet to receive a nod of forgiveness.

And so my reflections went through the two hours or so of batting practice. I sat pretty much uninterrupted. Baltimore was in town, and soon they emerged in their gray-and-orange suits from the first-base dugout. When the gates opened, I was soon surrounded by fans big and small, and I made my way back to the press box for dinner. I enjoyed the chicken and rolls alone.

Just minutes before the game, I left the press box. It is new and sleek, but still no place to watch a game. It is too high a perch, sterile behind the glass, and full of paid observers. I prefer to roam Fenway—sit with the scouts behind home plate, or just stand behind the last row of seats along the first or third lower deck with a beer and an open ear. The fans from South Boston and points beyond provide the insight and the amusement. There is no more candid bunch in baseball.

Once out of the press box I wandered, climbed, mingled with the nattering crowd, and soon I found my way to the upper grandstand in faraway right field. I turned and looked out of the stadium through the screen behind the top row. Across the street, looking east, I spotted the old Latin Academy, the squat buildings and parking lots beyond, the Howard Johnson Motel on Boylston and car-choked, urban streets beyond that. It was all city, like the neighborhood around Wrigley in Chicago, a place where people washed their cars at the curbs and kids wedged baseball cards in their bicycle spokes, where dogs chased alley cats. This Fenway Park in which I stood was a part of their block. It was their ballyard, the aura of its lights and the caterwaul of its crowds as much a part of their lives as mail carriers and landlords. It was they who knew Criger, Schreckengost, and Cuppy as Lou, Ossee, and Mace, guys who played here for a few years and parked in the lot on Ipswich. Did they also know the source of their doom?

I was puzzling over this as the innings passed, still wandering like a camel around the park, occasionally sitting in an empty seat behind a pole, enjoying the odd, different angles each seat provided. I even enjoyed the blind spots, the seats with restricted views that made you guess what was happening when the ball went out of sight. Like an old car with one windshield wiper, it was part of the bargain. The game was close but unexceptional save for a play or two that sent a buzz through the crowd because it was pure big league, effortless, simple. On one of them—an unassisted double play by a slick little Venezuelan shortstop—it hit me: Keep it simple. Simple. Eye on the ball. Head in.

Then I watched as the long black kid came up to hit. Still droopy-eyed, still so loose he seemed unconnected, he raised the bat over his head and absently lifted his fingers off the handle. I stared, mesmerized by those fingers. Lifting and dropping like an insect's tentacles, lifting and dropping.

Again it was simple: Jack Slattery's fingers. Broken fingers. Why in hell break them? Why?

The game was hard into the seventh inning, the Sox up by a run, when I was beeped. For the first time in my life the annoying sound came from a gadget in *my* pocket, something I was unaware of until the lady next to me nudged my arm. I felt like a codger whose hearing aid had shorted out, and I awkwardly wrestled with the little electronic pest. Its screen flashed a telephone number. It was mine at the hotel. Petey, no doubt.

I lumbered off to a pay phone and dialed the room.

"Unk! Finally, dammit!" Petey said. "We've been robbed. Somebody broke into the room. They tossed everything."

In minutes I was out of the park and into a cab.

"Cripes!" I said upon seeing the mess.

The suite had not so much been burgled as ransacked. The mishmash of notes, police reports, and newspaper articles that we'd left on the table had become an unholy mess strewn about the suite. Beyond the table I could see that drawers had been opened, the closet rifled, even the bed had been pulled apart.

Petey stood with her hands on her hips.

"Don't touch anything—Fred's on his way," she said.

"Your room too?" I asked.

"They got in. The door between the suites was open, but I can't see that they touched anything. Whatever they wanted, it was in here," she said, surveying the litter.

"This guy knows us, Pete. He's right on our tails."

She exhaled loudly and bit her lip.

"Let's get out of here!" she said. "Let's move."

We waited almost half an hour before Parent showed up, an evidence technician in tow.

"Dammit," he muttered when he got a look. He gingerly moved through the suite. His companion went to work on the knob of an open dresser drawer.

"What's missing? Can you tell?" Parent said.

"Some of your police reports, I think," Petey said.

"You see our notes anywhere?" I asked, looking into the mess.

Petey looked, pushed aside some newspaper clippings, lifted and probed, and finally said, "No. They're gone."

Parent's evidence guy looked up at him and shook his head. "Nothing," he said.

"Bastard's playing with us," Parent said.

"With us?" Petey said, throwing the cop from Homicide a sharp look.

"With you," he said.

—15—
The Morgue

"Hell, we just clean the joint up and go to bed," I said.

Petey wasn't buying it. She had her grips half filled and was hell-bent on checking out.

"He gets in once, he gets in again," she said. "I'm not laying me down to sleep in that room another night."

"So we change rooms. Another floor. There's dozens of them."

"He got to us here. And real easy. I want out."

"Where you going?"

"HoJo's by the ballpark if I have to," she said.

She was rattled, not the unflappable Petey I used to know. Of course, she was still sore and purple from the battering she took in Hartford. And she was steamed that somebody had the *cojones* to jimmy the lock and run through her belongings. Her expression was taut, the look of someone who sees a monster in the rearview mirror.

"You coming?" she said.

"Let me make a call," I said, and I got on the horn to the Lenox Hotel. I hated to leave the Parker House, and I certainly did not hold it responsible for the break-in, but Petey was adamant—and afraid. The Lenox was another venerable Boston inn, a nearby place we might slip into without notice. A clerk there said they were anxious to have us.

Fred Parent hung around, mostly watching his evidence man poke about, and even offered to take us over to the Lenox when we were ready. He looked tired, his clothes sagged on him, and he didn't smell too good. He was barely even able to make nice to Petey. Police work, I fear, wears people down. Cases like these weigh on them like yokes.

"There's not much for us here," he said, casting a glance on the carnage of my suite. "If this is our boy again, he's left us shit. Same as we got with Slattery. But he's too damn close, Duffy. He's playin' us for jerks. He broke in here as if to say, 'Hey, House, whattaya know? Lemme see your notes.' That's what he did, if you ask me."

"Does that mean we know him, Fred?" I asked.

"Or he knows us. It's like the firebug, Duffy. He'll be hangin' around when all the hook and ladders get there. We used to have a saying, 'Pinch the first guy who volunteers for a posse.' 'Cuz sometimes you get the perpetrator pushing it in your face. It's a thrill for him. He's saying, 'You stupid assholes. I did it and you don't even know it.' That's what I see with this guy."

I studied him, digesting what he'd said. "Is Tommy Dowd that slick?" I asked.

Parent shook his head. "Until we grab his ass, we don't know."

It took us a while to get packed. You don't stay in a place for a week and move out in a jiffy. But finally we were out of the Parker House, and with no forwarding address. In his unmarked detective pool car, Parent shuttled us over to the Lenox at Exeter and Boylston in the Back Bay. It was late now, near midnight, and he was calling it a night. We slipped into the canopied Exeter entrance with the help of a single bellhop. Had we been in the mood, we would have taken in the Lenox's ambience, the formal "salon" look and feel to it. Old, small, filled with Oriental lamps and deep-blue tones, the Lenox was a place suited to troubled characters peopling literary novels. George Washington and his pals looked out over the lobby and the foyers from oil paintings. Beethoven sonatas caressed the background din.

In a few moments we were escorted to a pair of eighth-floor rooms on the Boylston Street side. The rooms were small, even cramped when compared to the Parker House suites, but a recent face-lift made them quite elegant and cozy. We padded on thick, emerald-green carpeting. Floral-print wallpaper, glossy white woodwork, tiny but sparkling white bathrooms, a simple table and chairs in front of a window looking out over Boston.

Petey was satisfied, and with a wave she turned in.

"Sleep tight," I said.

"No way," she said as she closed her door, snapped the dead-bolt lock, and slid the door chain into place.

The bed was fine, the hotel tomblike, but I couldn't sleep worth a damn. At dawn I was in the Lenox Grill eating eggs and poring over the papers. Parent was coming over for breakfast later on. At seven I placed a call to the private line of the commissioner in New York. An old bean trader accustomed to being on the trading floor at dawn, Chambliss could be counted on to be in his office, alone, unbothered.

"House? I pay his bills but I don't hear from him," Chambliss replied after I'd offered a simple hello.

I informed him of the room invasion and our new location—at reduced rates—and we talked baseball and Boston and misery.

"It all distracts us from the core issues of the game," he said. "Salaries, urine tests, and Japanese ownership."

I rang off after a while and dialed a local number. Mrs. Dougherty was also up and suggested I join her for breakfast. I opted for dinner instead, and she obliged. She said she was eager to see me again, that it had been too long. *Oh my,* I thought.

An hour later I was joined by the redhead and the detective. Parent had nicked his adam's apple, used a piece of tissue paper to blot it, and the scrap hung there on his neck like a fly's wing. Otherwise, he was up and at 'em.

"I'm two-faced on this thing," he said, digging into a seafood omelet that covered his plate.

He and Petey had joined me just about the time I was getting sick of sitting. Parent had brought along the latest batch of detective reports on the Slattery scene and gave them to me.

"Ambivalent, Fred," Petey said. "You're ambivalent about it."

"That too," he said, frowning at her. "Point is, you ready for this? Here we are: hard on Dowd's ass. I mean, I just heard 'fore I come here the boys say they found a bag full of caffeine pellets, like super No-Doz, in Tommy's car. The kind of stuff that blew out Mace Cuppy's meter. It's preliminary, but that's the word."

"Now that digs Tommy even deeper. His watch. The dented

car. Now the drug. The little shithead is dead meat. *If* we could pinch him."

Petey worked on a bagel. I picked my teeth and perused the Slattery reports.

"Then again, we got *your* episode," he went on. "Your place gets tossed. Notes, reports grabbed. Now that doesn't fit. If Tommy Dowd so much as went out for a newspaper his ass would be *nailed*. That's how hot it is for him out there. If I'm Tommy, hey, I may get away with slipping into the Park Plaza for Slattery but after that there's no way I'm in the Parker House sniffing through your underwear—"

"Hey!" Petey snapped.

"Sorry, but shit, there's no way this kid, whose face is on every TV in New England, moonwalks into a big hotel, downtown Boston, gets up on your floor, jimmies his way into both your rooms like some goddamn cat burglar and then walks out. And *nobody* sees him? C'mon. People saw Lee Harvey Oswald runnin' down the street and they hadn't even seen his picture on TV yet. And right now in this town, Tommy's a lot more famous than Oswald. So I can't buy it."

"Good. I can't either," said Petey.

"What do you buy, Fred?" I asked.

"Thought you'd never ask. Try this. Let's say Tommy's our killer in Fenway. Perfect. The little worm can walk around the park and nobody pays attention to him. Why does he do it? Maybe he works for Slattery, or somebody in Slattery's group who wants the competition whacked. I don't know. But it goes down, and now the heat's on. Then Slattery gets it. Now wait a minute. There's no way Dowd takes out Jack Slattery. If I'm Slattery I don't let the prick do anything but shine my shoes. But some other bastard, somebody real close, somebody, say, who gets screwed by Jack, this guy sees he can get Slattery and put it on Dowd. The watch . . . the car . . . the nicotine shit. I mean, the kid is set up like a duck."

He talked and chewed with purpose, his system working overtime.

I had to break in. "This guy? How about Patsy Dougherty? Where does she fit in here, Fred?"

He gave me a pained look.

"She don't. Look, Duffy, Patsy's got motive coming out her eyebrows, and we've been all over her case, especially after Slattery's murder, but we got nothing. She's as clean as the Virgin Mary."

"With her money she'd have connections," said Petey. "She'd hire somebody."

"She could. No question about it," Parent replied. "But what I'm sayin' is, we haven't found a *thing* on her and we got a shitload on everybody else. Whoever set up Tommy Dowd is who we want."

"You're saying Tommy's dumb enough to let this happen? He's too dumb to catch on?" Petey asked.

"No. Tommy's dead."

He paused for a moment and we stared at him.

"That's right," he said. "If you ask me, Tommy Dowd'll come floatin' in on Revere Beach one of these days. You watch. They just took him out, that's all."

He liked that. And well he should. Even though it smacked of an inspiration that had hit him in the shower while he was rinsing a second time, it was one of the first original thoughts in the whole investigation. And it had made his day. Petey measured him from across the table.

"Sure takes the heat off you guys, Fred," she finally said.

"Hey, it's a scenario. We're still dragging the streets for Tommy Dowd. But in the meantime it makes a whole lot of sense. And on top of that—"

Parent was now leveling a stack of wheat toast. For a skinny guy, he ate a ton.

"What? There's more?" Petey said. "Come on, Uncle Duffy. Jump in here. You're sitting like a stone."

Maybe I was. Or maybe I was still bothered by what Parent had said about Patsy and her role in this. If he could not place a smoking gun in her possession, was there none?

"It's Fred's floor," I finally said.

"Thank you, sir," he said. "And yes, there's more. Try this: As far as I'm concerned, you're hot. Critical mass. Both of you. This guy *knows* you. He knows what you do and where you go. He knows what you've done. In Chicago, L.A. He knows you're tied into the department, chapter and verse. And he thinks you're blind to him so that's why he's staying close."

"Like the firebug who loves the firehouse," I said.

"You got it. I know these guys . . . there's a mentality there," Parent went on. "So I say we all stop going separate ways and stay together. Draw him in. Put both of you front and center."

I smiled, but not gaily.

"It's called bait, Pete," I said.

She knew. She wadded up her napkin and stuffed it into Parent's juice glass.

"Forget it, Fred. You want chum, go to a fishery," she said. "This maniac's killed four people, maybe even five if you think Tommy Dowd's croaked. I got my car flipped and my nose broke and my room broken into. And you want us front and center. What are we now, Fred, decoys or drones or just plain sacrificial lambs?"

She turned to look at me.

"I agree, and my nose wasn't even broken," I said.

"Wait a minute, the point is—" Parent began.

"Hold it, Officer, my turn," I said. "Seems to me it's time we figured out if our boy is done yet. He may be, you know. He may have had his own personal agenda and that's that. No more mayhem . . ."

"Wouldn't a broken into your room then," Parent cut in.

"Just the opposite," I said. "He breaks in to make sure we're stymied. If he's satisfied, he sits tight. Job done, and he's the happiest killer alive. And we're shut out. We'll never catch him."

They both chewed on that. Drank to it with more coffee.

"But you don't think so, do you?" Parent finally said.

He was sharp this morning.

"Not for a minute," I said. "I think this guy gets a thrill killing ballplayers. He's as driven as the worst serial killer. Psychotic. In his mind he's got a score to settle, except it isn't with young women or little kids or homosexuals like those other sick bastards, it's with guys who played in Fenway. Red Sox."

"That means he kills again," Parent said.

I nodded. "Has to. There's too many devils left."

Petey made a face, but she did not contest the call.

"Then why don't we pinch Buck Freeman's ass?" Parent said. "Sounds right up his alley."

"Not bad, Fred," I said. "Who called Slattery's hit? We were all standing right there. Remember? If you ask me, Freeman's very much in this ball game."

"And who's next?" he asked.

"Get out your old yearbooks," I said.

By now I was almost as sick of sitting in a restaurant booth as the waitress was sick of me sitting there. I tipped her mightily, and that made me feel better. Waitresses who work breakfast, earning their dough on two-buck coffee and English-muffin orders, are the backbone of this country, everybody knows that. The guilt I felt at monopolizing her booth was appropriate, and the indulgence paid insufficient.

Parent broke away and left Petey and me to our devices.

"I knew you couldn't resist," she said as we rode the elevator back to the rooms.

"How's that?"

"Oh, you know. Your way of looking at things, Mr. Holmes. The spin you put on murder. I should call it something. Maybe like 'the Hot Stove League Method,' or . . . ah . . ."

"Cork it, Watson," I cut in. "I'm a baseball writer. Always have been. I didn't invite these homicidal jerks into the garden. When they show up, I only have so many weapons in the bag."

"What now? You serious about combing the Red Sox yearbooks?"

"No. I'm gonna look over what Fred gave me here, then see where we're at. Then cast a serious arm out for Buck Freeman."

"You get him. I'll get Charlie Hemphill. Wish me luck."

I chuckled. "Freeman and Hemphill. We're on the Chock Full o'Nuts detail," I said.

Then I stopped chuckling.

"It's dumb for us to work apart, Petey," I said.

"Agreed. But right now he doesn't know where we are, does he?"

I couldn't answer that. As Petey left for her room, we agreed not to go out alone, not to be valiant or stupid.

Before I got on the horn, I took a closer look at the reports on Slattery's homicide. Most of them were field reports—including the cop's interview with me—and they didn't say much. The autopsy was clean except for that old devil prostate and the broken fingers. Toxicology could find no trace of anything toxic, and while they weren't finished yet, it appeared as if Slattery was the first victim devoid of any poison.

The last report was from the scene, and it told me pretty much that what we saw was what we got. No fingerprints, no smudges, no residue of whatever struggle Slattery had put up. In the carpeted area around the corpse, evidence detectives had found a few odd hairs and lint, but no buttons or fabric or anything that one would not ordinarily find in any carpeting.

Then the report stated: "Portions of subject's sleeve and

shoulder area contain numerous epidermal scales or flakes. Similar substances found on back of victim's hand and finger areas. Subject exhibits no evidence of dandruff or dermatitis. Scales consistent with dandruff, psoriasis, related rashes."

I read the paragraph again, then looked for a follow-up report but found none. I was struck, however, tripped by something, and I strained to recollect the sight of Slattery's outstretched, lifeless hands. I saw the broken fingers—how could I forget them?—but nothing more. Not any sign of the flaking or scaling of psoriasis or "related rashes" that the technician had described.

I *had* seen it though. I had seen chafed, flaking hands. But where?

I was tempted to call Parent and ask for more. I wanted to talk to the evidence man, or see if any detective had looked into Slattery's medical past. Had anyone even checked his shower stall for a bottle of Head & Shoulders?

I rubbed my own hands, the joints of the fingers, the bone and the cartilage, and stared off like a dreamer. In my mind I saw fingers being rubbed the same way, fingers chafed, irritated, and, yes, flaking. And then I suddenly remembered the person itching them. Indeed, an old man in his tattered bathrobe, a growling, phlegmy cough, whose fingers as they held his brandy and cigar were red and scaly: Chick Stahl.

Chick Stahl. The old *Herald* sportswriter, the dying man in the smoky apartment on Joy Street. And I shook my head back and forth like a lost tourist.

I sat on the notion for a while, then put the police reports aside. Buck Freeman was still my boy, and I wanted to find him. I knew baseball people who had been close to him, old coaches and general managers, a few caring souls here and there who had burned through Buck's craziness for a time. I made a list and started calling. I got to some, and missed others. I got some leads, some phone numbers that produced still other numbers, yet all the while I was dialing I had Chick Stahl on my mind. It bothered the hell out of me.

I called Hobe Ferris, not sure of what I was going to ask him, then was almost relieved when I got no answer. I called Parent in homicide, thinking I might grill his laboratory man on the nature of the skin flakes found at the scene, but Parent wasn't there. Even Petey's phone was busy. When I walked down the hall with the report and showed it to her, I explained Stahl and his condition.

"But he's what—seventy, seventy-five years old?" she said.

"Somewhere in there."

"Strong enough to strangle somebody?"

"I don't think so. I just remember his fingers, and it jumps out at me. And he was at the Old-Timers' Game. We jawed some," I said, thinking out loud.

"I don't know, Unk. It's a little weird, if you ask me."

"That's why it bothers me," I said.

"So why don't you ask him then? Confront the old horse."

Petey had a point. I could feel Stahl out, see what he had to say about Jack Slattery, maybe sense something there. So I considered a strategy, a plausible inquiry because Chick was no dummy, and gave him a call.

"Whattaya got on Slattery?" I said. "Let me pick your brain."

He snorted.

"Brain's rusted out, Duffy. I can't remember how to open a soup can."

"How bad was it between you two, Chick?" I asked. "How personal? There's more in your stuff than the cops'll ever come up with."

It was as long a stroke as I could muster.

"He was the best we had, and he never—" Chick stopped there.

"Never what?" I pressed.

"Ah, hell, Duffy, it's sliced baloney," he said. "You knew the bastard as well as me."

"No, I didn't, Chick. Nobody did."

I got nothing with that. Some breathing, because with his bad lungs you could always hear the rale. He coughed, and I thought I could hear the clanking of one of his heavy ashtrays. I pictured those chafed hands of his.

"I know what you're after, Duffy," he said, and stopped with that too.

I waited for more. Exactly what was I after? I asked myself. I could feel the empty air between us.

"Good-bye," Stahl finally said.

I nodded, agreeing.

Moments later Petey knocked and said she was waiting for a

return call from Charlie Hemphill. I told her of my conversation with Stahl.

"So I'm going to the *Herald*," I said. "To the morgue."

"Why?" she asked.

"To read Stahl's book. I'm not gonna drop this thing."

"Is it worth the time?" she asked.

I could not answer that. Most of this detecting business is a waste of time, sniffing and tracking, talking to people who are probably lying to you. At least Chick Stahl's written words would be straight, maybe even telltale.

I cabbed over to the *Herald* and they let me into the archives. Like just about every major newspaper, the *Herald*'s morgue was computerized now, for better or worse. A young fellow helped out enough to show me that only the tail end of Stahl's career had been indexed. A few years' worth of random columns. I wasn't sure where to start so I punched in "Slattery" as a cross-reference. That was fertile enough.

Slattery was mentioned dozens of times in various columns. A single command printed them, and in minutes I had a sheaf of Stahl columns printed out in dot matrix as if they were dispatches from Arabia. There was no sense of the column to them, no snarling Stahl mug shot at the top, no context of the sports page and its collective energy. Just printouts. But that was enough.

As I sat and read his words, the paper curling in my hands, I could almost feel his rancor. It told me everything and nothing. Like so many in the Boston sports press over the years, Stahl intermittently extolled and vilified the Red Sox. With a blunt, fan-in-the-seats style, a writer long on opinion and short on metaphor, Stahl scored his points. To him, Jack Slattery was everything and nothing, gifted but arrogant, inspiring but vapid, splendid but dour. And, of course, like the hapless Red Sox through the ages, Slattery was never the grand champion. For these and hundreds of other sins—he devoted one salty column to Slattery's habit of drumming his fingers on the bat handle as he awaited each pitch—Stahl came to resent him. Perhaps that was too mild a word.

I was finishing up, making a few notes in the margin, when my attendant, a lad who said his name was Melvin, came over with a fat oversized envelope. It was frayed at the edges and smacked of the old clip files I used to know.

"Got this from obits," he said.

He left me to figure that out, and I decided that some industrious obituary writer had been planning ahead. Inside the envelope were dozens of other Stahl columns, stories, and dispatches. Some of them were brittle and faded, stuck together with cellophane tape as yellow as honey, and went back forty years. This was the man's output, his career in slices and grunts, and I delicately culled through the clips.

This was what I wanted. If Stahl had a palm print it was here. I read story after story, column after column, on all sports but mostly on baseball, from spring training in Sarasota, Scottsdale, and Winter Haven to the regular season, the stretch runs, the Series of '46 and '67 and '75, profiles and scouting reports, mid- and postseason summaries. Stahl had done it all, fed the insatiable goat that was his reading public, turned out thousands of words over thousands of days.

As I read, I got a clear sense of the man, a gruff but resonant writer, a true baseball man of the same school I had enrolled in, a Bostonian to the point where he almost denied Red Sox rooting rights to the rest of New England. And I saw, again and again, the kind of guy who referred to the Sox as "we." Same thing he'd done in conversation.

I was totting all this up when I came upon a column that snagged me. It was a piece on Mace Cuppy, the old infielder and manager, an off-season piece written at the end of Cuppy's career that looked like it would be all color and jabber. Cuppy was one of those reliables, a friendly guy who hit a little more than his weight and caught pop-ups with two hands, who played three positions and seldom embarrassed you, and somehow kept showing up on the counter every year like an old toaster. Nobody didn't like Mace Cuppy any more than you didn't like Eddie Bressoud or Rick Burleson.

Or so I thought. Stahl started slowly, chatting the reader up a bit, then changed his tone of voice with a jab, then a cut. A few sentences later he was building a case against Cuppy the way a prosecuting attorney mounts on a child molester. Cuppy, Stahl wrote, was *the master of indecision, the chronic double clutcher, the cut-off guy who never knew where the runner was or which base he was going to throw to.*

The piece went on like that, with Stahl ripping Cuppy as a fielder, sniffing at him as a hitter, maligning him for never having made a truly crucial play at a truly crucial time, ascribing to him the collective faults of the Red Sox through the ages. He cited examples in game after game over Cuppy's considerable career, most of them long-forgotten contests where Cuppy had lapsed, struck out swinging on a hit-and-run and gutted the runner, or bobbled a relay and cost a run, maybe two or three. Not erred grievously in a decisive, unforgettable inning as Pesky did, not performed horribly again and again, but lapsed.

A gap-toothed, nice-guy player with a name that rhymes with a fish, Stahl fumed, *a guy they always say has a "big heart." That's what they say about all the guys who end up killing you, just ripping out your guts. Heart, huh? Well, I'd take Leo Durocher picking his nose over Mace Cuppy with a heart the size of the moon.*

End of article. An acid bath on a career.

I slumped in my chair when I finished it.

—16—
Confession

I SLIPPED OUT OF THE *HERALD* WITH A THANK YOU AND A photocopy. Tucked into my sport-coat pocket like a summons, the Stahl column scalded my chest. I moved along quickly, wondering even then if Chick knew what I was about or had an eye on me from across the street somewhere. Then I caught myself. What nonsense! If Stahl was the stalker, why was I rattled, much less afraid? Fear is in the unknown, the stranger; the known entity sleeps down the hall or next door and seldom gets a second thought. I told myself that I was no more frightened of Stahl than I was of encroaching liver spots.

Back at the hotel I sought out Petey, eager to share my research with her. But she was gone, out for the night to a movie of all things, and with Fred Parent of all people. Even detectives working murder cases around the clock have lives of their own, they were telling me. The show was about some pull hitter named Hannibal Lector, who had somehow avoided my box score.

Left to my own thoughts, I found myself distracted and unsettled. I was lonely, and I knew damn well why. I mulled over something Petey had said. I'd been too harsh with my lady friend. It bothered me—enough, finally, to where I picked up the phone and dialed Patsy's number.

She was not making herself available, and her secretary could not tell me when she would. I left my name, of course, and a sentiment to the effect that I would like to see her. We were still collaborators, I hoped.

I tucked myself into bed alone.

The next morning I decided I wanted the homely detective and all his resources in my lap.

"That's dark, Fred," I said, displaying Stahl's column on Mace Cuppy.

"That's a Boston sportswriter. They're all weasels and they always were," he said after he and Petey had read it.

"This one has eczema," said Petey.

She was now more impressed with my case. She also respected my instincts on sports scribes.

"It's not enough for me to lean on him, but we can have a little talk," Parent said.

We decided to pay an unannounced call.

"I have a date with Charlie Hemphill," Petey announced, and grimaced. "If I'm lucky, he'll put me onto Tommy Dowd."

She had connected with Hemphill that morning, she explained, and he'd invited her out to his place in Wellfleet on the Cape.

"Told me to take the Provincetown ferry. 'Consumes less fossil fuel per rider than personal land vehicles,' he said."

"The ferry?" said Parent. "That'll take you three hours. Why don't you drive?"

I scowled at him, and acknowledged the purple shadow on the bridge of Petey's nose.

"On second thought . . ." Parent said.

With Stahl on our plate, Parent and I decided Petey would be safe enough in the hands of Hemphill and the sands of Cape Cod. What I did not know, but should have guessed, was that Petey was packing a .22. I had mixed feelings about the piece of lethal steel, but not about her ability to use it. It had saved my life once.

We drove her over to Commonwealth Pier near the World Trade Center, where she caught the *Provincetown II,* a spacious passenger ferry that made daily summertime runs out to the tip of the Cape. She was wearing her uniform: the leg-hugging jeans, running shoes, a windbreaker over a loose, short-sleeved top, sunglasses perched in her hair, which was loose and lying on each shoulder. An oversized canvas bag that hung on her right shoulder contained everything from a bathing suit and a novel about an olfactory murderer in eighteenth-century Paris to police reports on Tommy Dowd. She looked like a college kid off for a holiday at the beach, and we hoped that was the case. As she skipped off onto the boat, Parent sighed like a dog at the dinner table.

"Does she, uh, ever commit?" he said. "I mean, is there some guy she's really, uh, does she ever say anything about that sort of thing?"

"I'm her uncle, Fred," I said. "When's the last time you came clean with your uncle?"

It was a dodge, and he knew it.

Out of our sight, as she was to tell us in detail later, Petey checked her flanks and stayed among the crowd. In summer, Boston and the Cape exchanged patrons in droves, and there was no lack of passengers on the ferry. Petey spotted a woman with a toddler and a baby, offered to lend a hand with the woman's mountain of gear, and then sat across from the trio in a middle section. No maternal urges had surfaced—Petey simply felt the need to be secure and thought she might be safe in the company of a mom and her brood.

As she took her seat, she noticed a lone man, lean, with a beak nose and dark glasses, dressed in a tweed sport coat and what looked like a British sport cap, entering the interior seating area. He did not look around with suspicious eyes or make any subtle moves, and Petey immediately decided he looked like one of those Swedish actors they cast as assassins in spy movies. All he needed was an eye patch. He sat down a few rows away, facing Petey but staring at his *Wall Street Journal* instead of at her. Call it vanity, but Petey suspected men who did not even glance at her.

Between mugging at the woman's two-year-old and lifting a furtive eye at the man, she pulled out the police reports on Tommy Dowd. As she read, hunting for any mention of Charlie Hemphill, she decided that the man in dark glasses was dressed too warmly for the day. Fred Parent had told her that undercover cops always complained about having to wear sport coats in order to cover up their weapons. Ninety degrees in July, air humid enough to cut, and they were wearing polyester sport coats. This guy looked to be about forty; the *Journal* was a perfect cover.

Her personal sense of intrigue kept her from noticing the seascape easing past her window as the ferry headed southeast between Deer and Long islands. The day was windy and partially overcast, but very warm. The Cape beckoned, and on any other day and in any other circumstances, Petey would have reveled in it. Now she was unsettled, still sore from her injuries when she sat in the wrong position, wary of a guy reading a gray business newspaper through his shaded glasses, and wondering what Parent and I were up to.

Parent parked—illegally, of course—on Commonwealth, and we hiked up Joy Street to Stahl's place without saying much of anything to each other. We were going to visit one of my fraternity, suspecting the worst, and that bothered me. I wanted to put a cork on these killings, but the Massachusetts prison system didn't need a cancer-eaten old sportswriter, and I didn't want to be the person who sent them one. With Parent you couldn't tell. The only thing on him that betrayed any worry about fireworks or hostility was a rivulet of perspiration that leaked down his right temple. He let it leak.

At number 67 we entered and trekked up to the third floor without any interruption. Just as burglars do it, I presume. At 3A we knocked, and as we stood and waited I could smell the musty, smoky insides. But I didn't hear the growl. I didn't hear Fergie, Stahl's mutt, snarl and bump around like before. I didn't hear a thing. Parent rapped loudly, but we got nothing.

"Could be out in the park with the pooch," I said. "Big, moody old German shepherd."

Parent nodded blankly. He had spent a lot of his time knocking on doors and getting no answer.

"Now what?" I asked.

"Ask a neighbor. Find the super."

We backtracked a floor and knocked several times on a door that had some sound on the other side of it. A woman's face finally appeared through the crack of her partially opened doorway. In answer to Parent's flashed badge and our question, she said she'd heard Stahl early this morning but had heard nothing since then.

"He went up and down with Fergie," she said.

That was all. We asked if we could use her phone, and she said she preferred we did not. Then she was gone.

I was amazed at her chill. We certainly didn't look threatening. He shrugged off her response.

"No clothes," he said matter-of-factly. "People never have any clothes on around the house."

I had no comeback on that, and then suggested we call Chick's kid, Jake. He lived nearby and he'd given me his number; in fact, in nagging me to come on his radio show, he'd left his number several times. We used the phone in a hardware store on Cambridge. Jake said he'd be right over.

For the entire trip, Petey realized, the woman's two-year-old had a running nose, something the little bugger, in her conniptions over Petey's smiles and snorks, dipped repeatedly into Petey's lap. It wasn't pretty, Petey saw, and her jeans looked like they'd been blotted with half-ripe mulberries. Nevertheless, the time moved quickly, the ferry chugged on, and by late morning they were approaching Cape Cod's sandy landscape.

The man in the dark glasses looked up twice at Petey. He had spent a lot of time in the *Journal*'s market tables. He was probably dull as a stump despite the fact that he wanted to kill her. On the other hand, if he was an assassin, he was unduly concerned about his portfolio. Her mind raced with anxiety, and when the ferry pulled into the pier at Provincetown, she pried the kid's nose off her knee and hurried down the aisle.

As the boat groaned and churned its way next to the pier, Petey nudged her way to the front of the crowd waiting to exit. Finally the gate was opened and Petey quickly moved off the ferry. Twisting and turning her head, looking for the guy in the dark glasses, she caught her foot on a weathered railing support. She stumbled and half sprawled onto the pavement.

"Safe!" came a shout, which she heard but was too intent on the pain in her scraped palms to acknowledge.

When she did look up, her eyes met a pair of billowing lime-green pants that looked like they'd been stolen from a snake charmer. They were connected to a rangy torso bedecked in a tie-dyed shirt topped off by a face that was mostly beard. The mouth through the hair was smiling like a horse about to whinny.

Petey was not. Her frame didn't need any more falls, and she picked herself up with the help of greenpants's strong left arm. She knew it belonged to Charlie Hemphill, the former Red Sox eccentric.

"Safe," she muttered, then decided she had last seen a shirt like his at a Grateful Dead concert. Hemphill was a Deadhead deluxe. He was also a stallion, thin but hung with great shoulders and long, muscled arms so brown and gristly Petey wanted to bite them. And hands, hands that had made a baseball look like an egg.

"Only the pope kisses the ground when he visits the Cape," he said, and chuckled. He had the Kennedy front teeth.

"I lost my head," Petey said.

"I'm Charles Judson Hemphill," he said.

"Prove it," Petey said.

He stood back, spread out his long wings, and chanted, "Themistocles, Thucydides, the Peloponnesian War, X squared, Y squared, H-2-S-O-4; who for, what for, who we gonna root for? Maroons!"

"What's that?" Petey said.

"The University of Chicago rally cry," he said. "My favorite."

"You *are* Charlie Hemphill," she said.

He helped her gather herself and showed her to a jeep, not a showroom product but a pea-soup-green U.S. Army–issue jeep that looked like it had been swiped from Dwight Eisenhower. Growling and moaning like a mule with a hernia, it barreled down Highway 6 toward Wellfleet. Petey, who had never been to Cape Cod, gawked at the expanse of ponds and sand dunes, which she had expected, and thick stands of pine trees, which she had not. The woods, Hemphill explained, were planted and now protected by the government.

"The lumber industry raped the Cape years ago! Never again!" he yelled, the wind buffeting his beard.

Petey stood up in the jeep and smelled the air. It was salty enough to rust the barrettes out of her hair. The wind whipped against her as she scanned the coastline, the horizon, the remarkable expanse of ocean blues. She was not a beach nymph, but this curled finger of sand beguiled her as it has visitors for centuries.

"This land is my land," Hemphill said when she'd sat down again. "Fouled, trespassed, and obscenely developed, but still my land."

They pulled off Highway 6 onto Main and the collection of shops that make up the business center of Wellfleet. Hemphill made a series of turns until they were on Chequesset Neck Road, which led them to Wellfleet's blue harbor with its buoys and boats and sticks marking shellfish beds. He drove on, crossing over onto

Griffin Island and Duck Harbor Road. A few hundred yards later he pulled up to a bilevel beach house, a low, long structure sided with rough-hewn pine and roofed with what looked like a colony of solar panels. The place had homemade written all over it. What took Petey's attention, however, was a front yard overgrown with weeds and wildflowers.

"Abode and gardens," Hemphill said as he hopped out of the jeep.

"Nice lawn mower on ya," Petey said, pausing at the jungle.

"Wildflowers, natural grasses . . . plants in harmony," he said, bending down and thrusting his face into the overgrowth. "They have a right to mature, pollinate, and spew their seeds. Why stunt them?"

"Bet the neighbors love you," Petey said.

Hemphill sighed. "In fact, they petitioned the selectmen to order a massacre. Reduce them to lawn stubble. My neighbors. Good but unrealized people."

Petey smiled. Hemphill was as cockamamie as when he talked to the baseball and threw screwballs in Fenway, flapping off the mound with legs and arms and hair flying like a kid falling out of a tree, as the scribes used to put it. Petey had anticipated nothing less, and eagerly followed him into the house.

Hemphill's digs were all glass and driftwood, macramé—which Petey hadn't seen in years—futons, and oversized pillows. Vases held bursting stalks of dried grasses and wildflowers, probably picked out of his front yard. Nora Gibson had said that Hemphill's wife had flown the place a few years back, and Petey decided the missus had taken the home's smooth edges along with her. Petey scanned the interior and did not see a baseball memento anywhere. Ten years with the Red Sox, the team's political and spiritual conscience as well as a damn good left-hander in a home park that is murder on that species, and there wasn't so much as a souvenir ticket stub to be had.

The living room opened to a remarkable cedar deck, which drew Petey and from which she gazed at a sandy, grassy decline leading to the bay. It was a stunning perch.

"You can actually feel the earth revolve from here," Charlie said. "It's a purely organic feeling." He came up from behind with two Mason jars filled with grapefruit juice. He was barefoot now, and shirtless, displaying a cocoa-brown, hairless torso of defined tendons and muscles—tissue, Petey guessed, free of the ravages of unrefined sugar, red meats, or MSG. In her current, somewhat starved and celibate state, this single scan of Hemphill made her want to attack him. He was gorgeous, all natural, and all male, and she swallowed hard.

For his part, Charlie was blissfully unaware. He had once defined lust as a mere matter of "pituitary secretions" that affected his progesterone level, and, Petey decided for the moment, no such effect was happening now. He stepped onto the deck and was there no more than a few moments when the sun suddenly blazed through what had been an overcast sky. He was transfixed, and he lifted his hairy face, his thick, chopped blond hair collapsing onto the back of his neck, closed his eyes, and faced the sun like an Indian chief.

Petey had to think: What was it she came to see this guy about?

"A pure evil spirit has gripped Boston," he answered.

Jake Stahl met us at Chick's front door with that big woodchuck grin, only now it was a little ragged around the edges.

"The ol' man doesn't answer?" he said. "Dammit, he gets in his moods . . ."

He trailed off, partly in anger and partly in worry. He led us around back. Even in midafternoon he had the wet head and the big, damp paws, and his aftershave wafted behind him. He muttered something about his father always screwing up the front-door dead-bolt lock.

By the time we got up to Chick's back door, I was sick of climbing stairs.

"Listen to this," Jake said, and he thumped the door with his foot. "Fergie'll—"

Then he stopped and listened.

"Where in hell's Fergie?" he said, his radio voice revealing an uncharacteristic crack.

"Use the damn key," Parent said.

Jake did and we made our way into the kitchen. The overhead light was on and there were dishes all over.

"Dad! Fergie!" Jake yelled.

We tentatively followed him into the hallway, past the bathroom, and into the cluttered, stuffy dining room. The place was still and stifling, and everything smelled like a cigar. At the living room Jake stopped, then reached up to the pocket door for support.

"Aw shit," he moaned.

In front of him, sitting motionless in an easy chair, his head lolled to one side and a foamy spittle smearing his chin, was his father. An empty snifter of brandy balanced on his chest, and a cold cigar lay on the floor where it had fallen from his grasp. On a small table was a bowl of gelatin capsules, caplets, and multi-colored pills that looked from afar like an exotic mix of jellybeans. None of us had to be told that Chick Stahl had imbibed and inhaled his last.

"Aw shit, Dad," Jake repeated, still glued to the spot.

He looked around, as did we, and then moved quickly over to the sofa. He leaned down into an area between the lamp and the wall.

"Dammit, dammit, dammit!" he yelled.

He was stroking the feathers of a dog's tail as he cursed. The tail wasn't moving either.

"Actually, it's a conflagration of demons," Charlie Hemphill said. "They've risen from the toxic muck of Boston Harbor and settled on Fenway. It was inevitable."

The grapefruit juice stung Petey's palate as she waited for Hemphill to go on. She'd forgotten to bone up on her Zen and her Calvinism, and she silently scolded herself.

"They'd been submerged since the witch trials," he went on, "but I could feel them rising when I played. The pitching mound is the uterus of the ballpark, you know. The core. The womb. The physical merges with the metaphysical, as Paramahansa Yogananda tried to teach us."

"I bet Don Zimmer loved to hear that," Petey said.

"A gerbil is a simple animal," he said.

"Evil spirits," Petey mused. "They don't even leave finger-prints."

"Not in the physical sense. But good point. I'm hearing a Midwest education."

"Oberlin."

"Superb."

"Thanks," Petey said, "but it hasn't done much for me lately. That's why I came to see you."

He pulled his face from the sun and smiled at her. She felt like the daughter of Grizzly Adams. Then he turned and made a sphere with his giant hands.

"Invert," he said. "Invert the universe. Disallow the necessity of 'givens,' and go from there."

"That Yogananda again?"

"No, Bill Veeck," said Hemphill.

She exhaled. "This could go on forever."

"Mmmmmmm," he said. "Like all true discourse . . . sentences have no ends, no periods. Only ellipses . . ."

"Is the evil spirit singular? Or plural?"

"A wave of them, actually, emanating from management, which, of course, cannot help itself. A basic lack of oneness, oneness with the coaches, players, fans. It's very shortsighted not to include all as part of one. There are inevitable ruptures and mutinies."

"I didn't understand a word of that," Petey said.

The sun slowly slipped behind clouds.

"Come," he said, and led her back into the front room. After she waved off more grapefruit juice, he rummaged about over by a pinewood bureau before turning and sparking a blaze in front of his face. Petey realized that he was cradling a bong pipe, and he had lit a small bowlful of marijuana. It had been a long time since Petey had seen someone light up grass in the middle of the day, and the sweet aroma swept over her like a breeze. Hemphill took a long, almost worshipful pull on the pipe and offered it to Petey. Pot, after all, has always been a communal experience.

Petey, having been around uncles and cops far too long, at first declined. Then she shrugged her shoulders and waved over the pipe. Research, she reasoned, the gumshoe's ultimate alibi. Insight, she added, a little buzz to help her translate Hemphill's musings. She sipped the stem, gingerly at first, trying not to let the fumes scorch her throat. She felt like a nun at a frat party. She was no virgin with a joint, or a pipe, for that matter; it had just been a while.

Not so for Charlie. With great inhalations he held the cottony smoke in his lungs. His eyelids fluttered. Then, without warning, he fluidly descended into the lotus position. It was obviously a practiced technique, betrayed only by the crackling of the joints in his knees and ankles.

"Petrinella," he intoned. "A karmic name. Truly lovely." The tone of his voice flattened as the drug seeped into his brain.

Petey giggled. *Oh no,* she thought.

"If I were you, I'd simply wait," Charlie said. "Baseball is a religion, you know. Pursuit of perfection. Twenty-seven outs. It brings out desire and desire brings suffering. Sooner or later the sufferer will show himself."

Petey fought her brain's oncoming fog.

"You know something I don't know, Charlie?" she asked.

"The killer is confused. He's forgotten one thing: All other humans exist in us, and we exist in them. *Bodhisattvas* consider everyone, friends and enemies alike, as equal. They don't condemn anyone's past, nor do they hate those who are presently doing evil." He paused and took a hit the size of a mushroom cloud.

Ah shit, Petey thought, watching Charlie climb Mount Rushmore.

A quiet held in the room, save for wind gusts that rustled the dried weeds. Distant, lulling sounds came from the bay.

"Tommy Dowd sure as hell didn't kill anybody," Hemphill suddenly said.

Petey straightened up. Hemphill's eyes were wide open, bloodshot but fixed on her as if they were staring at a catcher for a sign.

"Talk to me," Petey said.

"The watch was stolen," he said. "So was his car."

"How do you know?"

"He told me."

From the corner of the room Jake Stahl was weeping. Choking, tormented, slobbering sounds.

"Come on, Fergie. Big guy. You're a police dog!" he sobbed.

Parent and I attended to Chick Stahl. His pulse was as dormant as his cigar. The glass had dripped a spot of brandy onto his shirt, a blousy, long-sleeved wash-and-wear white shirt, no doubt left over from his reporting days. Just below the spot lay Chick's right hand, the thin, bony fingers slightly curled. I immediately noticed the skin once again: red, chapped, peeling. Flakes adhered to the side of the glass.

"There it is," I said to Parent.

Parent looked closely and nodded.

"Beautiful . . . our first real link, Duffy," he said.

By now Jake Stahl had pushed the table away from the sofa and was sprawled next to the fallen dog. He stroked its gray-black fur.

"What's the *point*, Dad?" Stahl blubbered. "Fergie had, what, a good two, three more seasons left. . . ."

I stepped up when I heard that.

"You think he did this himself, Jake? Killed himself and the dog?" I asked.

Parent caught my logic.

"Yeah. We're up to our ears in poisonings. Maybe we got another one here. Your father ever say he wanted to kill himself?" Parent asked, looking at the pharmacy next to the body.

"Every third day. He was a walking Hemlock Society," Jake muttered.

"Why didn't you do something about it?" I asked.

"I did," said Stahl, not leaving the side of his dog. "I told him to go ahead. Just leave my police dog alone."

Parent turned to me. "Plain grief. Don't you love it?"

"Where are we now?" I asked. "What do we do?"

"If this is a suicide, we should look for a note," Parent said. "Don't touch anything, but snoop around. I'll call this in."

I looked around. The rooms were dumps, and the Stahls, one whimpering and one cooling, added to the mess. My first inclination was to find a typewriter. Writers who delete themselves always leave farewells in typewriters, the paper sticking up from the platen like a last gasp. And Stahl would have a typewriter, not a computer. It struck me that writers who used computers would have to leave the machine turned on and the note on the screen. Not the same.

Stahl's typewriter, a dusty Royal, was propped on a stack of newspapers with an ashtray in the keywell. Nothing else. I kept hunting. Finally, I spotted something by the phone. It was handwritten, like a message just taken, scribbled with an inky ballpoint pen on a pad of paper advertising some marvelous and unpronounceable new drug. The words were stroked in an old man's hand, that beautiful Palmer-method cursive that we all learned back when desks had inkwells.

> To Duffy House:
>   As Ring said it, "You know me, Al." And you know me, Duffy, or you wouldn't be interested. I know when a good reporter is onto a story, and you're a good reporter. I'll make it easy for you.

When you read this, I will be dead of my own hand, having thrown all my overpriced pills into a bowl and swallowed a handful with my brandy. I'm good at this kind of thing, as you already know. Hope I can enjoy my last panatela before the stew kicks in. Who knows, maybe Washington can balance the budget now that they don't have to pay the jackasses who call themselves my doctors. Hah.

The real point here is the fact that you probably figured out that I did it. Both the boys at the park. Ossee, I'm sorry for. Criger I'm not. Mace was hardly worth the drive. And Jackie Ballgame. My ass. He won't be drumming his fingers on the bat handle anymore, that's for sure.

So now they're gone and I'm going too. I'm sorry for one thing: I never should have defiled Fenway Park. I apologize for that to Red Sox fans and to baseball. What's done is done.

They killed my dear father, Duffy, and they were killing me. Remember the old Bible verse, "Be sure your sins will find you out." Throw in plenty of errors and missed signs, too. Damn them to hell. I'll be there with Harry Frazee to greet them.

Sincerely,
Chick Stahl
—30—

I had not seen "-30-" for a long time. End of copy. I'd used it most of my career. As did Chick. Yet that was trivial compared to what flooded through my mind as I held the tortured letter. Had Chick written this after I'd called him? Had I stupidly prodded his unstable psyche? Had I pushed him over the edge?

I had no reply to my own queries. I only knew that here was the second person in a matter of days who may have heard my voice as his last on this earth.

"Whattaya got?" said Parent.

I handed him the note.

"Says he did it," I said.

As Parent was reading, Jake's bulk cast a shadow over us. He read over Parent's shoulder. He speed-read, breathing loudly, sweating, the grief over his departed canine now replaced by seething disbelief.

"Bullshit," he exclaimed, pounding his right fist into his left palm. "What fucking bullshit!"

"Sitting right where you are, Tommy was," Hemphill said.

"Where is he now?" Petey pressed.

"Can't reveal that. He's bummed out by the Boston police. They're agents, you know, very status quo. Herd-oriented."

"Would he talk to me?" Petey asked.

"You mean, could you bring him in from the cold?"

"That too . . ."

"Intriguing possibility. His is a simple cosmos, remember, but he knows things. He's spooked right now. The police. And Buck. Someone else. Who knows?"

"Buck? Freeman?"

"Maestro Freeman. The one who plays the music of the spheres."

"Come off it, Charlie. I saw him dive into the screen the other night and it wasn't music."

"His karma freaked. Firestorms of the brain. Still, it's one of the most unconventional minds I ever encountered. It's beautiful."

"Half the shrinks in New England wouldn't agree," Petey said.

"*Crazy* is a relative term," he said. "Badly misused."

By now he'd put his bong pipe aside. He seemed pleasantly elevated. What a life, Petey thought.

"Get back to Freeman and Tommy Dowd," Petey said.

"Tommy's axis is shaken because there's a killer out there and he knows he's in the loop. Buck threatened to peel his face off in the clubhouse one time. Tommy, unequipped as he is, didn't see the statement as metaphorical. Now Slattery gets throttled and Tommy feels the sinister forces closing in on him."

"He told you this?"

"To an extent."

"Leaving the metaphysical on the rug for a minute, what's your feeling on this, Charlie?"

Hemphill smiled like a yogi. Then, like a mime, he pulled some imaginary beings out of the air and laid them on the rug. It was cute, Petey thought.

"I'm a port in this storm," Hemphill said. "As far as Tommy

is concerned, I'm the only person who's not sinister right now. He trusts me."

"He trusts you?"

"Bingo."

"Can I get in on that trust?" Petey asked.

Hemphill did not smile. Instead he stretched, his arms forming a remarkable wingspan. Then he stood up and looked out over the bay. The sun was shining again.

"Let's get out on that water!" he said.

"What about Tommy Dowd?" Petey said.

"Right time, right place," Hemphill said.

The same evidence man who'd combed Jack Slattery's body showed up for Stahl. He spent a lot of time around Chick's hands. Two of Parent's fellow detectives also arrived, and while one of them grilled Jake, the other joined us in rummaging through the apartment. Most of what we found was evidence that Stahl spent too much of his time fighting with doctors and bureaucrats over his medical bills. After an hour of searching, there didn't seem to be anything else on the murders.

"I don't know," said Parent, motioning toward the confession. "I'd expect more than this."

"It's all in the newspaper morgue, Fred," I said. "He spent a career venting his spleen."

"Maybe. In the meantime, let's work on this piece of paper before it goes public."

He went over to Jake with the note.

"What do you think of this?" he asked. "You're part of it. And you're media."

Stahl ran his hands through his slick hair. He was sitting sideways on a dining-room chair, staring at the rug, looking like an overgrown kid who had just lost a pet.

"He was a sick, sick old man," Jake said. "He killed my dog. I can't deal with anything else right now."

Parent exhaled.

"We won't go public with this until all the pieces fit. Stay close. You understand?"

Stahl lifted both his palms and shrugged.

Parent turned to me. I was fiddling with my beeper.

"How far do these things go?" I asked, displaying it. "Petey should know what we found."

"She's where—Wellfleet?" he said. "Give her a call now. Chick's phone line is wide open. We'll be outta here before long."

But long it was. After an interminable, exhausting afternoon, Chick Stahl's body was gently inserted into a vinyl body bag. Parent slid the confession into a clear plastic evidence bag. And we left the old man's musty home. Stahl was carried out behind us. Fergie, in Jake Stahl's arms, after him. Buffalo head.

—17—
Front Page

"THIS SMELLS ALL THE WAY TO THE CHEAP SEATS, DUFFY," Parent said.

"I'm glad you think so too," I said.

We were on our way back to Parent's home base, pushing the pastel cop car through stop-and-go late-afternoon traffic, playing and replaying the plausibility of the cranky, cancer-ridden, calcified Chick Stahl as self-designated hitter. It fit and it didn't fit. He had access. He could have laced the potato salad as easily as anybody. And the scales from his fingers were too incriminating to discount.

But *damn*. Since when do you leap out of your paragraphs? Since when do you transform the love of a kid's game into something deadly? Or was I kidding myself? Had I known it all along? Heard it in Chick's acid tongue over brandy, read it in his yellowed columns, detected it in his eyes that afternoon in his apartment?

There's nothing so benign as a sportswriter. Or so I thought. It's all a game: Be there and don't bore. And tell them how the weather was. In my eyes, the Chick Stahls of this world are no more suspects than they are gods. And sportswriters aren't gods.

Parent slapped me on the knee as he pulled into the cop shop on Berkeley, and I figured I had been staring into my navel. We hustled up to his department via the elevator, a remarkable convenience, where he immediately got into a huddle with his boss.

This was a young guy named Hughes, who waved us into his corner office and didn't seem to mind my being there. Parent handed him Chick Stahl's confession. Before Hughes finished reading, Parent had already started his beef.

"There's not much there," he said. "No details. No chapter, no verse. Nothing that says the old shit didn't flip out and decide to go out with a bang. That, or maybe there's something between the lines."

"Such as?" said Hughes.

"He knew something and he's taking the dive."

"Can you put him at the scenes?"

"Yeah, sure," Parent replied. "Fenway's a lock. Slattery's hotel depending on what evidence says. But Tim, this guy didn't have the legs for it, you hear what I'm saying? Duffy says he was missing half a lung and had a cough like to knock you over."

"Who knows about this?" Hughes asked, waving the note.

"Only his kid, Jake."

"Jake Stahl. Radio guy? Does the sports show on RKO?"

"That's him," I said.

"Can't stand the show and can't stand him," Hughes muttered, then looked sideways and thought about it. "But I'd hate to go public with the confession and pick egg off our face if it's bogus. Make us look like we're grasping at any straw."

"Makes three of us," Parent said.

"How's the son sit on this? How'd he react?" Hughes asked.

"He was glazed," Parent replied. "Said it was bullshit, then said the old man was sick in the head. When we left him he was more shook up over his dead dog than anything else."

"Huh?"

"The old man doped the German shepherd too," Parent said. "Jake was pissed big time about that."

"So we don't have to worry about Jake Stahl broadcasting his old man's confession," Hughes said.

"Wait a minute there," I said. "Breaking the confession story is a real scoop. The kid's a radio sports jock, don't forget, and he doesn't get something like this very often. Not only that, but things weren't real close between him and Chick. So don't think he wouldn't run with it."

Hughes lifted his eyebrows and sighed.

"All right," he said. "Put it together, Fred. Don't go home until we got a case either way."

We returned to Parent's desk. I wasn't sure where Hughes had left us.

"I'll translate," Parent said, reading my mind. "Boss is sitting on the confession until he has no choice. Unless we can prove that it's fake, he goes public with it. Chick Stahl will be our bogeyman, the Fenway Park killer. Hughes has to do something quick 'cuz we're getting beat up on this thing."

"And Chick is better than nothing, right?"

"You got it."

"What now?"

"Wait till Evidence gets back and see if the skin flakes match. That's first of all. If Stahl's rash is what we found on Slattery, that's concrete stuff. From there, we backtrack. You tell me: Did you see Chick get around Fenway at the game? I mean, enough to pull it off?"

"I think so, Fred. If he was anything like me that afternoon, the adrenaline was tapped and he was spry."

Parent grimaced, then spotted his evidence man entering the office from the hallway. He came right over. A frail, mopey guy named Landsman, maybe fifty, with the heaviest eyelids this side of Bette Davis, he had obviously been around too much rigor mortis.

"I don't like it, Fred," he said. "I'll wait for the microscopes but as far as I'm concerned, this guy's condition don't match with what they took off Jackie Slattery. I mean, this guy is a mess. Leprosy. If he'd a done it I could have picked up skin flakes with a snow shovel. And we only got a few with rug fibers. It's the same itch, but not anywhere near the concentration."

Parent looked at me, thinking.

"Another thing," Landsman went on, "you think this old guy had the rocks to strangle Jack? I don't. Not unless he put him under first. And it looks like that didn't happen."

Parent riffled through the folders scattered on his desk and came up with the Slattery photos. It was a gruesome portfolio, especially the shots of the angry ligatures around Slattery's neck. Parent studied one after another; there were dozens of them.

"That was one strong bastard did that," Landsman said. "Hey, I seen Jack play. Seen him break bats in two with his bare hands. Powerful, powerful man, and he was taken out like that? Piece of leather, if you ask me, maybe a belt. We're waiting on that too. Could be a necktie—I don't count that out, no way—but my money's on leather now, just looking at the way it grooved into the tendons in the neck."

"Leather . . ." I mused.

Parent stopped his photo shuffling and looked at me.

Landsman shrugged and began to walk off.

Then he turned. "By the way, Fred, we got a match on the paint that you wanted," he said. "The kid's car and that rental wreck you gave us. I'll get the paper right over to you. We're doin' good, huh?"

That jogged Parent back into the room.

"Dowd's car and Petey's, right, Fred?" I said. "That puts Tommy in Hartford."

"He got around," said Parent.

"Or somebody driving his heap . . ." I added.

I wanted Petey in on this, but she had not answered my beep. I thought you had to answer these things. What good are they? I called back to the Lenox, but no message had been left there. She'd given me Hemphill's number on Cape Cod, but nobody picked up on that either. It was now suppertime, and Parent was not going home. Hughes had scheduled a seven P.M. huddle with his task force, during which they'd throw the whole case up for grabs in light of Chick Stahl's confession.

There was a palpable buzz in the air when I left homicide, as Joe Friday used to say, the start of a headfirst slide into home by the Boston cops. I, on the other hand, was still rounding third, cleats in the baseline, not sure that anybody was served by a rush to pinch. But Parent and his fellow dicks were pestered and pressured by every politician and cheap-shot columnist in town on the Red Sox murders, and they wanted to close them.

The Lenox Hotel was maddening with its quiet and privacy. Petey was nowhere to be found, and I needed her noise. The ferry from the Cape arrived at half past six, and I decided to meet it. In the meantime I called the Parker House for my messages, and had four: an earlier one from Jake Stahl, and three calls from somebody named "John Frank," who said it was urgent and left a number with a suburban Boston area code. I rattled and scraped and chased moths out of my brain, but could not figure out who that might be. And I had no intention of calling back until I did.

Just then my phone rang.

"I got your beep, Unk, but I was out on Charlie's skiff. I

missed the ferry, so I'm catching a ride with one of Hemphill's girlfriends, okay? See you around eight or nine. I *got* something, Unk," she gushed.

I had no sooner cradled the receiver when the phone rang again. My hand felt its vibration.

"I hate to eat alone," Patsy said.

"I could remedy that," I replied.

"I mean right about now," she said.

"So do I," I answered.

I had a window of time before Petey would be back, and Patsy's invitation landed nicely on my ears. In less than a half hour I met her at the Bostonian Hotel, where Seasons was the restaurant of choice. We chatted amiably over smoked Nantucket scallops and striped bass.

"I appreciated your call, Duffy," she said. "You're a forgiving man."

Patsy seemed to have recovered from the strain of our exchange after Slattery's murder. I had never been called forgiving before.

"I don't think extraneous events should interfere with our work together," she added.

"I'm not so sure," I said. "The murders have interfered with everything in this town."

She raised her beautiful eyebrows slightly.

"I've spent a lot of time batting this around, Patsy—what's happened and how and to whom—and I may be some half-cocked, narrow-minded old sportswriter, but as far as I'm concerned, this whole ungodly mess, all these good men dying, has come about because of something right there in Fenway Park. Your ballpark. The old rusty girders and the green sod and the turnstiles on Yawkey Way."

I needed a drink of water. With a tine of her fork, she flaked off a morsel of bass.

"When the police get the Dowd boy," she said, "it will all be over, you know. Life will go on, Duffy."

It was as easy as that, at least to her. She mentioned something about her sister and wondered if she deserved a chapter in the memoirs.

"You can't mean that," I said.

"Oh, yes, she was very important in my life," she replied.

I exhaled.

"Did you know Chick Stahl of the *Herald?*" I asked.

She shrugged.

"Not really," she murmured, and added something about sweet butter versus salted.

"He killed himself today," I said.

"That's too bad, it really is," she replied, looking directly at me. "But if you're talking about the same creature who went out of his way to be a thorn in our side, then you can't expect us to get maudlin. R.I.P.—and tell me about your scallops. Confess, are they as good as they look? You know, it's such a shame that Jasper is gone. He was chef here. All the good young Boston chefs move about like free agents."

It was no use.

"You don't want to talk about the murders, do you?" I asked.

"No," she replied.

No, I said to myself. It was no more complicated than that. The chord that we had enjoyed, the harmony of thought and time, had dissolved. I made a stab at a scallop and missed. I looked up at this lovely lady and her understated elegance, and realized that I had nothing to say to her.

Suddenly I had little appetite. I felt tired and craved the company of my niece.

"Tommy Dowd—he's alive," Petey said the moment she spied me back in the lobby of the Lenox. "He's been in touch with Hemphill, and Charlie's going to get him together with us."

She and I had arrived back at the hotel within minutes of each other. She explained that Hemphill had talked her into going on his sailboat, which, she noted, was dubbed *Yin and Yang.*

"It was beautiful and all—the ocean, the boat, the sunshine— but it was killing me! I wanted to get the hell back here and instead I'm out in the bay watching Charlie commune with the fish." She was talking a blue streak.

"Here's the thing: Hemphill says Dowd didn't do it. He swears it. But he says Tommy's scared stiff the cops will lay it on him anyway. The watch and all. So he's holed up somewhere, and Charlie's the only one Tommy trusts."

"Dowd's car ran you off the road," I said. "The lab matched the paint."

"It did?" Petey said.

"That's not all, kid. Chick Stahl committed suicide. Fred and I found him this afternoon. Left a confession and said he killed them all."

Petey stopped in her tracks and faced me. Her jaw literally dropped.

"Why didn't you call me?" she said.

"I tried," I said, and wagged the damn beeper at her. I went on to tell her what Parent had, the conflicting evidence of the skin flakes, and that as we spoke, Fred and his fellow detectives were sitting on the confession while they mounted a case against a dead man.

"Not that Fred thinks Chick did it. He certainly had help strangling Slattery."

"Dowd?"

"Don't know. Somebody with a piece of leather—that's all we got."

Petey rubbed her hands against her face. She was weary and windburned.

"By the way," I said. "Who in hell is somebody named John Frank? Left me messages at the Parker House. Urgent."

Petey looked sideways at me.

"C'mon, Unk."

"C'mon, Unk, what?"

"John Frank Freeman," she said. "Better known as Buck. He's calling home."

"*Jeeee-zus,*" I scolded.

Petey went to her room for a change of clothes and a second wind, and I called down for some room service. She'd eat standing up, and we'd try to assemble what we had and where to go. I was eager to know what Parent and his people were going to do. I put a call in to him and was told he was in a meeting. I knew that, but it was taking a long time.

Petey reappeared, having taken a quick shower and changed into a fresh pair of slacks and a long-sleeved top. With all the sun she'd taken, she was chilled by the hotel's conditioned air.

"How serious do you take the old guy's confession?" she asked right off.

"If he had help, real serious," I began. "He was bitter and sick. You read the column on Mace. He couldn't have strangled

Jack Slattery, but he could have been the one who broke his fingers. Good Lord, Petey, think of it: Chick Stahl on his knees cracking Jack Slattery's knuckles!"

I clenched my own as I said it, and caught myself.

"But if he was there," I went on, "with *whom*? Tommy Dowd? Why would he have anything to do with Tommy Dowd?"

"If Dowd was his man in Fenway . . ."

"Was he? Now wait a minute, Pete. You just said it: Chick had help in the park. That'd mean two killers and that'd explain how Schreckengost and Criger both got it in two different places. Somebody laces the potato salad while the other guy—"

"The bench," Petey cut in. "You said Stahl was sitting in the dugout when you saw him."

"Right. He didn't get around too much, not with his condition."

"And Criger didn't eat in the clubhouse," she said. "He was in the dugout most of the time."

It was all stumbling together, the same hurly-burly speculating that Parent and his teammates were doing without us. I called him and finally got through.

"We sit on the confession for the time being," he said. Then he lowered his voice. "If we can. This place is a sieve as far as the press is concerned."

"Buck Freeman's called. Four times."

"He has? Oh, boy. There's people here who want a look at Buck as far as Slattery's murder is concerned. Those two hated each other, so talk to him. Talk him in."

"Sure, no sweat," I said, and shook my head.

"And Hughes still wants Tommy Dowd's ass pretty bad," Parent added. "He thinks he's alive, and you already know what I think. So that's the rundown. Bottom line, Duffy: If nothing breaks real quick with Dowd or Buck and the rest of this shit, then we got no choice but to put out the old man's suicide note. In this business, you take every little bit you get."

"Dowd's alive . . . we got a sighting," I said.

"What? Where? Whattaya got, Duffy?" he said.

"Petey just returned from the Cape. Hemphill told her he's heard from Tommy. But that's about all. Tommy's scared silly. Thinks you guys want to pinch him and throw away the key."

"He's right," Parent said, then added quickly, "She there? Can I talk to Petey?"

Of course he could, and I put Petey on and listened as she filled him in.

"That's all he'd tell me, Fred. I'm not holding out. You ever try talking to Charlie Hemphill? Well, all right then. Dowd's so scared, Charlie said he may never come up for air. No. No. Charlie wouldn't tell me where he is or when he saw him last. I tried. Trust me."

They talked on. I could almost feel Parent's heat. He was a good cop, a bulldog detective in the true sense, and he wanted his man. Petey held him off. First thing tomorrow, he said, he'd wring out the whole drama no matter what it took. Then the two of them hung up.

Petey looked up at me.

"We could be in a bind here," she said, and sat down on the bed. "Hemphill won't bring us Dowd if Parent and half of Boston Homicide are waiting just over the next sand dune."

"Right you are," I said.

There was nothing else for us to do that night, which was just as well.

"Make your call, Unk," Petey said. "John Frank Freeman."

That turned out to be easy. I had no sooner punched the last digit and introduced myself when the receiver fairly detonated in my hand. It was Buck all right.

"Duffy! Duffy! Duffy!" he wailed.

"Get me outta here, Duffy! I'm a rat in a hole. I didn't kill nobody. I'm on TV like a convict 'cuz I predicted Slattery would get it. I called it, didn't I, what the fuck!" he said, and laughed like he did the time he took out a squirt gun and doused home plate. "You know what I'm sayin', Duffy? You hear me? So get me out! Write somethin', you fuckin' Hall-of-Famer . . ."

I held the receiver away from my ear, and Petey leaned in. We both heard Buck very well. Then we heard a loud, hollow knock, like a dropped bottle, or a dropped telephone.

"I'm still here, Duffy. Don't worry," Buck continued, only now his voice was subdued. "I didn't kill nobody, for cryin' out loud. Come *onnnn*. Fuckin' Slattery was my meal ticket for ten years. That big prick, he'd rip my throat out I come near him. No way . . ."

And then nothing. The connection held, but we heard only a sea of quiet.

"Where are you, Buck?" I finally asked.

"I DIDN'T KILL ANY-FUCKIN'-BODY!" he suddenly screamed. "Put me on the machines! Or some truth serum, I'll drink that shit! So help me, I'll kill the first bastard says I killed a member of the Boston Red Sox Baseball Club! Past, present, or future!"

Then he went silent again. I had the feeling that this was life with Buck: The switch is on, the switch is off; the roller coaster strains to reach a crest, then it's hell-for-leather in the plunge.

"Come see me, Buck," I finally said. "Get the monkey off your back."

He didn't answer, didn't sputter, and I figured he was considering that.

"You gonna be at the park Friday night? Fuckin' Yankees, ya know," he said.

I paused. Friday's game was also to be tribute to the dead Sox, particularly Jack Slattery.

" 'Course, Buck," I said. "Wouldn't miss it."

"Buy me some peanuts and Cracker Jack," he said.

Then he laughed, just yucked like a hyena over a midnight kill. Then he hung up.

I looked at the receiver, and replaced it. My palm was moist, the hand trembling some. It was not due to age.

I turned to Petey.

"A sad, sad man," I said.

I slept soundly and long, I thought, until the phone rattled me awake. Before I started this business, nobody ever called me before seven.

"What, Fred?" I answered, knowing.

"The goddamn confession's in the paper," he said. "Front page of the goddamn *Globe*."

He was hot, calling from his office downtown where there was plenty of noise in the background. The skinny guy never slept.

"Where'd they get it?"

"Who knows? The broad Gibson broke it. One who got the peckers in her face—"

"I know, I know. Met her at Fenway on Buck's night," I said, rubbing my puss and trying to think.

"Well, we're blown out of the water now," he said. "The boss goes in front of the TV cameras with Stahl's confession in an hour or so, dammit!"

"I'll be down," I said.

I was bushed, and banked with one of those inexplicable morning headaches that seems punishment for having slept soundly, but I left the bed anyway. The Lenox had dropped a fresh *Globe* outside my door, and there was our Miss Gibson on page 1.

I read and scratched. In part, Parent had been wrong: Gibson did not reprint the confession but rather a paraphrase of it. She had spelled Chick Stahl's name right and communicated the gist of his tortured *sayonara,* but the paper did not publish the text of the confession. It was obvious to me that Nora Gibson did not have it, that someone had leaked its existence to her and she had run with it. A talky cop? Or a talkier sports reporter? Had Gibson tapped an old source, or had he tapped her?

Petey must have heard the phone and my clunking around.

"What's goin' on?" she asked, standing at my door in her bathrobe.

I handed her the paper. She squinted as she read.

"That bitch," she said.

—18—
The Curse of Fenway

THE MORNING BELONGED TO THE DICKS. BOSTON'S MURDER
boys hit the airwaves with a mixed revue of smug we-knew-it-all-
the-time pronouncements to vague we'll-tie-up-the-loose-ends-
soon promises. Hughes, Parent's young boss, did most of the
talking. He was glib and photogenic. He did not hold up the
confession. A point in his favor. Whenever he got a question he
could not answer, he simply said that "the ongoing investigation"
would not allow him comment. I wished I had had that out when
editors climbed all over me in years past. In all, the morning
homicide show was well done, even convincing, certainly as pla-
cating to the frothing Boston public as, say, an autumn firing of
a Red Sox general manager.

We were just about out the door on our way to Parent's office
when Petey's phone rang. Her eyes widened. Charlie Hemphill
was calling from his sailboat. It was a bad connection, but she
heard every word.

"I heard the news. Chick Stahl, huh? Bummer. He never liked
my stuff. Not my pitching either. But that takes the heat off
Tommy, don't ya think?"

"Helps a lot," Petey said.

"I'm gonna take him to the ballgame tomorrow night," he
said. "No moon. Strong interplanetary pull. Why doncha come
out? You can meet him."

"Wouldn't miss it," Petey said. "Where do we meet?"

"I'll find you," he said.

Though we went right up to Homicide—the Kelly cops at the door waved us through as if we were in uniform—we had to wait to see Parent. He was in an interview room, we were told. So we tarried, sitting next to his desk reading the morning papers.

Finally he appeared. He spotted us but did not come over. At his elbow, seemingly unbothered, was Jake Stahl. I got up from my chair and nudged Petey. Stahl gave me the high sign and came over.

He stuck out his paw and shook my hand while he coated Petey with a big-league glom.

"Duffy, good buddy, wish we didn't have to meet under these circumstances," he said, not making eye contact. His were still stapled on my niece. "Introductions are in order."

I obliged, finally prying my hand from his.

"This has been a shocker for me, but I still want you on my show, big guy," he said. "And this beauty must come with you."

I expected more gab, maybe a pause for a word from a sponsor, but Jake put a cork in it and he was out the door.

"He's a horse," Petey said.

"That's been said of him, yes."

Parent walked over.

"Our friend," he said. "We talked for over half an hour. He was very talkative."

"So does he buy his daddy's confession now?" I asked.

"That's what it looks like. He reeks of pity for the ol' man. Said Chick came to hate the Red Sox, that they were killing him— same thing as the suicide note. Said Chick was obsessed. Crazy. 'Cept Jake never thought crazy enough to actually murder anybody. He also pointed out that Chick knew a lot about prescription drugs because he took so many himself. Said his dad got around better than you'd think. And blah, blah, blah. He was real comfortable placing the blame right in his father's lap."

"You ask him how a seventy-year-old guy got the drop on Jack Slattery?"

"Yeah. He said he musta had help. Then he reminded me of Tommy Dowd's watch, thank you, and said his old man knew Tommy's dad real well."

"And Jake knows Tommy," I said.

"I mentioned that too. I didn't miss a thing, Duffy. He said he sure did. He says, 'Boy, I'd like to get him on the show.' "

"You ask him how the *Globe* got the confession?"

"No," Parent said. "He asked me."

We both mulled that one over.

"He's friendly," said Petey. "Big and friendly."

I absently ran my palms against my slacks. The last time I had shaken hands with Jake Stahl had left me with his aftershave. This time not. My hand seemed a little oily, but nothing worse.

"Told me to keep in touch," Parent said. "Gave me his card. Said he had to get to the station."

I stared into the front page of the *Globe,* the big headlines, the prominent mention of the fact that Chick Stahl had labored for the rival *Herald,* a less than flattering photo of Chick. It contrasted with son Jake's parting wave and his friendly smile.

"I guess Jake got over the dog," Parent said.

That afternoon Petey and I backhoed, digging at holes in the Chick Stahl picture, looking for a mistake, a footprint left somewhere in soft soil. Chick's confession aside, the only physical evidence we had that made Chick Stahl a murder suspect was skin flakes in Jack Slattery's apartment. And Landsman, the evidence guy, told us he didn't buy it, that the way Chick flaked, Slattery's place would have been a blizzard of dead skin. So why wasn't it? Why did just a few flakes show up under a microscope?

At the same time, Petey was still bothered by the assumption of Chick's guilt in Cuppy's murder in Hartford. For starters, the old man did not drive.

"Let me call my friend Tony," she said.

The next thing I knew she was asking an operator for the number to the Casa Loma in Hartford. I could follow the conversation without listening in. No, her friend said, he knew what Chick Stahl looked like and there was no Chick Stahl in his joint that night. He said he knew his customers and he was certain of it.

She followed that with a call to her friend George Winter, the assistant medical examiner. Yes, he insisted, Cuppy was decked with a caffeine overdose and he had to have gotten the fatal dose in his beer that night. That's how the stuff works, Winter insisted.

Then he jabbered on, reluctant to let Petey go. And did she have an extra ticket to the Yankee–Red Sox game tomorrow night? Finally, she cut him off.

"Whoever killed Mace," she said, looking over at me, "had to have been in Hartford and had to have been in the Casa Loma. And my man Tony says Chick wasn't there."

"So now what have we got?" I replied.

"We got Tommy Dowd's car in Hartford and the caffeine pills under the front seat and his old man's watch under Jack Slattery. Which means that even though Charlie Hemphill is in his corner, we have to have a good long talk with Tommy Dowd."

The next day we were hit in the face with weather. The air was full of water in the form of a warm, persistent mist. Dirty gray clouds hung so thick and low you could lose a pop-up in them. One of those rainmaking, I-got-it-pound-the-glove-eight-times Vern "Pop-up" Stevens pop-ups. It matched our production, for it had been a while since Petey and I had gotten good wood on anything.

It was not baseball weather, but the Yankees were in town for a Friday night series opener, strutting in first place like fat geese with their latest crop of mercenaries, and it would take air a lot heavier than this to dampen things at the ballpark. A tribute to Slattery, Criger, Schreckengost, and Cuppy had been bally-hooed, so tonight's game was a hot ticket.

But I personally didn't feel up to it. The weather soon seeped into my bones and brought my arthritis to a screaming head. The damn affliction is one of the bouquets of senior citizenry that smells rotten. I was soon feeling so bad that I called my sawbones back in Chicago and told him to wire a prescription to a pharmacy on Newbury Street.

An hour later I hobbled into the apothecary shop and was amazed to learn that my medicine awaited me. Technology some-times is what it's cracked up to be. The pharmacist, who with his wire-rimmed glasses reminded me of Dom DiMaggio, was a gabby guy who talked about arthritis as if it were a case of sunburn. He did a number with his knuckles, and I was just about to tell him what he could do with his knuckles when I thought of something.

"Hey," I said, "you're an expert. What do you give people with eczema?"

"Anything with cortisone. The higher the concentration, the better."

"What's it like?"

"It's a salve. Odorless. Although some are petroleum jelly based. Depends."

"Greasy?" I asked.

"Depends how often you put it on. Eczema can be nasty. Itchy. Patients will use a lot of it to control the itching and flaking."

I rubbed my hands together. My knuckles ached, but my prescription had been filled.

If Petey and I were certain of anything when we got to Yawkey Way early that evening, it was that we could plan on nothing. Petey worried about Parent and his dragnet. If he hung on our elbows, or we on his, if we looked like part of a Boston Homicide corps on a Fenway outing, Hemphill and Dowd, and even Buck Freeman, would not show themselves. I was worried about everything. We had them coming to the ballpark, but they were all loose cannons.

"Fred'll be hot when he finds out you didn't tell him about Dowd," I said.

"No choice, Unk," Petey said.

"Play it coy, kid," I said. "I'll try to block for you with Fred, but I'm not gonna fib. We're too stymied in this thing for that."

"Cross your fingers," she replied.

I was not sure what that meant, nor was she, and we made our way through the crowds dampened by the mist but as charged as Red Sox fans always are before Friday night games with New York. Mere mention of the Yankees brought a curl to the Boston lip. The stadium lights were on and they cut through the haze; the vendors and aromas and chatter were thriving despite the drizzle. The streets were clammy and traffic cops wore clear plastic covers over their hats. There would be no batting practices. The outfield grass would be as slick as jelly, the condition of the field a test of the grounds crew, Tommy Dowd's old cohorts.

We picked up our passes at the Yawkey Way gate near Van Ness Street. There were a pack of newsies clamoring for them, testimony to the interest in the memorial as well as the game. We finally got carded and entered a park not yet opened to ticket holders. Vendors, who were actually pink-eared college kids from the suburbs in red short-sleeved knit shirts, jockeyed for their stations. At the elevator Parent was waiting for us. He was wearing a vendor's red shirt. It was tight on him, and he looked like he'd been hired an hour ago, but with a walkie-talkie he could pass for a supervisor. It was a good costume, at least I thought so.

"Cool, Fred," Petey said.

Two of his detectives, Pickens and Kane, stood nearby wearing windbreakers and looking hungry. The five of us went up to the 600 Club on the second level. It was as good a place as any to wait out the damp, dull minutes until game time.

"They gonna play?" Parent asked.

"Unless a monsoon comes in," I said.

We were fidgety, Petey particularly. She was wearing a yellow slicker and carried her canvas bag over one shoulder. Parent tried but could not generate much small talk with her.

"You workin' beer or peanuts, Fred?" I asked.

"Workin' Buck, Duffy. Whattaya think he'll try?"

"I'd watch the back screen," I said. "He might do a half gainer instead of a swan dive."

He eyed me.

"You're Mr. Sarcasm. Petey is Miss Aloof. You guys got something goin'?"

"Sorry, Fred. Just don't feel too chipper in this park anymore. Petey's nervous too. We're out in the open here, you know."

"We'll help each other out then. I got eight guys in the stadium. We'll spot Buck before he spots us."

Petey and I stood around, searched for some high life out of Miller beer, and sampled finger food. We had a loose pact to stay together, one I knew would evaporate as quickly as an agent's promise were Petey to spy Charlie Hemphill. We watched as the park began to fill with fans. The mist was not enough to keep them from sitting in the open, but it took plenty of napkins to dry off the seats. With no pregame workouts, there was not much to watch. The vast center-field scoreboard was ablaze with a likeness of Jack Slattery. The sound system played rock music, the kind today's players liked and which Buck Freeman said was ruining baseball.

The pavane for dead ballplayers was scheduled for the half hour before the first pitch, and Petey and I moved over to the press box to watch. The place was crowded, with pockets of writers and radio guys hanging together waiting for the show. We got our share of eyeballs when we came in, but more attention was going to someone in blue jeans standing over near the broadcast booths. It was Gibson of the *Globe,* queen of the front page. Petey shot her an unrequited stare while I looked around for our favorite radio reporter. He wasn't to be seen.

We stood and shut up when the music changed to something with a lot of harps and oboes. The tributes to Criger, Cuppy, Schreckengost, and finally Jack Slattery reverberated through Fenway. Some smart guy in the promotions department had asked Curt Gowdy instead of Sherm Feller to do it, and Gowdy's familiar pipes richly narrated over the photos and footage that ran across the center-field screen. It was well done, even touching, backed by sad music, and it held the audience rapt. When the Slattery paean ran, with those famous images of Jack's unforgettable swing, his trot, the brief touch he gave a third-base coach when offered a congratulatory hand, his billowing pant legs, and that top-of-the-world smile, well, there was not so much as a breath of irreverence in the press box. The cheeks of Red Sox fans below us were streaming, and it wasn't the mist.

After it was all over—and the Red Sox had the good sense not to open a microphone and let a bunch of bores yap—I spotted a fellow from the Red Sox television broadcast crew. I recognized him because he'd run me in front of a camera on Old-Timers' Day. Seeing him just now gave me an idea. His name was Dick and he had a thin, receding scalp that looked like it had gotten that way from too many sets of headphones. I flagged him, and though he was harried he heard me out.

"If Charlie's gonna be here," he said quietly, "he'll sit with his people in right. Near the bullpen. Same jokers used to toss him grass when he warmed up."

He'd ask his cameramen to scan for him, and let me know.

Finally the infield tarp came off and it was time to play baseball. When the Red Sox ran out to their positions, their center fielder slipped on the wet grass behind second base and fell on his butt. Fans laughed, something they had not done for a while, and anticipated a good one in Fenway.

Petey stayed nearby. Both of us stood in an aisle, which bothered the press-box usher.

"I wanna get out of here," Petey said. "Walk around. Give Charlie a chance to spot me."

"Not on your life," I said. "He may not be the only one who's looking for you."

She snorted. She was nervous and making a pest of herself. The club let Parent set up in an engineer's booth just off to our left, and he popped his head out now and then. If any of the other denizens of the press box knew what was up, they didn't let on. The Yankees got their first three men on. The cleanup hitter then smacked one that would have landed in the Charles had not the Green Monster knocked it down first. After the carom and a flurry of relays seen only in Fenway Park, the Red Sox pulled off a double-play with tag-outs at third and then at second base. So what if two runs had scored? The action was spectacular and the bases were empty.

In their half of the inning, the Sox rallied with a walk and a shot that went so high to left that it must have taken on an extra pound's worth of water before it came down in the screen. Game tied, eight innings to go, and we'd already gotten our money's worth. I had almost forgotten why we were there when Dick, the TV guy, came over and nudged me.

"We got him," he said. "Right on the rail by the bullpen. Just like I thought. You can't miss him. He's wearin' a Hawaiian shirt."

Petey came alive. We leaned over and tried to get a look through the glass at the right-field stands. All we really saw was mist, and a wash of fans in the far recesses of seats. We had to get a better view. I went over to Parent.

"We're going behind the plate, lower level," I said, and did not give him a chance to argue.

As we left, I was certain he didn't buy it. Fenway Park was small. There were eyes everywhere.

On the ramp Petey said, "If he's there, I'm goin' out. Alone, Unk. It'll work if I'm alone."

She knew full well I did not want her to go alone.

"Dammit," I said.

At the lower level, in the beer-garden aisle behind the grandstand but open to the playing field, we stood among the sudsy fans and craned our necks in looking out toward right field. The second inning was on, but we had eyes only on the seats adjoining the Sox bullpen. Then we saw it: an aquamarine shirt that shouted Charlie Hemphill.

"Got him. I'm gonna go," Petey said, and gave me a quick peck on the chin.

Then she broke off, moving through the aisle crowded with distracted fans, winding her way toward right field. I watched as she went, something made easy by her bright hair and her yellow slicker as they moved among the reds and blues of Sox fans. When she got past first base, I'd shadow her. I am her partner, after all, her uncle and all that.

She moved rapidly along the curving aisle, and I began to follow. As I did I checked momentarily behind me. Near an exit ramp, my glance picked up someone I did not expect—or maybe I was half expecting him. Jake Stahl. I saw him and his great, intimidating cranium for a frozen moment before he ducked out of sight. I quickly turned back to find Petey and she was gone. *Dammit!* I groaned. The crowd suddenly cheered and jumped to its feet, and the hubbub made it even harder to locate that yellow slicker. I stepped lively but awkwardly down the aisle, bumping into fans, cursing myself.

And then everything went dark.

Everything around me, Fenway Park with all its raucous energy, suddenly had a curtain of black pulled over it. The huge banks of light above the park, the scoreboards and the billboards, the concession and stadium lights, the press box—all were dark, lifeless, bereft of even a single volt of current.

The crowd cheered. A few fans lit butane lighters. And nobody moved. Long, eerie seconds passed. I stood in the rear aisle unable to see my hand in front of my face, looking out at a field that was dark but not as dark as where I was. There is nothing so strange as being a prisoner of the night along with 35,000 others. Although the timing was suspect, power failures were not uncommon to Fenway. I knew that, but it didn't make things any less foreboding.

"Your attention, please," said Sherm Feller as if he were announcing a pinch hitter. With his words, a few bulbs beneath the stands and in the press box came alive, apparently from an emergency power source. The great expanse of the stadium, however, remained brown. "We've had a power failure. The lights will be back shortly," Feller said.

The crowd cheered again. But no lights followed. I tried to see what I could, and pushed on toward right field. I stepped on someone's foot and got an elbow in the chest.

*   *   *

Petey had reached the right-field corner and was wading across the seats toward Hemphill when the lights went. She was stunned like everybody else, but never took her eyes off the Hawaiian shirt and never stopped moving. Now, under the moonless, misty sky, she closed in on him as he stood along the railing looking down on the Sox bullpen. Next to him, hunched in a camouflage jacket with the hood pulled over his head, was a blocky kid who was staring at his shoes.

"Heyyyyy, my boat buddy," Hemphill said when Petey was almost in his face. He gave her a hug like a close relative and she nearly went blind from the shirt, which clung to him.

"Is this far out or is this far out?" he said, extending his arms above him and turning around to take in the confusion all around him.

Petey nodded and eyed the kid next to Hemphill, who in turn was eyeing her. He had grown a mustache, an uneven clump of hair that hung over his upper lip like a divot.

"Check the mound," Hemphill yelled, laughing and enjoying himself. "There's a giant fuse box right under the rubber. Take it from me." That got laughs from fans and a few of the Sox relief pitchers who were lined up along the fence waiting like everybody else.

Sherm Feller announced once again that the lights would be back on soon. The crowd booed. Hemphill raised his arms and called for more.

"Oh, yeah," he said, finally turning his attention to Petey and his companion. He lowered his voice and leaned close to her ear. "This is our fugitive."

Petey offered to shake Tommy Dowd's hand, but he did not raise his paw or make eye contact. He kept staring at his feet, looking like a kid about to be sentenced for shoplifting. Except that Dowd, whose shoulders were huge from what Petey could see of them in the gloom, was not a kid.

"Let's all sing 'Take Me Out to the Ballgame,' " announced Sherm Feller, and then started in without accompaniment. Though Feller sounded like he was singing from the inside of a can of kitchen cleanser, the crowd sang along. Except Charlie Hemphill.

"Redundant lyrics," he said. "We're here already."

The crowd, nevertheless, gave it a lusty rendition. Given the ditty's abbreviated lyrics, however, the a cappella exercise was over in no time. Soon the fans were left waiting and restless. By now the players had retreated to the dugouts, where they stood with their hands on their hips, idle millionaires held captive by bad wiring.

"Let's get outta here, Charlie," Dowd muttered.

"I assured him you're cool, Petey," Hemphill said.

"Keep assuring," she said.

"What's she gonna do for me?" Dowd said, just loud enough for Petey to hear.

"Hey," Hemphill said. "She may look funky but she's brass. Connected to the Lord of Baseball. They got a name for it in Chicago—"

"Clout," Petey said.

"Perfect," said Hemphill.

By this time, finding my way in the low light of the stadium's emergency power supply, I had reached the point in the stands where the seats curve around into fair territory. I had spotted Petey once again, and saw that she had made her way halfway up the aisle and was huddling with the Hawaiian shirt. It was enough; she'd made contact. I hung back and kept my eye out for the other guy.

"I was set up. I'm nothin' but a patsy," Dowd finally said to Petey.

He said it without looking at her, staring out into the expanses of the outfield instead. But it was a start, Petey knew, and she keyed on him. If Dowd was desperate enough, angry at having been played for a pooch, and sick of keeping a lid on it, they had a case.

"The watch and the car are killin' ya," Petey said.

"I sold the fuckin' watch! Four bills," Dowd snapped.

Before Petey could respond, the crowd began a rhythmic clapping mixed with boos and whistles. "Please be calm," begged Sherm Feller, and the booing increased. By now things had been stalled for more than ten minutes, and the novelty of the blackout had faded. The organist, whose repertoire had been most uninspiring during the lull, tried another "Take Me Out to the Ballgame" and got no takers.

Just then a flurry of cheers broke out behind Petey and Hemphill. Fans turned toward the bleachers as the cheering increased, and suddenly a figure in a Red Sox uniform bolted out of the runway cut into the right-field stands next to the Sox bull-pen. With a kick and a leap, he climbed atop the low outfield fence like Dewey Evans, hung there like a thief in a gangway, then hopped onto the warning track and sprinted into the outfield where he did a cartwheel and a perfect backflip.

The crowd went nuts, for the intruder, dressed in Red Sox home whites, was none other than Buck Freeman. He took off his hat, bowed deeply in all directions, and screamed, "It's a black day for the Red Sox!"

Then he danced and dashed and hopped and carried on in right field like a crazed mascot. The crowd cheered him wildly. A bullpen pitcher tossed him a ball and Buck flipped it up in the air behind his back and caught it in his hat. He took a bow and stuck out his tongue. Lights or no lights, Freeman was on his game.

Though the crowd was loving him—forgetting, obviously, that Buck had been a suspect in the Red Sox murders—I knew that Parent and his boys had gotten their wish. Suddenly clumps of sport coats dropped over the railings in several different spots and edged toward Buck. Parent was among them, having come onto the field near the Red Sox dugout, radio in hand. He hugged the fence along first base, proceeding past the rolled-up infield tarp and Canvas Alley, talking into his radio.

I moved instinctively closer to the field. Fans were standing now, clapping and hooting. Even in the dark, Buck was spreading his mania, and things were getting wild. If the cops grabbed him, all hell might break loose.

At the same time, Petey's conversation with Dowd was frozen. Hemphill was smiling beatifically at Buck's display.

"He's sent from the gods," he said. "He's everyman."

"What the fuck—!" Dowd sputtered, pointing at the cops on the field. Another pair of sport coats suddenly appeared in the aisle just to his left, causing him to swivel and search the stands around him for more. With Freeman concentrating his antics in deep right field, it looked to Dowd as if each advancing cop were coming toward him.

"Cool it, Tommy," Hemphill said.

"My ass! They're all over! I'm fucked!" he said.

Then he bolted.

He raced into the exit tunnel just a handful of seats away,

and Petey followed him. I was momentarily paralyzed, not knowing what to do. Parent had just about reached my position, and I decided to fetch him. Pushing through fans and vendors, I reached the low wall and struggled over it.

"Fred! It's Tommy!" I shouted, and got his attention.

He hesitated, looking first at me and then at Freeman, then hustled over. I told him what I saw and we took off. Just as we were leaving the stands, Buck Freeman dropped his pants and mooned everybody. His hams were luminescent within the murky depths of the outfield, and they provided an easy quarry for the pursuing gendarmes. As they closed in on him, Buck tried to sprint away, something that was not easy with his pants around his ankles, and soon he fell headlong in the grass. The fans went berserk. Parent's cohorts collared Freeman seconds later, pulled up his knickers, and led him off like a convict. As they did, the boos shook Fenway's beams.

Dowd was big—thick really—not particularly fast and in bad shape, but he knew the stadium well and he wanted out of it. He bulled his way toward the Yawkey Way service gate. Petey struggled to catch sight of him and catch up. The badly lit concourse was full of fans, most of them cranky and restless, paying fans unhappy at the game's delay and in no mood to be pushed or jostled. But push Petey did, moving and dodging as Dowd had toward the corner gate. It was a fight, but finally she got free of the crush and into the muggy air and the outdoor light of Yawkey Way just in time to see Dowd cut across the street and lumber down Van Ness.

Petey shot ahead like a spaniel after a bird, past the players' parking lot and the broadcast trucks that hugged the stadium wall, when she suddenly lost her footing. She tumbled down in a half fall, half slide on the clammy sidewalk, smearing her hands, her slicker, and one leg of her jeans with grime. She cursed and spat, and scrambled to her feet. As she did, her right ankle nearly went out from under her. She'd twisted it—the same ankle she'd injured in the rollover—and now it shot a jolt of pain up to her knee. She grimaced and cried out, half in anguish and half in a bewildered plea for help.

But there was no help around, and she pressed on, catching sight of Dowd's parka far ahead on Van Ness, a narrow side street of cyclone fences, muddy lots, and nondescript brick parking garages. As she went, limping and hopping, she spotted another figure loping just ahead of her on the other side of the street. It was a big, hulking man in a dark shirt and dark slacks whose wide, wet shoulders reflected light from each streetlamp. But it was his huge, glistening head of black hair that took Petey's breath away. It was Jake Stahl. He'd followed her, and she had led him right to Tommy Dowd.

Stahl, with his elephant strides, was making time, closing the gap between him and Dowd. He stayed on the right side of Van Ness, his legs shielded by parked automobiles. Up ahead, Dowd had slowed to a fast walk along the fence, dodging the stinkweeds, still apparently unaware that he was being followed. No matter how much she tried, Petey could not gain ground on either of them, particularly Stahl. He looked straight ahead, not knowing that Petey was behind him.

Suddenly he cut between parked cars and ran into the middle of the street. That's when she saw that he was carrying something in his left hand, something squat, almost lost in his giant mitt, but Petey could see it, its glint. She was certain she saw it each time his hand swung by his side.

"Stahl, you bastard!" she shouted.

He turned a shoulder and glanced back at her like a runner checking on an outfielder. As he did, Tommy Dowd turned around and spotted both of them. The sight spooked him and he lurched left, around the corner onto Kilmarnock Street, and dashed toward Boylston, now only seventy-five yards or so away. Stahl kept up his charge, a gorilla lumbering through the mist. Petey felt a surge of adrenaline, or maybe it was dread, and coaxed her ankle to do its stuff. As she did, frantic at what was taking place in front of her, yet slowed by the pain and the exhaustion of the dash, she suddenly had a clear picture of what this was all about, why Dowd was fleeing, why Jake Stahl was stalking.

She rushed on, the two bobbing figures framed in front of her. Tommy Dowd had nearly reached Boylston, and the main drag in this part of the city was racing with four lanes of traffic. But Dowd never came to a full stop. He threw another momentary glance behind him—Petey saw it, saw his wide, flat face—and then he barged into the street.

The sound followed, quickly and frighteningly loud, like the smacking of a heavy fist on a car's hood on a subzero night, a thud free of squealing tires or horns, and suddenly Dowd was down. Petey saw it all, and screamed.

A truck, a heavy Boston Edison lineman's truck, had struck Tommy like a bowling ball hitting a tenpin. He caromed off the truck and hurtled several feet in the air before landing and rolling in a heap on the wet pavement. He lay there faceup like a discarded bat bag, his legs splayed grotesquely.

Petey stopped in her tracks at the impact, stunned, choking from the horror she had just witnessed. The utility truck also stopped, its bib-overalled driver and his companion leaping out of the cab to see what they'd done. They went toward Dowd. But Jake Stahl got there first and crouched over him. He reached for Dowd's neck.

Petey saw him, saw his meat hook of a hand go for Dowd's throat, and she screamed.

"Stop him! Somebody! Get him away!"

She burst forward, now frantic at what she was seeing and the fact that several yards separated her from Jake Stahl's hand on Tommy Dowd's neck. She charged like a runner rounding third, gaining speed, intent on Stahl's immense, hideous form, her bruised body a convulsive, churning force of rage.

With one last surge, she rammed her entire body into Stahl, her knee slamming into his head, bone on bone, the impact knocking him back and onto the pavement. It was a teeth-jarring collision, a violent, bench-clearing hit, the likes of which Lou Piniella put on Carlton Fisk in '76. Stahl flopped on his back; Petey tumbled and rolled onto her side.

The Boston Ed men stopped, three bodies lying in front of them. Their massive truck blocked two lanes, its hood steaming in the mist. Cars pulled up and gawkers crowded in. Petey groaned and clutched her shoulder and her knee. Jake Stahl was out cold, his right arm extended, a small, silver tape recorder lying just outside his reach on the wet asphalt. Tommy Dowd lay where he was, bleeding from his ear and several other places, but still breathing.

Running is not the accurate term for what I did to get there, but I arrived, the debbil arthritis spearing my bones with every step. Parent's legs made better time, and he immediately took control of the scene. He filled in the dumbfounded Boston Ed guys, and made sure Jake Stahl did not recover and bolt. I went over to Petey, who was hurting anew, and gently pushed the hair out of her eyes.

"Is he still alive, Unk? Tommy?" she asked.

Just then a cheer rose from behind us. It was a tumult, a hosanna, and we looked behind us to see Fenway's lights flicker, then glow.

Box Score

In all, the blackout lasted eighteen minutes, and yet anybody who was there will tell you it went on no less than an hour, not including the Dowd boy, of course, who didn't see it lift. As the papers were to moan the next day, it was not the first power outage—in the literal or figurative sense—at Fenway, since there was a midgame blackout in a '91 game against the White Sox. That one did last nearly an hour. And, the papers went on, blackouts are nothing new to the Boston Garden, where they seem to happen during the Stanley Cup finals.

If all that were not enough of a lance in the vulnerable buttocks of Boston Edison, the gaff was twisted by photos of Tommy Dowd, Jake Stahl, and Petey spread out on the pavement in the shadow of the utility company's truck. Dowd made it to Mass General in one battered piece, and though he had a fractured skull and other severe injuries, he was a young, strong kid and he survived. Most of all, his memory was intact.

Jake Stahl's injuries were mostly to his ego, though Petey's knee had made his nose look like the shattered handle of one of Jim Rice's bats. When Petey got a look at him and his bandaged proboscis on a TV news report, she thrust her fist into the air and blurted something about "an eye for an eye and a nose for a nose." Then she groaned again, for her corpus ached as badly as his did.

Stahl, of course, denied any association with the murders,

and insisted he was pursuing Tommy Dowd in order to interview him. He knew a great story when he spotted one.

Those and other statements came to light the next day when Parent's team assembled the case against Jake Stahl. Petey and I sat with Fred in his Berkeley Street office and filled in the blanks.

"So is Jake our man? Can we put his fingers on every hit?" Parent began.

"No," I ventured. "Chick was in the ballpark. He could have salted the potato salad and tampered with the chewing tobacco."

"But you don't think so. . . ." said Parent.

"I hate the thought of old sportswriters killing old ball-players."

"Come clean, Duffy. We need something better than opinion. Jake's gonna have a good lawyer," Parent said.

"Okay, start with this," I said. "Your evidence guy said the skin flakes bothered him. Weren't enough to put Chick in Jack's hotel room. There were flakes, which means eczema, but not a bad case. And if you check it out, you'll probably find that Jake suffers with the rash too. It's hereditary. When I shook hands with him right here a couple days ago, he left my mitt as greasy as the pocket of an old fielder's glove. A pharmacist told me people with eczema control it with salves, and I'll put money down that that's what Jake does.

"And then try this, Fred. See if the ligature marks around Jack Slattery's neck could have come from a dog leash. How Jake loved that old mutt."

Petey looked at me and smiled.

"You holding out on me too, Unk?" she said.

She rubbed her sore knee once again.

"I have two questions; one small and one big," she went on. "Why did he burglarize our suite—?"

"I got that," Parent cut in. "He wanted whatever you had on the whereabouts of Tommy Dowd. He had to get to Tommy, the only guy who could put him away."

"Okay, I'll buy that," she said. "But why? Why did big ol' friendly, you're-on-the-air Jake Stahl turn into a killer?"

That word hung in the air after she'd uttered it. This time Parent did not rush to reply. The two of them turned to me.

"My turn, eh?" I said, rubbing my knuckles and the mottled backs of my hands. "You want eight column inches on another ballyard sapper. . . ."

"You wanna use my typewriter?" Parent said.

"Pipe down," I said. "If you ask me, which you did, Chick Stahl and his miserable rash, that itch he had but was too tight or too ornery to do anything about, just festered and infected what he touched. His life, from his old man, he told me, was the Red Sox. 'We, we, we,' he kept saying when he talked about the Sox. That's unhealthy, a disease, if you really think about it, and it piled up on top of all the diseases Chick already had.

"So throw the kid into that. Here's a ballpark brat. He inherits all the Red Sox stuff from the old man. He worships these guys. Becomes a radio guy, and that gives him a pass to commune with his heroes. But any two-bit talk-show shrink can tell you worship is never very far from loathing. He always knew he was only a jock-sniffer to them, a microphone jockey. Players always ask the radio guys when they're gonna make it to TV, and don't think they didn't rag Jake about that.

"But he also inherits the itch, the rash. We got a metaphor going here, folks. He keeps it medicated, right? Buys the creams that keep the flakes down. Can hardly see them unless you get a microscope. But he can't cure his problem with the old man. Chick laid it on with me about how his kid wasn't a writer, wasn't any kind of reporter at all in his eyes. He just didn't measure up. And if he threw that at *me,* you can only imagine what he threw at Jake.

"So now Chick is sick and wasted and he blames the Red Sox for his woes. He does it in print and he bitches about it when he's had too much brandy and he does it to me at the Old-Timers' game. But Chick's a print guy—he does it on the page. It's not *real,* it's figurative. Jake doesn't understand that. He's an over- grown kid still trying to prove himself to his father. So when Chick says somebody ought to put Ossee Schreckengost and Lou Criger and Mace Cuppy—the three guys who live in Chick's gallery of Red Sox infamy because of their costly blunders—out of their misery, Jake decides to do just that. But unless Jake comes clean, Fred, we may never know if he or Chick poisoned Ossee and Lou—"

"Don't worry, Duffy," Fred broke in. "Our guys are in his apartment and they tell me it's a mobile pharmacy. Including plenty of nicotine, caffeine, and the stuff that cleared Ossee's nose for good."

"But Jake doesn't stop with Mace Cuppy," I continued. "He

hates Jack Slattery like his old man did, and now he's whacked three guys and gotten away with it. He's starting to like the taste of blood in his throat. So he strangles Slattery. But he can't stop there. Chick once wrote a column about Slattery's hands on the bat—how he fluttered his fingers. It annoyed him. Kind of thing columnists nitpick at. I know about that. And Jake takes him up on it. Breaks Jack's fingers one by one. Can you imagine that? The sick bastard, breaking a ballplayer's fingers. That really struck me. There's something about an athlete's hands that sets him apart. Sets him apart from you and me. Take Williams or Yaz, Pete Runnels or Rice or Boggs—they played the bat handle like a fine instrument. And Jake can feel that. It's part of his worship and part of his hatred.

"He's smart, we'll give him that. And he's got a beard in Tommy Dowd. The kid is just as screwed up as Jake but not as bright. Jake knew he could use him like a talking dummy ever since he conned him into climbing into Fenway with his dad's ashes. So Jake uses his car and drives to Hartford, plants the caffeine in Mace Cuppy's beer, buys the watch off Tommy Dowd and plants it under Slattery. And having done that, he then has to get rid of Tommy. But Tommy's not as dumb as Jake thinks; he gets a gust of intelligence and hides out, the one thing he does well. Jake has to find the kid, has to find him bad because he is the only one who can nail his ass to the post on this. So he sticks on us, or Petey, I should say, and who calls Petey in Cape Cod from Chick Stahl's apartment while Jake is sitting right there? Yours truly. Which told Jake that Charlie Hemphill was connected. With Charlie, he knew, would come Tommy Dowd.

"To push that along, he made another shrewd move. You ask your friend Nora Gibson where she heard about Chick's confession. It didn't come from the Boston P.D., we know that. No, Jake tipped her to it, or my name's Pinky Higgins. A master stroke. If the confession's public, then the heat's off Tommy and he shows himself. And then Jake can get rid of him."

I was dry. I had not given a speech that windy since the Rotary Club in Braintree.

"Did you know Charlie Hemphill and Tommy Dowd were coming to the game?" Parent asked.

It was a pure homicide dick's question, which was not a question at all.

"Tell me, Fred, with Hemphill does anybody know anything?" I dodged.

He turned to Petey.

"Charlie said Tommy would freak at the sight of cops, Fred," she responded. "I knew you'd understand."

"Bullshit," he said. "If we knew Dowd was going to be there we wouldn't a wasted our goddamn time with Buck Freeman."

"You were under the gun of Chick's confession, Fred," I reminded him, "and we weren't."

"We knew Chick wasn't in Hartford and he wasn't in Slattery's hotel room either," Petey added.

"Since when?" said Parent.

"My restaurant guy knew Chick and said he was certain Chick wasn't there. But I'll bet he can put Jake there."

Parent ran a hand over his bloodhound face.

"Okay, I'll grant you that. Dowd did tell us Jake used his car a lot, and already my detectives have put him in Hartford the night Mace Cuppy went down. Next day too, according to the radio station, who told us they had him on the air from the medical examiner's office."

"And in my rearview mirror, the bastard," Petey said.

"I'll give you that too, Petey," Parent said. "He knew you were ahead of us, and he saw a chance to take you off the case."

"Cripes," I said, "he was going after anybody in his way."

"That's what these guys do," Parent said. "You're lucky, Petey, lucky he didn't turn around and break your neck."

"The oily creep . . ." Petey murmured.

"So how do you fit Chick's confession in?" Parent said. "Why would the old man go to his grave covering for that jamoke?"

"That jamoke's his kid, Fred. Whacking Chick's demons for him. You read his stuff yourself. Chick's the thinker. Jake's the doer."

"You're straining your milk now, Duffy. You'll point to anybody besides old Chick," he said.

"You're right," I said. "But don't forget the guilt factor here. A father's guilt. Chick was a smart guy. Even smart enough to realize that his kid had gone over the edge."

We all realized that. We were silent. The sounds of a busy police station clattered around us.

Parent looked at me and actually smiled, a tired, homely,

earnest smile. In a monotone of additional questions, Parent walked us through a few more reports on Dowd, Hemphill, and Jake Stahl. As I watched him filling out his reports with a ballpoint pen, I felt for the guy. His hair was matted on his head and a scab was evidence of another one of those damn shaving cuts. The city of Boston would never fully appreciate him, never even know him apart from his paycheck and his pension, so his gratification in life had to come from the street, from The Case. And the biggest one of his career had just cleared.

Then my brow tightened.

"Where'd you hear the word *jamoke*, Fred?"

"From you," he said.

Our Sunday started late. Petey's system had finally collapsed and she slept like a dead woman until nearly noon. In the meantime I made some mop-up phone calls. The one to the commissioner was easy. In a confab full of the usual sputters, wisecracks, and references to Honus Wagner, I simply said that this Boston scrod was in the net. Grand Chambliss, who never speaks in clichés, replied, "I'll call you Ishmael, Duffy." He then apologized. And I spoke with Marjorie, his marvelous assistant who also is normally a stranger to the hackneyed phrase. She said something about our case being "solved beyond a shadow of a doubt."

My calling was interrupted at midmorning by a knock at the door and the appearance of a messenger. He handed me a thick envelope. When I opened it, a scent of lilac came into the room like cats with big feet. It was a missive "From the pen of Patsy M. Dougherty . . ." The first sheaf of her memoirs. They were impeccably typed on paper as thick as wallcovering. I poured myself some brandy and started to read.

That night we had a dinner reservation. The date had been set a week earlier with Red Carney, the jowly Cubs play-by-play gabber and old friend. Coming up from New York where the Cubs had played a day game with the Mets, he wanted to revisit Locke-Ober's, that Winter Street culinary treasure.

Ever since the Braves left for Milwaukee in 1952, National League palates like Red's have been deprived of Locke-Ober's. And Red was still hot about it. Not thirty minutes after he gave the Cubs' losing totals and threw in an unsolicited plug for his sponsor's beer, he was out of Shea Stadium and heading for a shuttle flight to Logan. His cab got him to the Lenox and our doorstep at just after six, and what a welcome sight he was.

"Hold the ladder steady, my lady, we're elopin' tonight," he said, and gave Petey a bear hug.

"The big possum's out tonight," Petey said, and hugged back.

Red was the tonic Petey needed to help her forget her aches and get into a sleek, off-the-shoulder black number that rode her every curve until it got to mid-thigh, where it stopped dead. It was the dress she'd been waiting to wear in Boston, and Red's unabashed ogle was the payoff. Her new bruises were prominent, and she reminded me of Nelson Algren's reference to a woman with a broken nose: There may be some more beautiful, "but none so real."

"Lovely, lovely, lovely," Red said, as Petey thrust a hip good enough for a Bob Fosse number.

With her arms locked in ours, we hit the lobby. Petey wanted to walk to the restaurant, which was clear on the other side of the Common; but Red said his heart couldn't take it and his stomach was growling, so we flagged a cab.

Locke-Ober's restaurant has been around since 1875 and it looks like it. I say that with due admiration. Located just off Winter Street on what is really no more than an alley, the unassuming restaurant looks like the kind of inn John Hancock would have retreated to for sustenance just before going off to sign the Declaration. Inside, its bar is carved mahogany, its walls gold leaf, its chairs red leather, and its black-jacketed waiters men who can tell you when Curley was mayor and when Warren Spahn pitched for the team across town.

There are three floors, and we were seated on the first floor Men's Café, an anachronism not lost on Petey, at a round table set with white linen. We sat in full view of the venerable "rosy nude" painting on the far wall.

"She seems a little chunky in the hips this season," Red said.

"She's not the only one," I said.

"Speak for yourself," Petey said.

Locke-Ober's quiet, bordering-on-stuffy atmosphere was fine for our dispositions, and Red was all ears.

"Tell me ol' Chick Stahl didn't do it, Duffy," he said. "Start from the first inning. Don't leave out a thing."

"Not Chick, that kid of his . . ." I started.

"Tell me this, Duffy," Red cut in. "Did Lou Criger chew himself to death?"

Petey laughed.

"Sort of," I said. "Nicotine poisoning in the Red Man."

"Nicotine!"

"That's right," I said. "Laboratory guys told us it's so easy they're surprised more people don't try it."

Red frowned. "What's safe anymore? Not a damn thing. Okay, go on," he said, lifting a vodka gimlet to his lips. He'd get back to his beer a little later.

"Ever met his kid—Jake?" Petey said.

"Noooo," Red said, "I mean, yeah! I know the kid. Come *on*."

We paused to indulge in lobster bisque, oysters Rockefeller, and a platter of other appetizers taken offshore just hours earlier that reminded me of why Locke-Ober's owns my palate. While I ate, I considered the younger Stahl.

"He played us like bad actors the second we came into town," I said.

We filled Red in on the details of the case, from Petey's accident to the burgled hotel room to her Boylston Street dropkick of Jake Stahl's big head.

"You could tackle me anytime, doll," Red said, and I knew he was going.

By now the appetizers were finished and we got a second wind before we faced the heart of the menu's batting order. Red backhanded his vodka and drew a good guzzle from a glass of Sam Adams, his meal's companion.

"I hear ya, folks, but I'm wondering, I'm thinkin' out loud like you gotta in this business. I'm wonderin': 'Is anyone that good?' "

I could only shake my head at that.

Soon the real feast arrived: Lobster Savannah, a Locke-Ober's tradition where the tail is sautéed in a sherry cream sauce, Nantucket scallops, and a succulent rack of lamb. We gushed in unison: "Can anything be this good?"

Between bites Red began again. "What I don't understand is *why*, Duffy. You take a guy like Chick Stahl—I mean, he's one of *us*. Old school. How'd his kid go bad?"

"You want my honest opinion, Red, I think Chick Stahl was

a sick, deluded man. His kid fed off that, and it all got out of hand."

"The kid, that Jake sonuvabitch!" Red sputtered. "He makes Charley Manson look like a utility hitter!"

"That he does, Red," Petey said. "I saw him with his hands on Tommy Dowd's neck and I knew he was going to squeeze the breath out of him."

I eyed my niece as she spoke, her face agitated. It was a scene: the three of us eating sumptuously in a legendary Boston watering hole while talking of treachery and motive and madness.

"The curse of Fenway," Red said.

After that the waiter brought the Sultana Roll, a spumoni dessert no denizen of Locke-Ober's passes up, Indian pudding, and macaroons, those wonderful macaroons.

"It's time we got back to the ivy of Wrigley Field, Pete," I said after my first sip of coffee.

"Now that we can no longer call you Romeo," Petey said.

"Romeo? Why art thou Romeo?" Red said, getting all excited and dripping too much cream into his cup.

"Nothing, nothing—" I said, dabbing my lips with my napkin.

"Smitten, Red," Petey said. "My uncle here was smitten by the Grande Dame of Boston baseball—"

"Dougherty's wife?" Red queried.

"Widow, dammit," I said.

"She asked Uncle Duffy to be her Boswell . . . and it got steamy from there," Petey continued.

"What in hell does all this mean?" Red said.

I threw my linen on the table. Petey was grinning like a cockamamie cupid.

"Means Patsy decided he was the man to help her write her memoirs. And Unk took it from there," Petey said. The smirk on her face was criminal.

"Oh, calm down, both of you. I met the lady. I liked the lady. She's classy. But she's a little out of my league," I said. "You don't want the messy details . . ."

"Yes, we do," Petey said.

Red nodded, and waited.

"Ah well," I began. "Let's just say we got our signals crossed. Or maybe Patsy and I never were in the same rotation. She's from our vintage, Red, but she plays the game by the book—"

"Are we talking baseball or romance, Unk?" Petey asked.

"What's the difference?" I replied. "All I know is that the tables were turned. Mrs. Dougherty views life with a harder edge than I do. It's as simple as that."

"Leaves a hell of a lot open for interpretation," Red said.

"You bet it does," I said.

Petey's head tilted, and a hint of compassion replaced her sass. She had struck out a few times herself.

"Not only that, but I got the first installment of her auto-biography today. All wrapped in a bow. And that was the high point. I waded through fifty pages of it and my head was pounding. Awful stuff. Plain *awful*. Like Charlotte Brontë in the box seats."

Petey made a face.

"Heathcliff! Heathcliff!" she whispered.

Her education was too good for her britches. Red sat there looking at both of us as if we were speaking Urdu.

"It's best we leave Boston," I said. "Make a graceful exit from the Red Sox."

Petey patted my hand. She was a romantic at heart, had witnessed my renewed ardor, and offered me silent sympathy for its apparent passing.

"That I understand," said Red, and raised his glass. "You know," he added, "it's like the man said, 'They never should have taken out Willoughby.' "

Packing up the next day was easier than we expected. A late-morning flight back to Chicago had room for us.

Our cab to Logan was driven by a fellow whose name was Emile D'Arbanville. He was a shimmering black as skinny as Oil Can Boyd and looking just as agile. With an accent as thick as meringue, he told us that he was from Haiti and that he was glad to be in Boston. Very glad. He even wanted to learn about baseball. I asked him if his heart had ever been broken.

"*Beaucoup* . . . many times," he said.

He was ready for Fenway.